John Hookham Frere

Aristophanes

A Metrical Version of The Acharnians, The Knights and The Birds (Edition 2)

John Hookham Frere

Aristophanes
A Metrical Version of The Acharnians, The Knights and The Birds (Edition 2)

ISBN/EAN: 9783337002794

Printed in Europe, USA, Canada, Australia, Japan

Cover: Foto ©Andreas Hilbeck / pixelio.de

More available books at **www.hansebooks.com**

ARISTOPHANES

A METRICAL VERSION OF

THE ACHARNIANS, THE KNIGHTS
AND THE BIRDS

WITH OCCASIONAL COMMENT

BY

JOHN HOOKHAM FRERE

WITH AN INTRODUCTION BY HENRY MORLEY

LL.D., PROFESSOR OF ENGLISH LITERATURE AT
UNIVERSITY COLLEGE, LONDON

SECOND EDITION

LONDON
GEORGE ROUTLEDGE AND SONS
BROADWAY, LUDGATE HILL
GLASGOW AND NEW YORK
1887

INTRODUCTION.

ARISTOPHANES, son of Philippus, was born in Athens about
the year 444 before Christ, and lived probably to the age of
about seventy-six. He made social as well as political use of
his wit, and wrote (B.C. 427) his first comedy, "The Banquetters,"
when he was yet a youth below the legal age for competing for a
prize. That comedy was the satire of one fresh from the schools
upon the sophistries that had crept into the Athenian system of
education. There was a father whose two sons had been educated, one in the good old way, the other in the new way, and
the chorus, which gave its name to the play, was of a party who
had been feasting in the temple of Hercules. That play is
known only by tradition ; and the next play, "The Babylonians,"
produced in the next year in the name of Callistratus, is also
lost. It obtained the first prize, and was a political caricature
of the system of appointing to public offices by lot. Next followed, and in the next year (B.C. 425), also produced in the name of
Callistratus, "The Acharnians," the first play in this volume, produced when the poet's age was about nineteen. "The Knights"
—the second play here given—followed a year later, and was the
first play produced by Aristophanes in his own name. Each of
these plays won the first prize in competition. The other plays
—omitting those which have been lost and are known only
by tradition—were : "The Clouds" (B.C. 423); "The Wasps"
(B.C. 422) ; "Peace" (B.C. 419) ; "The Birds" (B.C. 414) ; "Lysistrata" (B.C. 411); "Plutus" (B.C. 408) ; "The Frogs" (B.C. 405);
"Ecclesiazusæ (B.C. 392). But Aristophanes is said to have
written in all fifty-four plays. His three sons, Philippus, Araros,
and Nicostratus, were all poets of what is called the Middle
Comedy; Aristophanes himself being the only one of many
writers of the Old Comedy of whom any complete work is left.

Frere's translations of some of the plays of Aristophanes have
a permanent place in English literature, and are entitled to wide
popularity. John Hookham Frere was not only a fine scholar,
but a man of genius, with wit and humour of his own, whose
writings are too good to be reserved for the enjoyment of a few.

He was born in May 1769, of a family that had lived for some time at Thwait Hall, near Finningham, in Suffolk, before it changed its seat to Roydon Hall, near Diss, in Norfolk. The father of John Hookham Frere was a John Frere, who was second wrangler at Cambridge in 1763, when the senior wrangler was William Paley. In 1768 John Frere married a lady who had been unusually well educated, Jane Hookham, only child of a rich London merchant; and in the following year John Hookham Frere was the first child of the marriage. John Frere's sister, who was also a very accomplished woman, married Sir John Fenn, editor of " The Paston Letters."

Hookham Frere was sent to Eton, from a school at Putney, when sixteen years old; he established there a close and life-long friendship with George Canning. In November 1786, in his second year at Eton, Frere was with Canning among those Eton boys who started " The Microcosm," perhaps the most famous of school magazines. From Eton, Frere went to Caius College, Cambridge, and he was a freshman there in 1790, when there appeared in Ellis's " Specimens of the Early English Poets " a metrical version of the Anglo-Saxon poem on the Battle of Brunanburgh, of which James Mackintosh said in his History of England, " it is a double imitation, unmatched perhaps in literary history, in which the writer gave an earnest of that faculty of catching the peculiar genius and preserving the characteristic manner of his original, which, though the specimens of it be too few, places him alone among English translators." Frere wrote it when at Eton. Scott spoke of it also in his " Essay on Imitation of the Ancient Ballads " as the only poem he had met with which, if it had been produced as ancient, could not have been detected on internal evidence." Frere graduated B.A. in 1792, Canning in 1793. Frere took his M.A. in 1795; and was made a Fellow of his College. He then entered the Foreign Office, and in 1796 became member for a Cornish pocket borough.

In 1797 John Hookham Frere joined Canning, George Ellis, and others in establishing the " Antijacobin," and in the poetry of the "Antijacobin" contributed his full share to the light battery of wit with which it assailed what it took to be revolutionary extravagances.

In 1799 Frere became Under-Secretary of State in the Foreign Office, succeeding Canning, who went to the Board of Trade. In October 1800 he was appointed Envoy Extraordinary and Plenipotentiary to Portugal; and in September 1802 he was transferred from Portugal to Spain. He remained there as British Minister at Madrid till August 1804, when he was succeeded by the Marquis Wellesley. The Ministry at home made him a Privy Councillor and gave him a pension. Walter Scott's " Sir Tristrem " was published in that year 1804:

Frere, who delighted in old ballad and romance, spoke with admiration of it to George Ellis. Ellis reported this to Scott, who replied, " Frere is so perfect a master of the ancient style of composition that I would rather have his suffrage than a whole synod of your vulgar antiquaries." Frere's contact with Spain caused him to translate parts of the " Poem of the Cid," and Southey in April 1808 wrote to Scott : " I saw Frere in London, and he has promised to let me print his translations from the ' Poema del Cid.' They are admirably done. Indeed, I never saw anything so difficult to do, and done so excellently, except your supplement to Sir Tristrem." In 1807 Frere's father died, and he inherited the family estates ; his mother and an unmarried sister, Susan, maintaining home for him at Roydon Hall. In 1808 Hookham Frere was sent to Spain again, accredited as British Envoy and Plenipotentiary to the Central Junta. The King of Spain recognised Frere's services in critical times by conferring on him a Castilian title of honour—Marquez de la Union. In 1809 he returned, and withdrew at the age of forty, from active political life. In September 1816 he married the Dowager Countess of Erroll, to whom he was strongly attached, and who had, beyond beauty, wit and wisdom of her own for the appreciation of his genius. It was she who urged him to print his first part of the " Monks and Giants," as " prospectus and specimen of an intended national work by William and Robert Whistlecraft, of Stowmarket, in Suffolk, harness and collar makers, intended to comprise the most interesting particulars relating to King Arthur and his Round Table." This piece of pure and delightful playfulness was published in 1817. Byron —who recognised Frere's hand—wrote of it : " Mr. Whistlecraft has no greater admirer than myself. I have written a story in eighty-nine stanzas in imitation of him, called ' Beppo.' " And again he wrote of " Beppo " to Murray: " The style is not English, it is Italian : Berni is the original of all ; Whistlecraft was my immediate model." Southey afterwards wrote of poems in this manner : " Frere began it ; what he produced was too good in itself and too inoffensive to become popular, for it attacked nothing and nobody."

In July 1820 appeared in the " Quarterly Review " an article on " Aristophanes" that attracted much attention. It was Frere's only contribution to the " Quarterly," and it included doctrine and illustration of his own principles applied to such translation. Frere had been translating Aristophanes from time to time for his own pleasure and the entertainment of friends. In June 1817, when Coleridge at Highgate wanted somebody to meet the German poet Tieck, he wrote to Crabb Robinson : " I should be most happy to make him and that admirable man Mr. Frere acquainted. Their pursuits have been so similar ; and to convince Mr. Tieck that he is *the* man among us in whom taste at its maximum has vitalized itself into productive power—Genius.   You need only show him the incomparable translation annexed to Southey's 'Cid,' and I would finish the work off by Mr. Frere's Aristophanes."

In 1820 the failing health of Lady Erroll caused Frere to quit England, and he settled with his wife and sister at Malta in 1821.   His best friend, Canning, died in 1827 ; his wife died in January 1831.   In the November of that year, Sir Walter Scott, on his way to Naples, when his life was ebbing, was affectionately received by Frere at Malta.   Coleridge, whom Frere held in high esteem, died in 1834; and to Mr. Gillman, who had watched over his last years, he said in his will : "As the most expressive way in which I can only mark my relation to him, and in remembrance of a great and good man, revered by us both, I leave the manuscript volume lettered 'Arist. Manuscript—Birds, Acharnians, Knights,' presented to me by my dear friend and patron, the Right Hon. John Hookham Frere, who, of all men I have had the means of knowing during my life, appears to me eminently to deserve to be characterized as ὁ καλοκἄγαθος, ὁ φιλόκαλος."   Frere's sister and house companion died in 1839, and was buried by the side of his wife.   He also was laid beside her in the English burial-ground at Malta in January 1846.

The present edition of Frere's translation of " The Acharnians," "The Knights," and " The Birds " has been printed direct from copies printed for himself at Malta in 1839, and published by Pickering in 1840.   " The Works of John Hookham Frere, in Verse and Prose, now first collected, with a Prefatory Memoir by his nephews, W. E. and Sir Bartle Frere," were published in 1872, in volumes of which a handsome popular edition would be a delight to many readers.

H. M.

April 1886.

THE ACHARNIANS.

DICÆOPOLIS, whose name may be interpreted as conveying the idea of
honest policy, is the principal character in the play. He is represented as a humorous, shrewd countryman (a sort of Athenian
Sancho), who (in consequence of the war, and the invasion of Attica
by the Peloponnesian army) had been driven from his house and
property to take shelter in the city. Here his whole thoughts are
occupied with regret for the comforts he has lost, and with wishes
for a speedy peace. The soliloquy in which he appears in the
first scene, represents him seated alone in the place of Assembly,
having risen early to secure a good place, his constant practice (he
says), in order " to bawl, to abuse and interrupt the speakers," with
the exception of those, and those only, who are arguing in favour of
an immediate peace. But the magistrates and men of business,
not having so much leisure on their hands as the worthy countryman, are less punctual in their attendance, and he is kept waiting,
to his great discomfort ; their seats are empty, and the citizens in
the market-place are talking and idling, or shifting about to avoid
a most notable instrument of democratic coercion—namely, a cord
coloured with ochre, which the officers stretch across the market-
place in order to drive the loiterers to the place of Assembly ; those
that are overtaken by the rope, being marked by the ochre, besides
the damage to their dress, becoming liable to a nominal fine. To
avoid the sense of weariness, he is in the habit (as he tells us), upon
such occasions, of giving a forced direction to his thoughts ; and he
gives a sample of his mode of employing this expedient, in the very
first lines : he is tasking himself to recollect and sum up all the
things that had occurred of late either to gratify or to annoy him.
At length, however, he is relieved from the pursuit of this unsatisfactory pastime. The magistrates arrive and take their seats—the
place of Assembly is filled, and silence is proclaimed—when a new

personage enters hastily.   Here we have an instance of the peculiar
character of invention which belongs to the ancient comedy; in
which a bodily form and action is given to those images which have
no existence except in the forms of animated or fanciful language.
"If a deity were to come down among the Athenians and propose
to conclude a peace for them, they would not listen to him"—this
phrase is here exhibited in action; for the personage above mentioned is a demigod (descended immediately from Ceres herself, as
he proves by a very rapid and confident recitation of his genealogy),
but his offer of his services as a mediator are very ill received, and
he very narrowly escapes being taken into custody.

The next persons who present themselves to the Assembly are two
Envoys returned from a mission to the Court of Persia, which they
have contrived to prolong for several years.   They relate all the
hardships which they had undergone in luxurious entertainments
and in tedious journeys with a splendid equipage : they moreover
had been detained by an unforeseen circumstance on their arrival at
the capital.   The state of things was such as Autolycus describes :
"The King is not at the palace, he is gone to purge melancholy and
air himself:" but the King of Persia was not gone, like the King
of Bohemia, "on board a new ship;" he was gone with a magnificent military retinue to the Golden Mountains, where, according to
the Ambassadors' report, he continued for eight months in an
unremitting course of cathartics.   On his return to the capital, they
had the honour of being presented, and entertained at a most
singular and marvellous banquet ; finally, they had succeeded in
their mission, and had brought with them a confidential servant of
the Crown of Persia (a nobleman of high rank, though rather of a
suspicious name), Shamartabas, commissioned to declare His
Majesty's intention to the people of Athens.   Shamartabas holds
the distinguished office and title of the King's Eye: of course the
mask which is assigned him is distinguished by an eye of enormous
size, the appearance of which and the gravity of gesture suited to
such an exalted personage excite the rustic republican spleen of
honest Dicæopolis.   The communications of the great Persian
courtier, being in his own language and consequently unintelligible,
are variously interpreted.   Dicæopolis takes upon himself to question him peremptorily, and in the course of the examination dis-
covers a couple of effeminate Athenian fops, disguised as eunuchs,
in his train ; this discovery, however, creates no sensation.   The
King's Eye is invited with the usual honours to a banquet in the
Prytaneum ; but when Dicæopolis sees these impostors and enemies
of his country upon the point of being rewarded with a good dinner,
the indignation which is excited in his independent spirit decides at

once his future destinies and the conduct of all the scenes which follow. In that tone which a person is apt to employ when he fancies that the zeal of his friends gives him a right to command their services, he calls out very peremptorily for Amphitheus, and without any preamble or prefatory request, directs him to proceed to Sparta without loss of time, and to conclude a separate peace for him (Dicæopolis), his wife and family, advancing to him at the same time the principal sum of eight drachmas for that purpose.

Another Envoy now appears, returned from a Court of a different description. He has not, like the former, any complaints to make of having been overwhelmed with an excess of ostentation and and profusion from the Grand Monarque of those times; he has resided with a sort of contemporary Czar Peter, the Autocrat of Thrace, having lived (of course according to his own account) in a most jolly barbarous intimacy with that rising potentate, and inspiring him with the sincerest hearty zeal in favour of the polished state of Athens. His son, the heir apparent, had been admitted by the Athenians to the freedom of their city, an honour which, in their opinion (as well as in that of Mr. Peter Putty in Foote's farce), any prince ought to be proud of; and the Assembly are accordingly informed of the delight and enthusiasm with which the compliment had been accepted. They are presented moreover with a specimen of the auxiliary troops, somewhat singularly equipped, which their new ally is willing to employ in their service, but at a rate of pay which Dicæopolis exclaims against as scandalous. He has soon other causes of complaint; for attracted by the passion for garlic, which it seems is predominant amongst them, the Odomantians (for that is the name of the tribe to which the new warriors belong) begin their operations by plundering the store which Dicæopolis had provided for his own luncheon; outrageous at this injury, after reproaching the magistrates with their apathy in suffering it, he takes, what it seems was an effectual mode of dissolving the Assembly, by declaring that a storm is coming on, and affirming that he has felt a drop of rain. This sort of Polish veto nullifies the proceedings of the Assembly, which is accordingly dissolved. Dicæopolis is left lamenting over the pillage of his provisions, but his spirits are soon revived by the appearance of Amphitheus, who has returned with samples of treaties of peace or truces. These treaties or truces are typified by the wines employed in the libations by which they were ratified; a conceit, which in the language of the original appears less extravagant, the Greeks having only one and the same word by which they expressed the idea of a truce and that of the libation by which it was rendered valid. Amphitheus is in a hurry, having been (as he says) discovered and pursued by a

number of old rustics of Acharnæ, who since the ruin of the vineyards of their village by the invading army, had become furious
against a peace. Dicæopolis tastes and discusses the qualities of
the wines, and having fixed upon a sample of thirty years' growth,
goes away with a determination to avail himself of the change
in his affairs, by keeping the Feast of Bacchus once more in his own
village ; while Amphitheus runs off to avoid the Acharnians whom
he had outrun, but who are still in quest of him.

SCENE.—*The Pnyx.*

DICÆOPOLIS.

How many things there are to cross and vex me,
My comforts I compute at four precisely,
My griefs and miseries at a hundred thousand.
Let's see what there has happened to rejoice me
With any real kind of joyfulness ;
Come, in the first place I set down five talents,
Which Cleon vomited up again and refunded ;
There I rejoiced ; I loved the knights for that ;
'Twas nobly done, for the interests of all Greece.
But again I suffered cruelly in the theatre
A tragical disappointment—There was I
Gaping to hear old Æschylus, when the Herald
Called out, " Theognis,* bring your chorus forward."
Imagine what my feelings must have been !
But then Dexitheus pleased me coming forward
And singing his Bœotian melody :
But next came Chæris with his music truly,
That turned me sick, and killed me very nearly.
But never in my lifetime, man nor boy,
Was I so vexed as at this present moment;
To see the Pnyx, at this time of the morning,
Quite empty, when the Assembly should be full.
There are our citizens in the market-place,
Lounging and talking, shifting up and down

---

* A bad tragic poet, ridiculed in this play.

To escape the painted twine that ought to sweep
The shoal of them this way ; not even the Presidents
Arrived—they're always last, crowding and jostling
To get the foremost seat ; but as for peace
They never think about it—Oh, poor country !
As for myself, I'm always the first man.
Alone in the morning, here I take my place,
Here I contemplate, here I stretch my legs ;
I think and think—I don't know what to think.
I draw conclusions and comparisons,
I ponder, I reflect, I pick my nose,
I make a stink—I make a metaphor,
I fidget about, and yawn and scratch myself ;
Looking in vain to the prospect of the fields,
Loathing the city, longing for a peace,
To return to my poor village and my farm,
That never used to cry " Come buy my charcoal ! "
Nor, " Buy my oil ! " nor " Buy my anything ! "
But gave me what I wanted, freely and fairly,
Clear of all cost, with never a word of buying,
Or such buy-words. So here I'm come, resolved
To bawl, to abuse, to interrupt the speakers,
Whenever I hear a word of any kind
Except for an immediate peace.   Ah there !
The Presidents at last ; see, there they come !
All scrambling for their seats—I told you so !

HERALD. Move forward there !   Move forward all of ye
Further ! within the consecrated ground.

AMPHITHEUS. Has anybody spoke ?

HER.   Is anybody
Prepared to speak ?

AMP.   Yes, I.

HER.   Who are you and what ?

AMP. Amphitheus the demigod.

HER.   Not a man ?

AMP. No, I'm immortal; for the first Amphitheus
Was born of Ceres and Triptolemus,
His only son was Keleüs, Keleüs married
Phænarete my grandmother, Lykinus
My father, was their son ; that's proof enough
Of the immortality in our family.
The gods moreover have dispatched me here
Commissioned specially to arrange a peace
Betwixt this city and Sparta—notwithstanding
I find myself rather in want at present
Of a little ready money for my journey.
The magistrates won't assist me.

HER.   Constables !

AMP. O Keleüs and Triptolemus, don't forsake me !

DIC. You Presidents, I say ! you exceed your powers ;
You insult the Assembly, dragging off a man
That offered to make terms and give us peace.

HER. Keep silence there.

DIC.   By Jove, but I won't be silent,
Except I hear a motion about peace.

HER. Ho there ! the Ambassadors from the King of
    Persia.

DIC. What King of Persia ? what Ambassadors ?
I'm sick of foreigners and foreign animals,
Peacocks* and coxcombs and Ambassadors.

HER. Keep silence there.

DIC.   What's here ? What dress is that ?
In the name of Ecbatana !† What does it mean ?

---

* Peacocks had been introduced at the public charge, and were exhibited
monthly.   It is to be supposed that the exhibition had become rather
stale.

† The name of an unknown and extraordinary place is sometimes used to
express wonder.   In New England a thing is said to be "Jerusalem fine."
Flanders in the time of Philip III. served the Spaniards for a phrase of
wonder, "No hay mas Flandes."

AMB. You sent us when Euthymenes was Archon,
Some few years back, Ambassadors to Persia,
With an appointment of two drachmas each
For daily maintenance.

DIC.   Alas, poor drachmas !

AMB. 'Twas no such easy service, I can tell you,
No trifling inconvenience to be dragged
Along those dusty dull Caystrian plains,
Smothered with cushions in the travelling chariots,
Obliged to lodge at night in our pavilions,
Jaded and hacked to death.

DIC.   My service then
Was an easy one, you think ! on guard all night,
In the open air, at the outposts, on a mat.

AMB. .·. . . At our reception we were forced to drink
Strong luscious wine in cups of gold and crystal . . . .

DIC. O rock of Athens ! sure thy very stones
Should mutiny at such open mockery !

AMB. [*in continuation*]
. . . . with the barbarians 'tis the test of manhood.
There the great drinkers are the greatest men . . . .

DIC. As debauchees and coxcombs are with us.

AMB. [*in continuation*]
. . . . In the fourth year we reached the royal residence,
But found the Sovereign absent on a progress,
Gone with his army to the Golden Mountains,
To take his ease, and purge his royal person ;
There he remained eight months.

DIC.   When did he close
His course of medicine ?

AMB. With the full of the moon
He rose, and left his seat, returning homeward :
There he admitted us to an audience,
And entertained us at a royal banquet
With a service of whole oxen baked in crust.

Dic. Oxen in crust! what lies, what trumpery!
Did ever any mortal hear the like?

Amb. Besides they treated us with a curious bird,
Much bigger than our own Cleonymus.
'Tis called the Chousibus.

Dic.   Ay, by that same token
We're choused of our two drachmas.

Amb.   Finally,
We've brought you here a nobleman, Shamartabas
By name, by rank and office the King's Eye.

Dic. God send a crow to pick it out, I say,
And yours the Ambassador's into the bargain!

Her. Let the King's Eye come forward.

Dic.   Hercules!
What's here? an eye for the head of a ship!* what point,
What headland is he weathering? what's your course?
What makes you steer so steadily and so slowly?

Amb. Come now, Shamartabas, stand forth; declare
The King's intentions to the Athenian people.

> [Shamartabas *here utters some words, which Orien-*
> *talists have supposed to be the common formula*
> *prefixed to the edicts of the Persian Monarch—*
> Iartaman exarksan apissonai satra.]

---

* The imaginative spirit of antiquity had transformed the head of a ship into the likeness of a human face; the keel served for a nose, a painted eye being inserted on each side, and a portion of the convex projections of the bow was coloured red, to represent a pair of cheeks, whence the epithet "red-cheeked" is applied to ships in Homer. The face thus produced was appropriated to Medusa by the addition of two snakes *diverging from it,* and running along the gunwale (according to Hipponax's description "as if they were going to bite the head of the steersman"). The whole vessel was thus converted into the form of a protecting amulet. It appears by what Herodotus says of the oracle addressed to the Siphnians, that the "red cheeks" must have gone out of fashion in his time; but the "eye" is still universal in the Mediterranean, and the writer of this note has seen the snake in its proper position and direction, on the gunwale of small craft in the harbour of Valletta and in the Bay of Cadiz.

AMB. You understand it?

DIC.   No, by Jove, not I.

AMB. [*to* DICÆOPOLIS] He says the King intends to
send us gold.

[*to* SHAMARTABAS] Explain about the gold; speak more
distinctly.

SHAMARTABAS. Sen gooly Jaönau aphooly chest.

DIC. Well, that's distinct enough!

HER.   What does he say?

DIC. That it's a foolish jest for the Ionians
To imagine that the King would send them gold.

AMB. No, no!—He's telling ye of chests full of gold.

DIC. What chests? you're an impostor.—Stand away,
Keep off; and let me alone to question him.

    [*to* SHAMARTABAS]
You Sir, you Persian! answer me distinctly
And plainly, in presence of this fist of mine;
On pain of a royal purple bloody nose.
Will the King send us gold, or will he not?

    [SHAMARTABAS *shakes his head*]
Have our Ambassadors bamboozled us?

    [SHAMARTABAS *nods*]
These fellows nod to us in the Grecian fashion;
They're some of our own people, I'll be bound.
One of those eunuchs there I'm sure I know:
I'm positive it's Cleisthenes the Siburtian.
How durst you, you baboon, with such a beard,
And your designing wicked rump close shaved,
To pass yourself upon us for a eunuch?
And who's this other? Sure enough it's Strato!

   HER. Silence there! Keep your seats!
The Senate have invited the King's Eye
To feast with them in the Prytaneum.

   DIC.   There—
An't it enough to drive one mad? to drive one

To hang himself? to be kept here in attendance,
Working myself into a strangury;
Whilst every door flies open to these fellows.
But I'll do something desperate and decided.
Where is Amphitheus got to?

    AMP.   Here am I.

    DIC. There—Take you these eight drachmas on my
        part,
And make a separate peace for me with Sparta,
For me, my wife and children and maidservant.
And you—Go on with your embassies and fooleries.

    HER. Theorus, our ambassador into Thrace,
Returned from King Sitalces!*

    THEO.   Here am I.

    DIC. More coxcombs called for! Here's another coming.

    THEO. We should not have remained so long in
        Thrace . . . .

    DIC. If you hadn't been overpaid I know you wouldn't.

    THEO. But for the snow, which covered all the country,
And buried up the roads, and froze the rivers.
'Twas singular this change of weather happened
Just when Theognis here, our frosty poet,
Brought out his tragedy. We passed our time
In drinking with Sitalces. He's your friend,
Your friend and lover, if there ever was one,
And writes the name of Athens on his walls.†
His son, your new-made fellow-citizen,
Had wished to have been enrolled in proper form
At the Apaturian festival; and meanwhile,
During his absence, earnestly desires

---

* Theorus is noted in the "Wasps" as a flattering, super-civil, parasitical person. See his efforts at reconciliation in the next page.

† The common practice of lovers both in ancient and modern times; but in this instance there is probably an allusion to some public monuments which recorded the king's alliance with the Athenians in terms flattering to their national vanity.

That the Apaturian sausages may be sent to him.
He is urgent with his father to befriend
His newly adopted countrymen ; and in fine
Sitalces has been so far worked upon,
He has sworn at last his solemn Thracian oath,
Standing before the sacrifice, to send
Such an army, he said, that all the Athenian people
Shall think that there's a flight of locusts coming.

DIC. Then hang me if I believe a word about it,
Except their being locusts ; that seems likely.

THEO. And now he has sent some warriors from a tribe
The fiercest in all Thrace.

DIC.   Well, come—That's fair.

HER. The Thracians that came hither with Theorus !
Let them come forward !

DIC.   What the plague are these ?

THEO. The Odomantian army.

DIC.   The Odomantians ?
Thracians ? and what has brought them here from Thrace
So strangely equipt, disguised, and circumcised ?

THEO. These are a race of fellows, if you'd hire 'em,
Only at a couple of drachmas daily pay ;
With their light javelins, and their little bucklers,
They'd worry and skirmish over all Bœotia.

DIC. Two drachmas for those scarecrows ! and our
        seamen
What would they say to it ?—left in arrears,
Poor fellows, that are our support and safeguard.
Out, out upon it ! I'm a plundered man.
I'm robbed and ruined here with the Odomantians.
They're seizing upon my garlic.

THEO. [*to the* THRACIANS] Oh, for shame,
Let the man's garlic alone.   You shabby fellow,
You countryman, take care what you're about ;
Don't venture near them when they're primed with garlic.

Dic. You magistrates, have you the face to see it,
With your own eyes—your fellow-citizen
Here, in the city itself, robbed by barbarians?
But I forbid the Assembly.　There's a change
In the heaven!　I felt a drop of rain!　I'm witness!

Her. The Thracians must withdraw, to attend again
The first of next month.　The Assembly is closed.

Dic. Lord help me, what a luncheon have I lost!
But there's Amphitheus coming back from Sparta.
Welcome Amphitheus!

Amp.　　　　　　　　I'm not welcome yet,
There are the Acharnians pursuing me!

Dic. How so?

Amp.　　　　　　　I was coming here to bring the treaties,
But a parcel of old Acharnians smelt me out,
Case-hardened, old, inveterate, hard-handed
Veterans of Marathon, hearts of oak and iron,
Slingers and smiters.　They bawled out and bellowed:
" You dog, you villain! now the vines are ruined,
You're come with treaties, are you?"　Then they stopped,
Huddling up handfuls of great slinging stones
In the lappets of their cloaks, and I ran off,
And they came driving after me pell-mell,
Roaring and shouting.

Dic.　　　　　　　　Aye, why let them roar!
You've brought the treaties?

Amp.　　　　　　　　　Aye, three samples of 'em;
This here is a five years' growth, taste it and try.

Dic. Don't like it!

Amp.　　　　　　Eh?

Dic.　　　　　　　　Don't like it; it won't do;
There's an uncommon ugly twang of pitch,
A touch of naval armament about it.

Amp. Well, here's a ten years' growth, may suit you
　　better.

Dic. No, neither of them.   There's a sort of sourness
Here in this last, a taste of acid embassies,
And vapid allies turning to vinegar.

Amp. But here's a truce of thirty years entire,
Warranted sound.

Dic.   O Bacchus and the Bacchanals !
This is your sort ! here's nectar and ambrosia !
Here's nothing about providing three days' rations ;
It says, " Do what you please, go where you will."
I choose it, and adopt it, and embrace it,
For sacrifice and for my private drinking.
In spite of all the Acharnians, I'm determined
To remove out of the reach of wars and mischief,
And keep the feast of Bacchus in my farm.

Amp. And I'll run off to escape from those Acharnians.

Masses of men, when in a state of excitement, whatever may be their
collective character or purpose, are apt to separate into two divi-
sions; those of a milder and more reasonable temper taking the
one side, and the more ardent and intractable taking the other. This
is exemplified in two Semichoruses. The first are upon the point of
abandoning their pursuit, while the second persevere in it with
unabated eagerness, indefatigable and (as they afterwards show
themselves) implacable. The first, on the contrary, are by degrees
pacified and induced to listen to reason.

This difference of feeling finally produces a struggle between them, in
which those who are of "milder mood" obtain the advantage ; and
their opponents are obliged to call for assistance from Lamachus, a
romantic, enthusiastic military character, and, of course, as decided
an advocate for war as Dicæopolis (the poet's dramatic representative) is for peace. Lamachus appears in his gorgeous armour.
Dicæopolis, under the affectation of extreme terror and simplicity,
contrives to banter and provoke him. Lamachus proceeds to
violence, and is foiled ; after which a dispute is carried on for some
time between them upon equal terms ; and they finally separate
with a declaration of their respective determinations ; the one
looking forward to military achievement, and the other to commer-
cial profit and enjoyment.

It may be necessary to say something of an attempt that has been
made in the translation of the following Chorus to convey to the

English reader some notion of the metrical character of the original. The poet himself has described the metre as bold and manly, expressive of firmness and vehemence, and, as such, suitable to the persons of whom his Chorus is composed. The Cretic metre (for that is its name) consists of a quaver between two crotchets (— ‿ —), and may be considered as a truncated form of the Trochaic, differing from it only by the subtraction of a short or quaver-syllable ; the Trochaic itself consisting of four syllables, a crotchet and quaver alternately (— ‿ — ‿). In consequence of this affinity, we find that the two metres frequently pass into each other.

In the instance before us, the Chorus begins with the Trochaic, but after the first four lines passes into the Cretic ; the second Cretic line exhibits a variety of frequent occurrence in the Greek, the last crotchet being resolved into two quavers (— ‿ ‿ ‿). Moreover, the altercation between Dicæopolis and the Chorus is kept up for some time in Trochaics and Cretics alternately.

CHORUS.

Follow faster ! all together ! search, inquire of every one.
Speak, inform us, have you seen him ? Whither is the rascal
   run ?
'Tis a point of public service that the traitor should be
   caught
In the fact, seized and arrested with the treaties that he
   brought.

SEMICHORUS I.

He's escaped, he's escaped—
Out upon it ! Out upon it !—
Out of sight, out of search.
O the sad wearisome
Load of years !
. Well do I remember such a burden as I bore
Running with Phayllus* with a hamper at my back,
Out alack,
Years ago.

---

* An eminent conqueror in the foot-race at Olympia. There was probably some story of his having been matched (under certain disadvantages) against an active man who had been used to run under a burden.

But, alas, my sixty winters and my sad rheumatic pain
Break my speed and spoil my running,—and that old
    unlucky sprain.
He's escaped—

SEMICHORUS II.

    But we'll pursue him. Whether we be fast or slow,
He shall learn to dread the peril of an old Acharnian foe.
O Supreme Powers above,
Merciful Father Jove,
Oh, the vile miscreant wretch ;
How did he dare,
How did he presume in his unutterable villany to make a
    peace,
Peace with the detestable, abominable Spartan race.
No, the war must not end—
Never end—till the whole Spartan tribe
Are reduced, trampled down,
Tied and bound, hand and foot.
    CHOR. Now we must renew the search, pursuing at a
    steady pace.
Soon or late we shall secure him, hunted down from place
    to place.
Look about like eager marksmen, ready with your slings and
    stones.
How I long to fall upon him, the villain, and to smash his
    bones !

Enter DICÆOPOLIS, *his* WIFE *and* DAUGHTER, *a*
SLAVE, *&c.*

    DIC. Peace, Peace.
        Silence, Silence.
    CHOR. Stand aside ! Keep out of sight ! List to the
    sacrificial cries !
There he comes, the very fellow, going out to sacrifice.

Wait and watch him for a minute, we shall have him by
  surprise.

DIC. Silence! move forward, the Canephora;
You, Xanthias, follow close behind her there,
In a proper manner, with your pole and emblem.

WIFE. Set down the basket, daughter, and begin
The ceremony.

DAUGHTER.   Give me the cruet, mother,
And let me pour it upon the holy cake.

DIC. Oh, blessed Bacchus, what a joy it is
To go thus unmolested, undisturbed,
My wife, my children, and my family,
With our accustomed joyful ceremony,
To celebrate thy festival in my farm.
Well, here's success to the truce of thirty years.

WIFE. Mind your behaviour, child; carry the basket
In a modest proper manner; look demure
And grave; a happy fellow will he be
That gives more than an eye to ye.—Come, move on.
Mind your gold trinkets, they'll be stolen else.

DIC. Follow behind there, Xanthias, with the pole,
And I'll strike up the bacchanalian chant.
Wife, you must be spectator; go within,
And mount to the housetop to behold us pass.

DIC. [*Sings*]
Leader of the revel rout,
Of the drunken roar and shout,
Crazy mirth and saucy jesting,
Frolic and intrigue clandestine!
Half a dozen years are passed,*
Here we meet in peace at last.

---

* This comedy was produced in 425 B.C., the sixth year of the Peloponnesian war.

All my wars and fights are o'er :
Other battles please me more,
  With my neighbour's maid, the Thracian,
Found marauding in the wood ;
Seizing on the fair occasion,
  With a quick retaliation
Making an immediate booty
Of her innocence and beauty.
If a drunken head should ache,
Bones and heads we never break.
If we quarrel overnight;
At a full carousing soak,
In the morning all is right ;
And the shield hung out of sight
In the chimney smoke.
  CHOR. That's the man.   Mind your aim ;
Pelt away—Pelt away.
    DIC. Heaven and Earth ! what's here to do ? You'll
      break the pitcher, have a care !
  CHOR. We'll break your head,
We'll break your bones,
We'll pummel you to death with stones.
    DIC. Tell me, most serene Acharnians, wherefore, upon
      what pretence ?
  CHOR. Impudence ! Insolence !
Infamous traitor, do ye dare to ask ?
In despite
Of duty and right,—
Duty to the state,
Duty to the laws,—
You've presumed to separate
Your private cause,
With the villainous abuse
Of a treasonable truce.

And you dare,
Standing there,
Void of shame, void of grace,
To look us in the face.

Dic. But my motive—Once again, let me be heard, and
I'll explain.

Chor. No reply. You shall die,
Stoned and buried all at once,
Buried in a heap of stones.

Dic. Have patience, do ! forbear a bit !
You've never heard my reasons yet.

Chor. We've forborne, long enough ;
Say no more. Trash and stuff !
We detest you worse than Cleon, him that, if he gets his
dues,
We shall cut up into thongs to serve the knights for straps
and shoes.
We'll not hear ye ; your alliance with the worst of enemies,
With the wicked hated Spartans, we'll avenge it and chastise.

Dic. Don't be talking of the Spartans; 'tis another
question wholly,
All my guilt or innocence depends upon the treaty solely.

Chor. Don't imagine to cajole us with your arguments
and fetches ;
You confess you made a peace with those abominable
wretches.

Dic. Well, the very Spartans even,—I've my doubts and
scruples whether
They've been totally to blame, in ev'ry instance, altogether.

Chor. Not to blame in every instance ! Villain, vagabond,
how dare ye,
Talking treason to our faces, to suppose that we should
spare ye.

Dic. Not so totally to blame ; and I would show that,
here and there,

The treatment they received from us has not been absolutely fair.

CHOR. What a scandal ! what an insult ! what an outrage
on the state !

Are ye come to plead before us as the Spartans' advocate ?

DIC. I'm prepared to plead the cause, and bring my neck
here for a pledge,

Placed upon the chopping-block, ready to meet the axe's
edge.

CHOR. Don't be standing shilly-shally, comrades, let the
traitor die.

Pummel him with stones to pieces, pound and maul him
utterly,

Mash the villain to a jelly, like a vat of purple dye.

DIC. I'm astonished at your temper. Won't you give me
leave to say

Something in my own defence, my good Acharnians ? Hear
me, pray !

CHOR. We're determined not to hear ye.

DIC.   That will be severe indeed.

CHOR. We're determined.

DIC.   Good Acharnians, give me time
and hear me plead.

CHOR. Death awaits you, death this instant.

DIC.   Then the quick resolve is taken.

Know that I've secured a hostage destined to redeem my
bacon.*

He, your homebred kindly kinsman, he with me shall live
or perish.

CHOR. What's the matter ? Is there any child or infant
that you cherish,

Missing here amongst you, neighbours, whom he keeps
confined in durance ?

---

* The extravagant burlesque which follows, turns upon the occupation of
the Acharnians as charcoal-burners.

What can else inspire the man with such a confident
assurance ?

Dic. Strike, destroy me then, while I shall act in turn
the assassin's part,

If the native love of charcoal moves not your obdurate
heart.

> [Dicæopolis *discovers a hamper of charcoal, and
> stands over it in a menacing theatrical attitude,
> with a sword drawn.*]

Chor. O forbear ! see there !
See the poor natural Acharnian hamper of our own,
Ready to be overthrown.
Spare it, I beseech thee, spare.*

Dic. I'll not hear ; the word is passed.   Poor thing, this
instant is its last.

Chor. Spare it as our only joy,
Our solace and employ,
The staff of our declining years.

Dic. You, when I besought a hearing, armed your hands
and shut your ears.

Chor. Yes, but now we'll permit,
We'll dispense, we'll allow
Your defence.
Our beloved
Darling is at stake.
We submit
Wholly for his sake.

---

* A burlesque of some scene in a contemporary tragedy in which the
actors were "brought to a dead-lock." It should seem as if in the original
here parodied, the assailants had been kept at bay by the counter-menace
of destroying some royal infant in a cradle, which suggested the substitute
of a hamper of charcoal. In one of the existing tragedies of Euripides
there is an instance of a dead-lock quite as decided as the one which seems
to be parodied here.

Dic. Before we parley or compound, cast me those
  pebbles to the ground.
Chor. See there, all's fair.
    But keep your word, sheath the sword.
Dic. Other pebbles may be lurking in the lappets of your
  jerkin.
Chor. Never fear, never doubt;
See them here shaken out.
There's none behind : only mind,
Keep your word, sheath the sword.
And here I fling stone and sling,
Sling and stone, both away,
Both in one ; both are gone.
    Dic. Well now, will you please to have done with your
      noise and nonsense,
And fling them away, too, both.   Fine work you've made,
A pretty business ! Look there at your hamper.
What a taking the poor creature has been in,
Voiding its coal-dust, like a cuttle-fish,
For very fright ; nearly destroyed, in short,
Merely from a want of temper and discretion
On the part of its own friends.*   'Tis passing strange,
That human nature should be so possessed
With a propensity to pelt and bawl ;
When gentle easy Reason might decide
All their debates with order, peace, and law ;
When I myself stand here resigned, and ready
To plead my cause before a chopping-block,
To vindicate the Spartans and myself.
Yet I, forsooth, can feel the fear of death,
And hold my life as dear as others do.
    Chor. Bring the block ! Bring it here !
      Rogue, for I long to hear

---

* Parody of the rhetorical style of Euripides.

Speedily whatever you can have to say.
Speak away.

SEMICHORUS.

'Twas your own choice, your own appointed pledge.
Bring forth the chopping-block, and speak away.
Dic. Well, there it is. See, there's the chopping-block!
And little I myself am the defendant.
Depend upon it, I'll fight manfully.
I'll never hug myself within my shield;
I'll speak my mind, moreover, about the Spartans.
And yet forsooth a secret anxious fear
Appals me; for I know the turn and temper
Of rustic natures, then delighted most
When from some bold declaimer, right or wrong,
They hear their country's praises and their own;
Delighted, but deluded all the while,
Unconsciously bamboozled and befooled.
And well I know the minds of aged men,
And the malignant pleasure that they feel
In a harsh verdict or an angry vote.
And well I recollect my sufferings past
From Cleon, for my comedy last year; *
And how he dragged me to the senate house,
And trod me down, and bellowed over me,
And licked me with the rough side of his tongue;
And mauled me, till I scarce escaped alive,
All battered and bespattered and befouled.
Permit me, therefore, first to clothe myself
In a pathetical and heartrending dress.
Chor. It's no use! mere excuse!
Mere pretence!
Take what you will for your defence,

---

* The Babylonians.

Anything you think of use,
Even the invisible huge hobgoblin helmet
Of the learned Hieronymus,* if you choose.

     I care not, I;
     You may try
The tricks and turns of Sisyphus in the play ; †
We grant free leave for all, but no delay.

  DIC. Well, I must try then to keep up my spirits,
And trudge away to find Euripides.
Holloh!

  SERVANT. Who's there?

  DIC.   Euripides within?

  SERV. Within, yet not within. You comprehend me?

  DIC. Within and not within! why, what do ye mean?

  SERV. I speak correctly, old sire ! his outward man
Is in the garret writing tragedy ;
While his essential being is abroad,
Pursuing whimsies in the world of fancy.

  DIC. O happy Euripides, with such a servant ;
So clever and accomplished !—call him out.

  SERV. It's quite impossible.

  DIC.   But it must be done.
Positively and absolutely I must see him ;
Or I must stand here, rapping at the door.
Euripides ! Euripides ! come down,
If ever you came down in all your life !
'Tis I, 'tis Dicæopolis from Chollidæ.‡

  EUR. I'm not at leisure to come down.

  DIC.   Perhaps—
But here's the scene-shifter can wheel you round.

---

  * A lyrical and tragic poet particularly studious of the terrific.

  † This play is lost, but Sisyphus had been represented in old poetic legends as so artful a person, that he had persuaded Proserpine to consent to his release from the infernal regions.

  ‡ A mark of rusticity. Dicæopolis mentions his demus in addition to his name.

EUR. It cannot be.

DIC. But however, notwithstanding.

EUR. Well, there then I'm wheeled round ; for I had not
    time
For coming down.

DIC. Euripides, I say !

EUR. What say ye ?

DIC. Euripides ! Euripides !
Good lawk, you're there ! upstairs ! you write upstairs,
Instead of the ground-floor ? always upstairs.
Well now, that's odd !   But, dear Euripides,
If you had but a suit of rags that you could lend me.
You're he that brings out cripples in your tragedies ;
A'nt ye ?   You're the new poet, he that writes
Those characters of beggars and blind people.
Well, dear Euripides, if you could but lend me
A suit of tatters from a cast-off tragedy.
For mercy's sake, for I'm obliged to make
A speech in my own defence before the Chorus,
A long pathetic speech this very day ;
And if it fails, the doom of death betides me.

EUR. Say, what do ye seek ? is it the woeful garb
In which the wretched aged Œneus acted ?

DIC. No, 'twas a wretcheder man than Œneus, much.*

EUR. Was it blind Phœnix?

DIC.   · No, not Phœnix, no,
A fellow a great deal wretcheder than Phœnix.

EUR. I wonder what he wants ; is it the rags
Which Philoctetes went a begging with ?

DIC. No, 'twas a beggar worse than Philoctetes.

EUR. Say, would you wish to wear those loathly weeds,
The habiliments of lame Bellerophon ?

---

* This and the names which follow refer to personages in those dramas
of Euripides in which his object had been (what in poetry, as in real life, is
the meanest of all), to excite compassion.

Dic. 'Twas not Bellerophon, but very like him.
A kind of a smooth, fine spoken character;
A beggar into the bargain and a cripple,
With a grand command of words, bothering and begging.

Eur. I know your man; 'tis Telephus the Mysian.

Dic. Ah, Telephus! Yes, Telephus! do, pray,
Give me the things he wore.

Eur.   Go fetch them there.
You'll find 'em next to the tatters of Thyestes,
Just over Ino's. Take them, there, and welcome.

Dic. O Jupiter, what an infinite endless mass
Of eternal holes and patches! Here it is,
Here's wherewithal to clothe myself in misery.
Euripides, now, since you've gone so far,
Do give me the other articles besides
Belonging to these rags, that suit with them,
With a little Mysian bonnet for my head.
For I must wear a beggar's garb to-day,
Yet be myself in spite of my disguise;
That the audience all may know me; but the Chorus,
Poor creatures, must not have the least suspicion
Whilst I cajole them with my rhetoric.

Eur. I'll give it you; your scheme is excellent,
Deep, subtle, natural, a profound device.

Dic. " May the heavens reward you; and as to
    Telephus,*
May they decide his destiny as I wish ! "
Why, bless me, I'm quite inspired (I think) with phrases.
I shall want the beggar's staff, though, notwithstanding.

Eur. Here, take it, and depart forth from the palace.

Dic. O my poor heart! much hardship hast thou borne,
And must abide new sorrows even now,

---

* In the play which is here burlesqued, Telephus had been speaking in
an assumed character, and had appeared, with a similar ambiguous form,
to be imprecating evil upon himself.

Driven hence in want of various articles.
Subdue thy nature to necessity,
Be supple, smooth, importunate, and bend
Thy temper to the level of thy fortune.—
Yet grant me another boon, Euripides ;
A little tiny basket let it be,
One that has held a lamp, all burnt and battered.

　　Eur. Why should you need it ?
　　Dic.　　　　　　　　　　'Tis no need, perhaps,
But strong desire, a longing, eager wish.

　　Eur. You're troublesome.　Depart.
　　Dic.　　　　　　　　　　　　　Alas, alas !
Yet may you prosper like your noble mother.*

　　Eur. Depart, I say.
　　Dic.　　　　　　　Don't say so !　Give me first,
First give me a pipkin broken at the brim.

　　Eur. You're troublesome in the mansion.　Take it, go !
　　Dic. Alas, you know not what I feel, Euripides.
Yet grant me a pitcher, good Euripides ;
A pitcher with a sponge plugged in its mouth.

　　Eur. Fellow, you'll plunder me a whole tragedy.
Take it, and go.

　　Dic.　　　　Yes ; aye forsooth, I'm going.
But how shall I contrive ?　There's something more
That makes or mars my fortune utterly ;
Yet give them, and bid me go, my dear Euripides ;
A little bundle of leaves to line my basket.

　　Eur. For mercy's sake ! . . . . But take them,　There
　　　　they go !
My tragedies and all ! ruined and robbed !

　　Dic. No more ; I mean to trouble you no more.
Yes, I retire ; in truth I feel myself
Importunate, intruding on the presence

---

* His mother was of very low condition.

Of chiefs and princes, odious and unwelcome.
But out, alas, that I should so forget
The very point on which my fortune turns;
I wish I may be hanged, my dear Euripides,
If ever I trouble you for anything,
Except one little, little, little boon,
A single lettuce from your mother's stall.

    EUR. This stranger taunts us.   Close the palace gate.

    DIC. O my poor soul, endure it and depart,
And take thy sorrowful leave, without a lettuce.
Yet, knowest thou yet the race which must be run,
Pleading the cause of Sparta : and here you stand
Even at the goal ; time urges, arm yourself !
Infuse the spirit of Euripides,
His quirks and quibbles, in thine inmost heart !
'Tis well.   Now forward, even to the place
Where thou must pledge thy life, and plead the cause
As may befall thee.   Forward, forward yet ;
A little more.   I'm dreadfully out of spirits.

SEMICHORUS II.*

Speak, or are ye dumb,
    Thou rogue in grain,
    Iron brain !
    Heart of stone !
Villain, are ye come,
    Venturing your head alone,
    Singly to support a treason of your own.

SEMICHORUS I.

He's resolved,
    Confident,
    Firm in his intent,

---

* See p. 23, for the characters of the two Semichoruses.

Ready to the day.
—Well, my man !
Since that's your plan,
Speak away !
[*In the following lines there is an intentional imi-
tation of the dry drawling style of* EURIPIDES'
harangues.]
DIC. Be not surprised, most excellent spectators,
If I that am a beggar, have presumed
To claim an audience upon public matters,
Even in a comedy ; for comedy
Is conversant in all the rules of justice,
And can distinguish betwixt right and wrong.
The words I speak are bold, but just and true.
Cleon, at least, cannot accuse me now,
That I defame the city before strangers.
For this is the Lenæan festival,
And here we meet, all by ourselves alone ;
No deputies are arrived as yet with tribute,
No strangers or allies ; but here we sit
A chosen sample, clean as sifted corn,
With our own denizens as a kind of chaff.
First, I detest the Spartans most extremely ;
And wish, that Neptune, the Tænarian deity,
Would bury them in their houses with his earthquakes.
For I've had losses—losses, let me tell ye,
Like other people ; vines cut down and injured.
But, among friends (for only friends are here),
Why should we blame the Spartans for all this ?
For people of ours, some people of our own,
Some people from amongst us here, I mean ;
But not the people (pray remember that) ;
I never said the people—but a pack
Of paltry people, mere pretended citizens,
Base counterfeits, went laying informations,

And making a confiscation of the jerkins
Imported here from Megara; pigs moreover,
Pumpkins, and pecks of salt, and ropes of onions,
Were voted to be merchandise from Megara,
Denounced, and seized, and sold upon the spot.
   Well, these might pass, as petty local matters.
But now, behold, some doughty drunken youths
Kidnap, and carry away from Megara,
The courtesan Simætha.   Those of Megara,
In hot retaliation, seize a brace
Of equal strumpets, hurried force perforce
From Dame Aspasia's house of recreation.
So this was the beginning of the war,
All over Greece, owing to these three strumpets.
For Pericles, like an Olympian Jove,
With all his thunder and his thunderbolts,
Began to storm and lighten dreadfully,
Alarming all the neighbourhood of Greece ;
And made decrees, drawn up like drinking songs,
In which it was enacted and concluded,
That the Megarians should remain excluded
From every place where commerce was transacted, ·
With all their ware—like " old care "—in the ballad :
And this decree, by land and sea, was valid.*
   Then the Megarians, being all half starved,
Desired the Spartans, to desire of us,
Just to repeal those laws ; the laws I mentioned,
Occasioned by the stealing of those strumpets.
And so they begged and prayed us several times ;
And we refused ; and so they went to war.
You'll say, " They should not." Why, what should they
    have done?

---

* The rhymes in the text are intentional. The Scholiast tells us that the
original contains an allusion to the words of a well-known drinking song.

Just make it your own case ; suppose the Spartans
Had manned a boat, and landed on your islands,
And stolen a pug puppy from Seriphos ;
Would you then have remained at home inglorious?
Not so, by no means ; at the first report,
You would have launched at once three hundred galleys,
And filled the city with the noise of troops ;
And crews of ships, crowding and clamouring
About the muster-masters and pay-masters ;
With measuring corn out at the magazine,
And all the porch choked with the multitude ;
With figures of Minerva, newly furbished,
Painted and gilt, parading in the streets ;
With wineskins, kegs, and firkins, leeks and onions ;
With garlic crammed in pouches, nets, and pokes ;
With garlands, singing girls, and bloody noses.
Our arsenal would have sounded and resounded
With bangs and thwacks of driving bolts and nails ;
With shaping oars, and holes to put the oar in ;
With hacking, hammering, clattering, and boring ;
Words of command, whistles and pipes and fifes.
    " Such would have been your conduct.   Will you say,
That Telephus should have acted otherwise ? "
    2ND SEMICH. Really ! is it come to that? You rogue,
        how dare ye,
A beggar, here to come abusing us,
Slandering us all, inveighing against informers ?
    1ST SEMICH. By Jove, but it's all true ; truth, every
        word ;
All true ; not aggravated in the least.
    2ND SEMICH. And if it is, what right has he to say so ?
None in the world ; and he shall suffer for it.
    1ST SEMICH. Hands off there ! what are ye after? Leave
        him go !
I'll grapple ye else, and heave ye neck and crop.

2ND SEMICH. Lamachus! Lamachus!
Lamachus arise!
Let the gaze,
Of thine eyes,
In a blaze,
Daunt and amaze
Thine enemies.
Bring along
All the throng,
Hardy comrades, bold and strong,
For assault or standing fight;
Hasten and assist the right.

LAMACHUS. Whence came that noise of battle on mine
ears?
Where am I summoned? whither must I rush?
To the rescue or assault? what angry shout
Rouses the slumbering Gorgon on my shield?

DIC. O Lamachus, with your glorious crests and con-
quests!

2ND SEMICH. O Lamachus! if there an't this fellow here
Abusing us and all the State this long while

LAM. How dare ye, sirrah, a beggar to talk thus?

DIC. O mighty Lamachus, have mercy upon me,
If, being a beggar, I prated and spoke amiss.

LAM. What were your words? repeat them, can't ye?

DIC.   I can't.
I can't remember; I'm so terrified.
The terror of that crest quite turned me dizzy;
Do take the hobgoblin away from me, I beseech you.

LAM. There then.

DIC.   Now turn it upside down.

LAM.   See there.

DIC. Now give me one of the feathers.

LAM.   Here, this plume.
Take it.

Dic. Now clasp your hands across my forehead,
For I feel that I shall strain in vomiting.
Those crests turned me so sick !
Lam.   What are you doing?
You varlet, would you use my plume for a vomit?
Dic. A plume, do you call it?   What does it belong to?
Lam. To a bird—
Dic.   To a cock lorrel, does it not?
Lam. Ah, you shall die.   [*A scuffle, in which* LAMACHUS
   is foiled.]
Dic.   No, Lamachus, not so fast.
That's rather a point above you, stout as you are.
Lam. Is this the sort of language for a beggar
To use to a commander such as me?
Dic. A beggar am I?
Lam.   Why, what else are you?
Dic. I'll tell ye ! an honest man ; that's what I am.
A citizen that has served his time in the army,
As a foot soldier, fairly ; not like you,
Pilfering, and drawing pay, with a pack of foreigners.
Lam. They voted me a command.
Dic.   Who voted it?
A parcel of cuckoos ! Well, I've made my peace.
In short, I could not abide the thing, not I ;
To see grey-headed men serve in the ranks,
And lads like you despatched upon commissions ;
Some skulking away to Thrace, with their three drachmas ;
Tisamenus's, Chares's, and Geres's,
Cheats, coxcombs, vagabonds, and Phænippus's,
And Theodorus's sent off to Gela,*
And Catana, and Camarina, and the Catamountains.

---

* The Scholiast mentions all these persons as disreputable intriguers.
The Athenians were already extending their views to Sicily.

LAM. It passed by a vote.

DIC. But what's the reason, pray,
For you to be sent out with salaries always,
And none of these good people? You, Marilades,*
Have you been ever sent on an embassy?
You're old enough. He shakes his head. Not he!
Yet he's a hard-working steady sober man.
And you, Euphorides, Prinides,* and the rest,
Have you ever been out into Chaonia,
Or up to Ecbatana?—no, not one of ye.
But Megacles, and Lamachus, and such like,
That, with their debts and payments long since due,†
Have heard their friends insisting and repeating,
"Get off,"—"Keep out of the way;" like the huswife's
    warning,
That empties a nuisance into the street at night.

LAM. And must we bear all this,—in the name of
    democracy?

DIC. Yes, just as long as Lamachus draws his salary.

LAM. No matter! Henceforth I devote myself
Against the Peloponnesians, whilst I live,
To assault and harass them by land and sea.

DIC. And I proclaim for all the Peloponnesians
And Thebans and Megarians, a free market;
Where they may trade with me, but not with Lamachus.

The Parabasis, in which the Chorus was brought forward to speak in
    praise or defence of the author, was a portion of the *primitive*
    satirical undramatic comedy. In the times of the *ancient* or (as we
    should call it, from the name of the only author whose remains
    have reached us) the Aristophanic comedy, it seems to have been
    regarded as nearly superfluous; and is seldom introduced without
    some alleged motive, as in the instance before us; sometimes a
    burlesque one, as in "The Peace."

* Names allusive to their occupation as charcoal-burners.
† Monthly payments to their club.

The present, which is the oldest of the existing plays of Aristophanes, was, as he tells us, the first in which he had introduced a Parabasis. Since his alleged, and probably his real, motive was the circum·stance to which he had already alluded when speaking in the assumed character of Dicæopolis, he had reverted to his

> "sufferings past
> From Cleon, for my comedy last year" (p. 32).

This comedy ("The Babylonians") seems, as far as we can judge of it from the few fragments that remain, to have been intended, in the first place, as an exposure of existing malpractices and abuses, and, secondly, as a *reductio ad absurdum* of the extravagant schemes of Athenian ambition ; assuming them to be realized, and exhibiting the result.

The progressive aggrandizement of Athens had been marked, from the beginning, by the extortion and oppression practised (with a few honourable exceptions) by her military commanders ; Themistocles himself having set the first example. In process of time, as the inferior allied States became gradually subject to the more imme·diate dominion of Athens, they became exposed to the additional pest of professional informers and venal demagogues, subsisting or enriching themselves by extortion and bribery. This state of things, odious and offensive to the whole Grecian race, disgraceful to the Athenian people, and profitable only to the most worthless and un·principled among them, was the final unsatisfactory result of their vast efforts and indefatigable activity during two generations, the con·summation of the ambitious projects of the most able statesmen of a former age. Meanwhile, at the time when this play ("The Baby·lonians") was produced, the same scandals and abuses continued to be perpetrated in the subject States, under the cover of the Athenian supremacy; while the avidity for further conquest and dominion still remained predominant in the minds of the Athenian people.

The poet then, in the fervour of youthful patriotism and the pride of conscious genius ; not as he was soon afterwards tempted to become and to constitute himself, a professional playwright, the poetical serf of the community ;* but with the option of active life still open before him, comparatively therefore independent of his audience, and confident in his own wit and courage as a defence against the resentment of the most powerful opponents; had ventured an appeal to the Athenian people against their whole system of imperial policy both internal and external, against the grievances

---

* These inferences are distinctly deducible from the Parabasis of "The Knights."

which they authorized or overlooked, and against their insatiable avidity for empire, tending, if attainable, in its unavoidable results, to the wider extension and aggravation of a system of abuses disgraceful to the name and character of the Athenian people.

With this view therefore, taking for his canvas an imaginary empire, extending to the furthest limits to which the wildest ambition of his countrymen would have aspired, he had transferred to its remote localities the practices of the most notorious Athenian characters, and the most flagrant instances of existing oppression and corruption. The demagogues and informers of Athens (under this supposed unlimited extension of Athenian supremacy) were represented as transacting business on a larger scale, and extending to the richest and most distant regions of the East the practices which had hitherto been limited to the islands of the Archipelago and the shores of Asia Minor.

The poet, however, must have been aware that he had undertaken a task of extreme difficulty and hazard ; one in which, more than in any other theatrical attempt, it was necessary for him, at the first outset, to secure the sympathy of his audience ; or, more properly speaking, to excite an antipathy against the objects of his attack, similar to that by which he himself was animated. It seems probable, therefore, that the order of subjects in the comedy must have been the same as that which is observable in the Parabasis which follows, and which may be considered as an apologetical analysis of the preceding play. It had begun then with the least criminal perhaps, but to the feelings of the Athenians the most invidious and irritating topic of accusation—namely, the occasional instances of undue advantages obtained for a subject State, by the hired agency of Athenian statesmen and orators, co-operating with the panegyrical cajolery of its deputies and envoys. A fragment has been preserved, evidently belonging to what was called a "long rhesis," a narrative speech, in which a character of this kind is making a triumphant report to his employers; describing his success in captivating the attention of an Athenian auditory, and giving a ridiculous picture of the effect which his oratory had produced upon them.

> Then every soul of them sat open-mouth'd,
> Like roasted oysters, gaping in a row.*

But the general plan of the play must have included a picture of the abuses and insolence, under which the subject States were suffering ; an exhibition of the processes of extortion and intimidation which

---

* Ap. Athen. p. 86. Compare this with "Knights," v, 651, and the whole passage to which it belongs.

were practised upon them; an exposure of the persons most
notoriously guilty of such practices, and probably also of some
flagrant instances which were known to have occurred, and which
might have been represented on the stage with no other disguise
than that of a remote fanciful locality assigned to them in the new
imaginary universal Empire of the Athenian Commonwealth.

This must have been the service, which, as he says, had excited the
grateful feelings of the subject States, and their just admiration of
the courage of the man "who had risked the perilous enterprise of
pleading in behalf of justice, in presence of an Athenian auditory."
It is observable that the poet, after having, with a just feeling of
pride and self-estimation, ventured in this way to assert his own
merits, immediately after, as if alarmed at his own boldness (like
Rabelais or the jesters in Shakespeare, when they are apprehensive of having touched upon too tender a point) makes a sudden
escape from the subject, and hurries off into a strain of transcen-
dental nonsense, about the high consideration with which his
character and services to the country were regarded by the Persian
monarch, and how the Spartans insisted upon obtaining the island
of Ægina, from no other motive than a wish to deprive the Athenians of the advantage which they might derive from his poetical
admonitions.

PARABASIS OF THE CHORUS.

Our poet has never as yet
Esteemed it proper or fit,
To detain you with a long
Encomiastic song,
On his own superior wit.
But being abused and accused,
And attacked of late,
As a foe to the State,
He makes an appeal in his proper defence
To your voluble humour and temper and sense,
　　With the following plea ;
　　Namely, that he
Never attempted or ever meant
　　To scandalize
　　In any wise

Your mighty imperial government.
    Moreover he says,
    That in various ways
He presumes to have merited honour and praise,
Exhorting you still to stick to your rights,
And no more to be fooled with rhetorical flights;
    Such as of late each envoy tries
    On the behalf of your allies,
That come to plead their cause before ye,
With fulsome phrase, and a foolish story
Of *violet crowns* and *Athenian glory;*
With *sumptuous Athens* at every word ;
Sumptuous Athens is always heard,
Sumptuous ever ; a suitable phrase
For a dish of meat or a beast at graze.
    He therefore affirms,
    In confident terms,
That his active courage and earnest zeal
Have usefully served your common weal :
    He has openly shown
    The style and tone
Of your democracy ruling abroad.
He has placed its practices on record ;
The tyrannical arts, the knavish tricks,
That poison all your politics.
    Therefore we shall see, this year,
The allies with tribute arriving here,
Eager and anxious all to behold
Their steady protector, the bard so bold :
The bard, they say, that has dared to speak,
To attack the strong, to defend the weak.
    His fame in foreign climes is heard,
    And a singular instance lately occurred.
It occurred in the case of the Persian king,
Sifting and cross-examining

The Spartan envoys. He demanded
Which of the rival States commanded
The Grecian seas ? He asked them next
(Wishing to see them more perplexed),
Which of the two contending powers
Was chiefly abused by this bard of ours ?
For he said, " Such a bold, so profound an adviser
By dint of abuse would render them wiser,
More active and able ; and briefly that they
Must finally prosper and carry the day."
Now mark the Lacedæmonian guile !
Demanding an insignificant isle !
" Ægina," they say, " for a pledge of peace,
As a means to make all jealousy cease."
Meanwhile their privy design and plan
Is solely to gain this marvellous man—
Knowing his influence on your fate—
By obtaining a hold on his estate
Situate in the isle aforesaid.
Therefore there needs to be no more said.
You know their intention, and know that you know it.
You'll keep to your island, and stick to the poet.
And he for his part
Will practise his art
With a patriot heart,
With the honest views
That he now pursues,
And fair buffoonery and abuse ;
Not rashly bespattering, or basely beflattering,
Not pimping, or puffing, or acting the ruffian ;
Not sneaking or fawning ;
But openly scorning
All menace and warning,
All bribes and suborning :
He will do his endeavour on your behalf ;

He will teach you to think, he will teach you to laugh.
So Cleon again and again may try ;
I value him not, nor fear him, I !
His rage and rhetoric I defy.
His impudence, his politics,
His dirty designs, his rascally tricks
No stain of abuse on me shall fix.
Justice and right, in his despite,
Shall aid and attend me, and do me right :
With these to friend, I ne'er will bend,
Nor descend
To an humble tone
(Like his own),
As a sneaking loon,
A knavish, slavish, poor poltroon.

STROPHE.

Muse of old
 Many times,
Strike the bold
 Hearty rhymes,
New revived
 Firm energetical
Music of Acharnæ ;
 Choleric, fiery, quick,
As the sparkle
From the charcoal,
Of the native evergreen
 Knotted oak,
 In the smoke
Shows his active fiery spleen.
 Whilst beside
 Stands the dish
 Full of fish
Ready to be fried :

Every face, in the place,
Overjoyed, all employed,
  Junketing apace.
Muse then, as a friend of all,
Hasten, and attend the call.
  Give an ear
    To your old,
    Lusty, bold
  Townsman here.

EPIRREMA.

We, the veterans of the city, briefly must expostulate
At the hard ungrateful usage which we meet with from the
  State,
Suffering men of years and service at your bar to stand
  indicted,
Bullied by your beardless speakers, worried and perplexed
  and frighted ;
Aided only by their staff, the staff on which their steps are
  stayed ;
Old, and impotent, and empty ; deaf, decrepit, and decayed.
There they stand, and pore, and drivel, with a misty pur-
  blind gleam,
Scarce discerning the tribunal, in a kind of waking dream.
Then the stripling, their accuser, fresh from training, bold
  and quick,
Pleads in person, fencing, sparring, using every turn and
  trick ;
Grappling with the feeble culprit, dragging him to dangerous
  ground,
Into pitfalls of dilemmas, to perplex him and confound.
Then the wretched invalid attempts an answer, and at last,
After stammering and mumbling, goes away condemned
  and cast ;
Moaning to his friends and neighbours, " All the little store

All is gone! my purchase-money for a coffin and my
   grave."

ANTISTROPHE.

   Scandalous and a shame it is,
      Seen or told;
   Scandalous and a shame to see,
      A warrior old;
   Crippled in the war,
   Worried at the bar;
   Him, the veteran, that of old
      Firmly stood,
   With a fierce and hardy frown,
   In the field of Marathon;
      Running down
      Sweat and blood.
   There and then, we were men;
   Valorous assailants; now
      Poor and low;
   Open and exposed to wrong,
      From the young;
   Every knave, every ass,
   Every rogue like Marpsyas.*

The Thucydides mentioned in the following lines is not the historian
   (the son of Olorus), but a much older man, and in his time of much
   greater personal eminence.   In the scanty historical notices which
   have reached us respecting the period in which he lived, he is distinguished from others of the same name, as the son of Milesius;
   and it should seem that he must have succeeded to Cimon, as the
   leader of an unavailing opposition to that system of innovation in
   domestic and foreign policy which Pericles introduced, and by which
   he secured for himself, at the expense of posterity, a life annuity of
   power and popularity.
A very characteristic anecdote is alluded to in the seventh and eighth
   lines.   Thucydides had been asked "which of the two (himself or

---

* Not known in history, but said by the Scholiast to have been noted by
the contemporary comic poets as a troublesome contentious orator.

Pericles) was the best wrestler,"—*i.e.*, the best debater. To which he answered, " I am the best wrestler ; but when I have flung him he starts up again and persuades the people that he was not thrown down."

ANTEPIRREMA.

Shame and grief it was to witness poor Thucydides's fate,
Indicted by Cephisodemus,* overwhelmed with words and prate.
I myself when I beheld him, an old statesman of the city,
Dragged and held by Scythian archers,† I was moved to tears and pity,
Him that I remember once tremendous, terrible, and loud;
Discomfiting the Scythian host, subduing the revolted crowd;
Undaunted, desperate, and bold, that with his hasty grasp could fling
A dozen, in as many casts, of the best wrestlers in the ring.
Three thousand archers of the guard, he bawled and roared and bore them down.
No living soul he feared or spared, or friends or kinsmen of his own.
Since you then refuse to suffer aged men to rest in peace,
Range your criminals in classes, let the present method cease.
Give up elderly delinquents to be mumbled, mouthed, and wrung
By the toothless old accusers; but protect them from the young.

---

* An orator famous, or rather infamous, as a bold and dangerous accuser.

† These were purchased slaves, the property of the State, employed by the magistrates as a police guard : see Thesm. v. 1001. They were also employed to maintain order in the public assembly, and to force disorderly speakers to descend from the bema. This part of their duties is alluded to e'sewhere : see Eccles. v. 143, 258.

For the younger class of culprits young accusers will be
fair,
Prating prostituted fops, and Clinias's son and heir.
Thus we may proceed in order, all of us, with all our
might,
Severally, both youths and elders, to defend and to indict.

/

DICÆOPOLIS.

Well, there's the boundary of my market-place,
Marked out, for the Peloponnesians and Bœotians
And the Megarians. All are freely welcome
To traffic and sell with me, but not with Lamachus.
Moreover I've appointed constables,
With lawful and sufficient straps and thongs,   .
To keep the peace, and to coerce and punish
All spies and vagabonds and informing people.
Come, now for the column, with the terms of peace
Inscribed upon it ! I must fetch it out,
And fix it here in the centre of my market. [*Exit.*

A writer in the *Quarterly Review* for July 1820 (not a very different
person from the writer of this note) adduces the two scenes immediately following, as instances, amongst others, of that tendency to
generalization which, as he contends, was no less predominant in the
mind of Aristophanes than in that of Shakespeare.
In reference to this principle it is observed of the following scenes, that
"the two country people who are introduced as attending Dicæopolis's market, are not merely a Megarian and a Theban distinguished by a difference of dialect and behaviour ; they are the two
extremes of rustic character—the one (the Megarian) depressed by
indigence into meanness, is shifting and selfish, with habits of coarse
fraud and vulgar jocularity. The Theban is the direct opposite—a
primitive, hearty, frank, unsuspicious, easy-minded fellow ; he comes
to market with his followers, in a kind of old-fashioned rustic triumph,
with his bag-pipers attending him : Dicæopolis (the Athenian, the
medium between the two extremes before described) immediately
exhibits his superior refinement, by suppressing their minstrelsy ; and
the honest Theban, instead of being offended, joins in condemning
them. He then displays his wares, and the Athenian, with a bur-

lesque tragical rant, takes one of his best articles (a Copaic eel) and delivers it to his own attendants to be conveyed within doors. The Theban, with great simplicity, asks how he is to be paid for it ; and the Athenian, in a tone of grave superiority, but with some awkwardness, informs him that he claims it as a toll due to the market. The Theban does not remonstrate, but after some conversation agrees to dispose of all his wares, and to take other goods in return ; but here a difficulty arises, for the same articles which the Athenian proposes in exchange happen to be equally abundant in Bœotia. The scene here passes into burlesque, but it is a burlesque expressive of the character which is assigned to the Theban ; a character of primitive simplicity, utterly unacquainted with all the pests by which existence was poisoned in the corrupt community of Athens. A common sycophant or informer is proposed as an article which the Athenian soil produced in great abundance, but which would be considered as a rarity in Bœotia. The Theban agrees to the exchange, saying, that if he could get such an animal to take home, he thinks he could make a handsome profit by exhibiting him."

The scene which immediately follows (that of the Megarian) has been slightly modified, without detriment, it must be hoped, to the genuine humour of the original, perhaps even with advantage; since the attention of the English reader is not distracted by that strange contrast of ancient and modern manners, which strikes the reader of the original with an impression, wholly disproportionate to the intention of the Author, and destructive of that general harmony and breadth of effect which he had intended to produce, and which, as far as his contemporaries were concerned, he had succeeded in producing.

Enter a MEGARIAN *with his two little girls.*

MEG. Ah, there's the Athenian market ! Heaven bless it,
I say; the welcomest sight to a Megarian.
I've looked for it, and longed for it, like a child
For its own mother. You, my daughters dear,
Disastrous offspring of a dismal sire,
List to my words ; and let them sink impressed
Upon your empty stomachs ; now's the time
That you must seek a livelihood for yourselves.
Therefore resolve at once, and answer me ;
Will you be sold abroad, or starve at home ?

BOTH. Let us be sold, papa! Let us be sold!

MEG. I say so too; but who do ye think will purchase
Such useless mischievous commodities?
However, I have a notion of my own,
A true Megarian* scheme; I mean to sell ye
Disguised as pigs, with artificial pettitoes.
Here, take them, and put them on. Remember now,
Show yourselves off; do credit to your breeding,
Like decent pigs; or else, by Mercury,
If I'm obliged to take you back to Megara,
There you shall starve, far worse than heretofore.
—This pair of masks too—fasten 'em on your faces,
And crawl into the sack there on the ground.
Mind ye—Remember—you must squeak and whine,
And racket about like little roasting pigs.
—And I'll call out for Dicæopolis.
Ho, Dicæopolis, Dicæopolis!
I say, would you please to buy some pigs of mine?

DIC. What's there? a Megarian?

MEG. [*sneakingly*].　　　　　Yes—We're come to market.

DIC. How goes it with you?

MEG.　　　　　　　　　　We're all like to starve.

DIC. Well, liking is everything. If you have your liking,
That's all in all: the likeness is a good one,
A pretty likeness! like to starve, you say.
But what else are you doing?

MEG.　　　　　　　　　　What we're doing?
I left our governing people all contriving
To ruin us utterly without loss of time.

DIC. It's the only way: it will keep you out of mischief,
Meddling and getting into scrapes.

MEG.　　　　　　　　　　Aye, yes.

---

* The Athenians could not claim the invention of comedy, which
belonged to the Megarians: they therefore indemnified themselves by
decrying the humour of the Megarians, as low and vulgar.

DIC. Well, what's your other news? How's corn? What price?

MEG. Corn? it's above all price; we worship it.

DIC. But salt? You've salt, I reckon—

MEG.   Salt? how should we?
Have not you seized the salt pans?

DIC.   No! nor garlic?
Have not ye garlic?

MEG.   What do ye talk of garlic?
As if you had not wasted and destroyed it,
And grubbed the very roots out of the ground.

DIC. Well, what have you got then? Tell us! Can't ye!

MEG. [*in the tone of a sturdy resolute lie*]. Pigs—
Pigs truly—pigs forsooth, for sacrifice.

DIC. That's well, let's look at 'em.

MEG.   Aye, they're handsome ones;
You may feel how heavy they are, if ye hold 'em up.

DIC. Hey-day! What's this? What's here?

MEG.   A pig, to be sure.

DIC. Do ye say so? Where does it come from?

MEG.   Come? from Megara.
What, an't it a pig?

DIC.   No truly, it does not seem so.

MEG. Did you ever hear the like? Such an unaccount-
able
Suspicious fellow! it is not a pig, he says!
But I'll be judged; I'll bet ye a bushel of salt,
It's what we call a natural proper pig.

DIC. Perhaps it may, but it's a human pig.

MEG. Human! I'm human; and they're mine, that's
all.
Whose should they be, do ye think? so far they're human.
But come, will you hear 'em squeak?

DIC. Aye, yes, by Jove,
With all my heart.

MEG.   Come now, pig! now's the time :
Remember what I told ye—squeak directly!
Squeak, can't ye?   Curse ye, what's the matter with ye?
Squeak when I bid you, I say; by Mercury
I'll carry you back to Megara if you don't.
  DAUGH. Wee wée.
  MEG.   Do ye hear the pig?
  DIC.   The pig, do ye call it?
It will be a different creature before long.
  MEG. It will take after the mother, like enough.
  DIC. Aye, but this pig won't do for sacrifice.
  MEG. Why not?   Why won't it do for sacrifice?
  DIC. Imperfect! here's no tail!
  MEG.   Poh, never mind;
It will have a tail in time, like all the rest.
But feel this other, just the fellow to it;
With a little further keeping, it would serve
For a pretty dainty sacrifice to Venus.
  DIC. You warrant 'em weaned? they'll feed without the
     mother?
  MEG. Without the mother or the father either.
  DIC. But what do they like to eat?
  MEG.   Just what ye give 'em;
You may ask 'em if you will.
  DIC.   Pig, Pig!
  1ST DAUGH.   Wee wée.
  DIC. Pig, are ye fond of peas?
  1ST DAUGH.   Wee wée, Wee wée.
  DIC. Are ye fond of figs?
  1ST DAUGH. .   Wee wée, Wee wée, Wee wée.
  DIC. You little one, are you fond of figs?
  2ND DAUGH.   Wee wée.
  DIC. What a squeak was there ! they're ravenous for the
     figs ;
Go somebody, fetch out a parcel of figs

For the little pigs ! Heh, what, they'll eat I warrant.
Lawk there, look at 'em racketing and bustling !
How they do munch and crunch ! in the name of heaven,
Why, sure they can't have eaten 'em all already !
　　MEG. [*sneakingly*]. Not all, there's this one here, I took
　　myself.
　　DIC. Well, faith, they're clever comical animals.
What shall I give you for 'em ? What do ye ask ?
　　MEG. I must have a gross of onions for this here ;
And the other you may take for a peck of salt.
　　DIC. I'll keep 'em ; wait a moment. 　　　　　[*Exit.*
　　MEG. 　　　　　　　　　　　　Heaven be praised !
O blessed Mercury, if I could but manage
To make such another bargain for my wife,
I'd do it to-morrow, or my mother either.

Enter INFORMER.

　　INF. Fellow, from whence ?
　　MEG. 　　　　　　　　From Megara with my pigs.
　　INF. Then I denounce your pigs, and you yourself,
As belonging to the enemy.
　　MEG. 　　　　　　　There it is !
The beginning of all our troubles over again.
　　INF. I'll teach you to come Megarizing here :
Let go of the sack there.
　　MEG. 　　　　　　　Dicæopolis !
Ho, Dicæopolis ! there's a fellow here
Denouncing me.
　　DIC. 　　　　Denouncing is he ? Constables,
Why don't you keep the market clear of sycophants ?
You fellow, I must inform ye, your informing
Is wholly illegal and informal here.
　　INF. What, giving informations against the enemy ;
Is that prohibited ?
　　DIC. 　　　　At your peril ! Carry
Your information to some other market.

MEG. What a plague it is at Athens, this informing!

DIC. O never fear, Megarian; take it there,

The payment for your pigs, the salt and onions :

And fare you well.

MEG. That's not the fashion amongst us.

We've not been used to faring well.

DIC. No matter.

If it's offensive, I'll revoke the wish;

And imprecate it on myself instead. [*Exit.*

MEG. There now, my little pigs, you must contrive

To munch your bread with salt, if you can get it. [*Exit.*

The following song consists merely of a satirical enumeration and
description of persons, now, for the most part, entirely forgotten.
An attempt has therefore been made to give some interest to it (an
interest of curiosity at least) by a close imitation of the metre of the
original. The Cratinus here mentioned is not the celebrated comic
author, but a cotemporary lyrical poet, of whom nothing, I believe,
is known. The name of Hyperbolus is upon record, as that of a
turbulent public speaker and accuser. Cleonymus is noted in this
and other comedies (see p. 18, v. 87-8), as a great overgrown coward,
and a voracious intrusive guest.

CHORUS.

Our friend's affairs improve apace; his lucky speculation

Is raising him to wealth and place, to name and reputation.

With a revenue neat and clear,

Arising without risk or fear,

No sycophant will venture here

To spoil his occupation.

Not Ctesias, the dirty spy, that lately terrified him;

Nor Prepis, with his infamy, will jostle side beside him :

Clothed in a neat and airy dress,

He'll move at ease among the press,

Without a fear of nastiness,

Or danger to betide him.

Hyperbolus will never dare to indict him nor arrest him.

Cleonymus will not be there to bother and molest him.

Nor he, the bard of little price,
Cratinus, with the curls so nice,
Cratinus in the new device
    In which the barber dressed him.
Nor he, the paltry saucy rogue, the poor and undeserving
Lysistratus, that heads the vogue, in impudence unswerving.
    Taunt and offence in all he says;
    Ruined in all kinds of ways;
    In every month of thirty days,
        Nine and twenty starving.

Enter a THEBAN *with his attendants, all bearing burdens;
    followed by a train of bagpipers.*

THEB. Good troth, I'm right down shoulder-galled; my
    lads,
Set down your bundles.   You, take care o' the herbs.
Gently, be sure don't bruise 'em ; and now, you minstrels,
That needs would follow us all the way from Thebes ;
Blow wind i' the tail of your bagpipes, puff away.
    DIC. Get out ! what wind has brought 'em here, I
    wonder ?
A parcel of hornets buzzing about the door !
You humble-bumble drones—Get out ! Get out !
    THEB. As Iolaus shall help me, that's well done,
Friend, and I thank you ;—coming out of Thebes,
·They blew me away the blossom of all these herbs.
You've sarved 'em right.   So now would you please to buy,
What likes you best, of all my chaffer here ;
All kinds, four-footed things and feathered fowl,
    DIC. [*suddenly, with the common trick of condescension, as
        if he had not observed him before*].
My little tight Bœotian ! Welcome kindly,
My little pudding-eater ! What have you brought ?
    THEB. In a manner, everything, as a body may say ;
All the good cheer of Thebes, and the primest wares,

Mats, trefoil, wicks for lamps, sweet marjoram,
Coots, didappers, and water-hens—what not?
Widgeon and teal.

Dic.   Why, you're come here amongst us,
Like a north wind in winter, with your wild fowl.

Theb. Moreover I've brought geese, and hares moreover,
And eels from the lake Copais, which is more.

Dic. O thou bestower of the best spichcocks
That ever yet were given to mortal man,
Permit me to salute those charming eels.

Theb. [*addressing the eel, and delivering it to* Dicæopolis].
Daughter, come forth, and greet the courteous stranger,
First-born of fifty damsels of the lake !

Dic. O long regretted and recovered late,
Welcome, thrice welcome to the Comic Choir;
Welcome to me, to Morychus,* and all.
(Ye slaves prepare the chafing dish and stove.)
Children, behold her here, the best of eels,
The loveliest and the best, at length returned
After six years of absence.   I myself
Will furnish you with charcoal for her sake.
Salute her with respect, and wait upon
Her entrance there within, with due conveyance.

     [*the eel is here carried off by* Dicæopolis's *servants*].
Grant me, ye gods ! so to possess thee still,
While my life lasts, and at my latest hour,
Fresh even and sweet as now, with . . . . savoury sauce.

Theb. But how am I to be paid for it? Won't you
tell me?

Dic. Why, with respect to the eel, in the present instance,
I mean to take it as a perquisite,

---

* At the close of the play, a splendid supper was given by the choregus
to the whole Comic Choir; authors, actors, and judges. Morychus was a
noted epicure.

As a kind of toll to the market ; you understand me.
These other things of course are meant for sale.

THEB. Yes, sure.   I sell 'em all.

DIC.   Well, what do you ask ?
Or would you take commodities in exchange ?

THEB. Aye ; think of something of your country produce,
That's plentiful down here, and scarce up there.

DIC. Well, you shall take our pilchards or our pottery.

THEB. Pilchards and pottery ! Naugh, we've plenty of
they.
But think of something, as I said before,
That's plentiful down here, and scarce up there.

DIC. [*after a moment's reflection*].
I have it ! A true-bred sycophant and informer.
I'll give you one, tied neatly and corded up,
Like an oil-jar.

THEB.   Aye ; that's fair ; by the holy twins !
He'd bring in money, I warrant, money enough,
Amongst our folks at home, with showing him,
Like a mischiéf-full kind of a foreign ape.

DIC. Well, there's Nicarchus moving down this way,
Laying his informations.   There he comes.

THEB. [*contemplating him with the eye of a purchaser*].
'A seems but a small one to look at.

DIC.   Aye, but I promise ye,
He's full of tricks and roguery, every inch of him.

Enter NICARCHUS.

NIC. [*in the pert peremptory tone of his profession as an
informer*].
Whose goods are these ? these articles ?

THEB.   Mine, sure ;
We be come here from Thebes.

NIC.   Then I denounce them
As enemies' property.

THEB. [*with an immediate outcry*]. Why, what harm have
they done,
The birds and creatures ?   Why do you quarrel with 'em ?
NIC. And I'll denounce you too.
THEB.   What, me ? What for ?
NIC. To satisfy the bystanders, I'll explain.
You've brought in wicks of lamps from an enemy's country.
DIC. [*ironically*]. And so, you bring 'em to *light ?*
NIC.   I bring to light
A plot !—a plot to burn the arsenal !
DIC. [*ironically*]. With the wick of a lamp?
NIC.   Undoubtedly.
DIC.   In what way ?
NIC. [*with great gravity*]. A Bœotian might be capable
of fixing it
On the back of a cockroach, who might float with it
Into the arsenal, with a north-east wind ;
And if once the fire caught hold of a single vessel,
The whole would be in a blaze.
DIC. [*seizing hold of him*]. You dog ! You villain !
Would a cockroach burn the ships and the arsenal?
NIC. Bear witness all of ye.
DIC.   There, stop his mouth ;
And bring me a band of straw to bind him up ;
And send him safely away, for fear of damage,
Gently and steadily, like a potter's jar.

The metre of the following song is given as a tolerably near approach
to that of the original ; in fact, the nearest which has been found
consistent with the necessity of rhyme.

CHOR. To preserve him safe and sound,
You must have him fairly bound,
With a cordage nicely wound,
Up and down, and round and round ;
Securely packed.

Dic. I shall have a special care,
For he's a piece of paltry ware;
And as you strike him, here—or there—[*striking him*
The noises he returns declare—[*the informer screamin*
                                   He's partly cracked.*
    Chor. How then is he fit for use?
    Dic. As a store-jar of abuse.
Plots and lies he cooks and brews,
Slander and seditious news,
            Or anything.
    Chor. Have you stowed him safe enough?
    Dic. Never fear, he's hearty stuff;
Fit for usage hard and rough,
Fit to beat and fit to cuff,
            To toss and fling.
You can hang him up or down,†
By the heels or by the crown.
    Theb. I'm for harvest business bown.
    Chor. Fare ye well, my jolly clown.
            We wish ye joy.
You've a purchase tight and neat;
A rogue, a sycophant complete;
Fit to bang about and beat,
Fit to stand the cold and heat,
            And all employ.
    Dic. I'd a hard job with the rascal, tying him up!
Come, my Bœotian, take away your bargain.
    Theb. [*speaking to one of his servants*].
Ismenias, stoop your back, and heave him up.
There—softly and fairly—so—now carry him off.
    Dic. He's an unlucky commodity; notwithstanding,

---

* The soundness of an earthen vessel is ascertained by striking a sm
blow upon it, and attending to the tone which it gives out.
    † The Informer being by this time fairly corded and packed, is flu
about and hung up, in confirmation of Dicæopolis's warranty.

If he earns you a profit, you can have to say,
What few can say, you've been the better for him,
And mended your affairs by the informer.

Enter a SLAVE.

SLAVE [*in à loud voice*].   Ho, Dicæopolis!
DIC.   Well, what's the matter?
Why need ye bawl so?
SLAVE.   Lamachus sends his orders,
With a drachma for a dish of quails, and three
For that Copaic eel, he bid me give you.
DIC. An eel for Lamachus?   Who is Lamachus?
SLAVE. The fierce and hardy warrior; he that wields
The Gorgon shield, and waves the triple plume.
DIC. And if he'd give me his shield, he should not
    have it :
Let him wave his plumage over a mess of salt fish.
What's more ; if he takes it amiss, and makes a riot,
I'll speak to the clerk of the market, you may tell him.
But as for me, with this my precious basket,
Hence I depart, while ortolans and quails
Attend my passage and partake the gales.   [*Exit.*

CHORUS.

An attempt has been here made to reproduce in English the peculiar
metre of the original, in which (after an irregular beginning) each
line is made to consist of four Cretic measures, of which it is requisite that the three first should be of the form already described
in p. 24 (namely, a crotchet followed by three quavers).   The
difficulty arising from the great scarcity of short syllables in the
English * language, as compared with the Greek, has led to some
infractions of this rule, in the unequal length of some of the lines,
and the substitution of the common Cretic measure, in its usual
unresolved form ; † not to mention one or two indefensible but

---

* The whole of the English Liturgy gives only one instance of five short
syllables in succession: In the three first lines of Herodotus we find a
succession of six and of five.
† As may be seen in v. 8, 9, 10, and 11.

C

unavoidable false quantities, together with certain hiatuses and semi-
hiatuses, which in a less restricted metre it would not have been
difficult to avoid.

EPIRREMA.

O behold, O behold
The serene happy sage,
The profound mighty mind,
Miracle of our age,
Calmly wise, prosperous in enterprise,
Cool, correct, boundless in the compass of his intellect.
Savoury commodities and articles of every kind
Pouring in upon him, and accumulating all around.
Some to be reserved apart, ready for domestic use ;
Some again, that require
Quickly to be broiled or roast, hastily devoured and
smoused,
On the spot, piping hot.
See there, as a sample of his hospitable elegance,
Feathers and a litter of his offal at the door displayed !
War is my aversion ; I detest the very thought of him.
Never in my life will I receive him in my house again ;
Positively never ; he behaved in such a beastly way.
There we were assembled at a dinner of the neighbour-
hood.
Mirth and unanimity prevailed till he reversed it all,
Coming in among us of a sudden, in a haughty style.
Civilly we treated him enough, with a polite request :
" Please ye to be seated, and to join us in a fair carouse."
Nothing of the kind I but unaccountably he began to
storm,
Brandishing a torch as if he meant to set the house afire,
Swaggering and hectoring, abusing and assaulting us.
First he smashed the jars, he spoilt and spilt the
wines ;
Next he burnt the stakes, and ruined all the vines.

ANTEPIRREMA.

An endeavour to develop with more effect a pretty fanciful allusion in
the original has led to another infraction of the metrical rule above
described. It is to be hoped, however, that the passage in question
(from v. 7 to 14) will not be found to exhibit any marked departure
from the general character which belongs to this peculiar form of
the Cretic metre. The picture, the work of Zeuxis, was an object
well known to all the inhabitants of Athens ; for the sake of the
modern reader, it was necessary to insert a slight sketch of it.

> Wherefore are ye gone away,
> Whither are ye gone astray,
>> Lovely Peace,

Vanishing, eloping, and abandoning unhappy Greece?
Love is as a painter ever, doting on a fair design.
Zeuxis has illustrated a vision and a wish of mine.

> Cupid is portrayed
> Naked, unarrayed,
> With an amaranthine braid
> Waving in his hand ;
> With a lover and a maid
> Bounden in a band.
> Cupid is uniting both,
>> Nothing loth.

Think then if I saw ye with a Cupid in a tether, dear,
Binding and uniting us eternally together here.
Think of the delight of it ; in harmony to live at last,
Making it a principle to cancel all offences past.
Really I propose it, and I promise ye to do my best
(Old as you may fancy me), to sacrifice my peace and
> rest ;
Working in my calling as a father of a family,
Labouring and occupied in articles of husbandry.
You shall have an orchard, with the fig-trees in a border
> round
Planted all in order, and a vineyard and an olive ground.

When the month is ended, we'll repose from toil,
With a bath and banquet, wine and anointing oil.

HERALD, *or* CRIER.

Hear ye ! Good people ! Hear ye ! A Festival—
According to ancient custom—this same day—
The feast of the pitchers—with the prize for drinkers,
To drink at the sound of the trumpet. He that wins
To receive a wine-skin ; Ctesiphon's own skin.*
   DIC. O slaves ! ye boys and women ! Heard ye not
The summons of the herald? Hasten forth,
With quick despatch, to boil, to roast, to fry ;
Hacking and cutting, plucking, gutting, flaying ;
Hashing and slashing, mincing, fricasseeing.
And plait the garlands nimbly ; and bring me here
Those, the least skewers of all, to truss the quails.

When Aristophanes cannot make use of his Chorus to sustain an efficient
part, he is apt to indemnify himself for the incumbrance they create,
by turning the essential characteristics of a Chorus into ridicule.
Here then, and at the close of the following scene (that between
Dicæopolis and the Countryman), they are represented as time-
serving and obsequious ; in "The Lysistrata," as dawdling, useless,
and silly (v. 319 to 49); and in "The Birds," as exciting the spleen
and impatience of the practical active man of business, by their vague
speculations and poetical pedantry (1313 to 36). In "The Peace,"
the absurdity of introducing such a Chorus is kept out of sight by
the absurd unmanageable behaviour of the Chorus itself (v. 309).

CHOR. Your designs and public ends
        First attracted us as friends.
        But the present boiled and roast
        Surprises and delights us most.

---

* The notion of a person's being flayed, and having his skin converted
into a wine-keg, appears to have been familiar to the imagination of the
Athenians, and of frequent recurrence in their low colloquial language.
Ctesiphon is only known as having been ridiculed by the comic poets for
his extreme corpulence. The conqueror, therefore, would be rewarded with
a prize of unusual magnitude.

Dic. Wait awhile, if nothing fails,
  You shall see a dish of quails.
Chor. We depend upon your care,
Dic. Rouse the fire and mend it there.
Chor. See with what a gait and air,
  What a magisterial look,
  Like a cool determined cook,
  He conducts the whole affair.*

Enter a Countryman, *groaning and lamenting.*

Countr. O miserable! wretched! wretched man!
Dic. Fellow, take care with those unlucky words.
Apply them to yourself.
Countr.   Ah, dear good friend,
So you've got peace; a peace all to yourself!
And if ye could but spare me a little drop,
Just only a little taste, only five years.
  Dic. Why, what's the matter with ye?
  Countr.   I'm ruinated,
Quite and entirely, losing my poor beasts,
My oxen, I lost 'em, both of 'em.
  Dic.   In what way?
  Countr. The Bœotians! the Bœotians! it was they.
They came down at the back of Phyle there,
And drove away my bullocks, both of 'em . . . .
  Dic. But you're in white, I see; you're out of mourning.
  Countr. [*in continuation*]
 . . . . That indeed were all my comfort and support:

---

* A dignified and authoritative demeanour is an essential requisite to the
perfection of the culinary character. The complete cook (as described in
that admirable piece of good-humoured parody, *L'homme des champs à
table*)

Donne avec dignité des loix dans sa cuisine,	Avec l'air d'un sultan qui condamne au cordon :
Et dispose du ort d'un coq ou d'un dindon,	Son maintien est altier, et sa mine farouche.

That used to serve for my manure and maintenance
In dung and daily bread ; the poor dear beasts.
 Dic. And what is it you want?
 Countr. I'm blind well nigh,
With weeping and grief. Derketes is my name,
In a farm here next to Phyle born and bred :
So if ever you wish to do what's friendly by me,
Do smear my two poor eyes with the balsam of peace.
 Dic. Friend, I'm not keeping a dispensary.
 Countr. Do, just to get me a sight of my poor oxen.
 Dic. Impossible ! you must go to the hospital.
 Countr. Do, pray, just only give me the least drop.
 Dic. Not the least drop—not I—go—get ye gone.
 Countr. Oh dear ! oh dear ! oh dear ! my poor dear
  oxen ! [*Exit.*

   Chor. He, the chief, is now possessing
     Peace as an exclusive blessing,
     Which he will not part withal.
 Dic. Mix honey with the savoury dishes !
Be careful with the cuttle-fishes !
Stew me the kidneys with the caul !
 Chor. Hear him shout there ! Hear him bawl !
 Dic. [*louder*]. Season and broil him there—that eel !
 Chor. You don't consider what we feel ;
  We're famished here with waiting ;
     While you choke
     Us with your smoke,
  And deafen us with prating.
 Dic. Those cutlets, brown them nicely—there—do ye
  mind.

   Enter a Bridesman.

 Brid. Ho, Dicæopolis !
 Dic. Who's there ! Who's that ?

BRID. A bridegroom, that has sent a dish of meat
From his marriage feast.

DIC.   Well I come I That's handsome of him;
That's proper, whoever he is; that's as it should be.

BRID. In fact, my friend the bridegroom, he that sent it,
Objects to foreign service just at present;
He begs you'd favour him with the balsam of peace;
A trifling quantity, in the box I've brought.

DIC. No, no! take back the dish; I can't receive it.
Dispose it somewhere else; take it away.
I would not part with a particle of my balsam,
For all the world—not for a thousand drachmas,
But that young woman there, who's she?

BRID.   The bridesmaid;
With a particular message from the bride;
Wishing to speak a word in private with you.

DIC. Well, what have ye got to say?   Let's hear it all!
Come—step this way—No, nearer—in a whisper—
Nearer, I say—come, there now; tell me about it.

[*after listening with comic attention to a supposed
    whisper*].

Oh, bless me; what a capital, comical,
Extraordinary string of female reasons
For keeping a young bridegroom safe at home I
Well, we'll indulge her, since she's only a woman;
She's not obliged to serve; bring out the balsam!
Come, where's your little vial?—but I say—
Do you know the manner of it?—no, not you.
How should you, a girl like you! what; I must tell you?
Yes—and you'll tell the bride; she must observe;
·When a ballot is on foot for foreign service;
At the hour of midnight, when he's fast asleep,
Then she must be particularly careful,
Without disturbing him, to anoint him.   There I

[*giving her back the vial*].   ‾*Exit* BRIDESMAID.

Now take the balsam back, and bring me a funnel
To rack my wine off.   I must mix my wine.
CHOR. See yet another ! posting here, it seems,
With awful tidings, anxious and aghast.
MESS. Ho, Lamachus, I say ! Lamachus, Ho !
Here's terror and tribulation, wars and woe !

> [LAMACHUS *appears, probably with some appendage,
> to mark the interest which he had been taking in
> the culinary operations supposed to be going on
> behind the stage.*]

LAM. What hasty summons shakes the castle gates ?
MESS. The generals have despatched an order to you
To muster your caparisons and garrisons,
And march to the mountain passes ; there to wait
In ambush in the snow : for fresh advices
Have been received, with a credible intimation
Of a suspicion of an expedition
Of a marauding party from Bœotia.
LAM. Generals I   Aye, generals I the more the worse.
DIC. Well, is not it hard that a man can't eat his dinner,
But he's to be disturbed and called from table,
With wars, and Lamachuses, and what not ?
LAM. You mock me, alas !
DIC.   Say, would you wish to grapple,
In single combat, with this mailed monster ?
                              [*showing a lobster*].
LAM. Alas, that dismal fatal messenger !
DIC. But here's a message too, coming for me.
2ND MESS. Ho, Dicæopolis !
DIC.   Well, what ?
2ND MESS.   You're summoned
To go without a moment's loss of time,
With your whole cookery, to the priest of Bacchus.
The company are arrived ; you keep them waiting,
· Everything else is ready—couches, tables,

Cushions, and coverlids for mattresses,
Dancing and singing girls for mistresses,
Plum cake and plain, comfits and caraways,
Confectionery, fruits preserved and fresh,
Relishes of all sorts, hot things and bitter,
Savouries and sweets, broiled biscuits, and what not;
Flowers and perfumes and garlands, everything.
You must not lose a moment.

LAM.   Out alas!
Wretch that I am!

DIC.   'Tis your own fault entirely,
For enlisting in the service of the Gorgons.
There, shut the door, and serve the dishes here.

LAM. My knapsack and camp service; bring it out.

DIC. My dinner service; bring it here, you lout.

LAM. Give me my bunch of leeks, the soldiers' fare.

DIC. I'm partial to veal cutlets; bring them there.

LAM. Let's see the salt fish; it seems like to rot.

DIC. I take fresh fish, and broil it on the spot.

LAM. Bring me the lofty feathers of my crest.

DIC. Bring doves and quails; I scarce know which is best.

LAM. Behold this snowy plume of dazzling white.

DIC. Behold the roasted dove, a savoury sight.

LAM. Don't mock these arms of mine, good fellow,
    pri'thee.

DIC. These quails of mine, don't think to take them with
    ye.

LAM. The case that holds my crest—bring it in haste.

DIC. And the hare-pie for me—bring it in paste.

LAM. My crest—have the moths spoilt it? no, not yet.

DIC. My dinner—shall I spoil it by a whet.

LAM. Fellow, direct not your discourse to me.

DIC. Aye, but this boy and I, we can't agree;
And we've a kind of wager, which is best,
Locusts or quails, forsooth.

LAM.   Sirrah, your jest
Is insolent.

DIC.   My wager's gone this bout :
He's all, you see, for locusts, out and out.

Various demonstrations of menace and defiance take place between
Lamachus and Dicæopolis. Lamachus has called for his lance in
anger; Dicæopolis calls for the spit: both are brought, but neither
of them in a state fit for service. Lamachus (after a hostile recon-
noitring look), conscious of his present disadvantage, proceeds to
unsheath his rusty weapon ; but, in the meantime, Dicæopolis has
succeeded in disengaging his spit from the roast meat, and appears
again ready to confront him upon equal terms. Here again are
reciprocal looks and gestures of hostility, which terminate in mutual
forbearance. Any amusement which this scene might have afforded
to the spectators, must have been derived from the humour of the
performers ; to the mere reader, and more particularly to the modern
reader, it must be uninteresting ; and might have been passed over,
but for a wish (which perhaps has been carried too far) to omit
nothing that was admissible.

LAM. Bring here my lance; unsheath the deadly point.
DIC. Bring here the spit, and show the roasted joint.
LAM. This sheath is rusted.   Come, boy, tug and try.
Ah, there it comes.
    DIC. [*unspitting his roast meat*].
                         It comes quite easily.
LAM. Bring forth the props of wood, my shield's support.
DIC. Bring bread, for belly timber; that's your sort !
LAM. My Gorgon-orbed shield ; bring it with speed.
DIC. With this full-orbed pancake I proceed.
LAM. Is not this insolence too much to bear?
DIC. Is not this pancake exquisite and rare ?
LAM. Pour oil upon the shield !   What do I trace
In the divining mirror?   'Tis the face
Of an old coward, petrified with fear,
That sees his trial for desertion near.*

---

* It was a common practice to anoint the shield before battle.   There
was likewise a species of divination practised by figures reflected from an

Dic. Pour honey on the pancake ! what appears ?
A comely personage, advanced in years ;
Firmly resolved to laugh at and defy
Both Lamachus and the Gorgon family.

Lam. Bring forth my trusty breastplate for the fight.

Dic. Bring forth the lusty goblet, my delight!

Lam. I'll charge with this, accoutred every limb.

Dic. I'll charge with this, a bumper to the brim.

Lam. Boys, strap the shield and bedding in a pack !
I'll bear myself my knapsack on my back.

Dic. Boy, strap the basket with my feasting mess ;
While I just step within to change my dress.

Lam. Come, boy, take up my shield, and trudge away.
It snows !—Good lack ; we've wintry work to-day.

Dic. Boy, take the basket. Jolly work, I say.

[Exeunt severally.

Chorus.

Go your ways in sundry wise,
Each upon his enterprise.
One determined to carouse,
With a garland on his brows,
And a comely lass beside him.
His opponent forth hath eyed him,
Resolute to pass the night,
In a military plight,
 Undelighted and alone ;
  Starving, wheezing,
  Sneezing, freezing,
 With his head upon a stone.

The action of the stage, and even all allusion to it, are suspended durin
the following songs, which serve to afford an interval of dramatic

---

oiled surface. These two usages are here alluded to. A similar mode of
divination appears from the report of modern travellers to be still employed
in Egypt.

time during which Dicæopolis may be supposed to have returned from his feast, and Lamachus from his expedition. The Chorus remain in possession of the stage, and of their primitive privilege of desultory individual satire. The latter is directed against Anti-machus, who, it seems, had given offence to the dramatic powers by the scantiness of his entertainments. I do not know whether it would be refining too much, to observe that even this capricious sally harmonizes with what has preceded, as well as with the interval which is supposed to elapse; by the culinary images in the first part, and by the description of a person returning home late at night, in the second. Some circumstances in the original are omitted in the translation, as they seem intended to account for what does not appear unaccountable to a modern; namely, that a man should walk home at night without a stick. In the passage which immediately follows, the Chorus commence their remonstrance in a calm sober tone which they are unable to maintain. This effect is produced in the original, by the quiet prosaic methodical form of words by which Antimachus is designated—a nicety of tone which it was impossible to attain or at least to render obvious in a translation.

CHORUS.

We're determined to discuss
Our difference with Antimachus,
    Calmly, simply, candidly;
Praying to the powers above,
And the just almighty Jove,
    To—Sink and blast him utterly.
He that sent us all away
T'other evening from the play,
    Hungry, thirsty, supperless;
Him we shortly trust to see
Sunk in equal misery,
    In the like distress,
With a pennyworth of fish,
And a curious eager wish
    To behold it fried;
Let him watch, and wait, and turn,
With a hungry deep concern,
    Standing there beside.

Let an accident befall,
Which shall overturn the stall,
 And the fishes frying;
There shall he behold the dish
Topsy-turvy, with the fish
 In the kennel lying.
As he stoops to pick and wipe it,
Let a greedy greyhound gripe it,
 Snatch and eat it flying.

Him let other ills befall,
Walking home beneath the wall,
Late at night, attacked by ruffians,
Orestes and his ragamuffins;
Unprotected and alone,
Groping round to find a stone,
Let him grasp for his defence
A ponderous sirreverence;
Furious, eager, in the dark,
Let him fling and miss the mark,
 Smiting upon the cheek, but not severely,
 Cratinus merely!

———

MESSENGER, SERVANT *of* LAMACHUS, LAMACHUS,
 DICÆOPOLIS, *and* CHORUS.

The following speech of the Messenger is a burlesque of the tragic
speeches in which the arrival of the wounded hero was announced
in the last act of a tragedy.

MESSENGER.

Ye slaves that dwell in Lamachus's mansion,
Prepare hot water instantly in the pipkin; *

———

* The "pipkin," in allusion to the scantiness of Lamachus's establish‑
ment. See p. 42.

With embrocations and emollients,
And bandages and plaster for your lord.
His foot is maimed and crippled with a stake,
Which wounded it, as he leaped across a trench.
His ankle-bone is out, his head is broken,
The Gorgon on his shield all smashed and spoiled.
But when the lofty plume of the cock lorrel
That decked his helm, fell downward in the dirt,
He groaned, and spake aloud despairingly:
"O glorious light of Heaven! Farewell, farewell!
For the last time; my destined days are done."
Thus moaning and lamenting, down he fell
Direct into the ditch; jumped up again;
Rushed out afresh; rallied the runaways;
Made the marauders run; ran after them,
With his spear point smiting their hinder parts.
But here he comes himself; set the door open.

Lamachus is brought in, wounded and disabled; his appearance and
attendants are caricatures of the exhibition of the wounded heroes,
whom it had become the fashion to introduce. The dialogue is a
burlesque of the lyrical agonies and lamentations of the same
personages.

LAM. Out, out alas!
I'm racked and torn,
With agony scarce to be borne,
From that accursed spear:
But worst of all, I fear,
If Dicæopolis beholds me here,
That he, my foe, will chuckle at my fall.
    DIC. My charming lass,
What joy is this!
What ecstasy! do give me a kiss!
There coax me, and hug me close, and sympathize;
I've swigged the gallon off; I've won the prize.

LAM. O what a consummation of my woes,
What throbs and throes !
 DIC. Eh there ! my little Lamachus !   How goes ?
 LAM. I'm in distress.
 DIC. I'm in no less.
 LAM. Mock not at my misery.
 DIC. Accuse me not of mockery.
 LAM. 'Twas at the final charge; I'd paid before
A number of the rogues ; at least a score.
 DIC. It was a most expensive charge you bore :
Poor Lamachus ! he was forced to pay the score !
 LAM. O mercy, mighty Apollo !
 DIC. What, do ye holloh
A'.er Apollo ? it an't his feast to-day.
LAM. [*to his bearers*].
    Don't press me,
     Dear friends !
    But place me
     Gently and tenderly.
 DIC. [*to the women*].
    Caress me,
     Dear girls !
    Embrace me
     Gently and tenderly.
 LAM. Strip off the incumbrance of this warlike gear,
And take me to my bed. . . . .
 DIC. Strip off incumbrances, my pretty dear,
And take me off to bed.
 LAM. Or bear me to the public hospital
With care.
 DIC. Bring me before the judges ; one and all
Look there !
I've won the prize ;
As this true gallon measure testifies.
I've drunk it off. " I triumph great and glorious."

CHOR. And well you may; triumph away, good fellow;
you're victorious.

DIC. To show my manhood furthermore, and spirit in the
struggle,

I quaffed it off within my breath; I gulped it in a guggle.[*]

CHOR. Then take the wine-skin as your due.
We triumph and rejoice with you.

DIC. Then fill my train,
And join the strain.

CHOR. With all my heart;
We'll bear a part.

ALL. We're triumphant, great and glorious,
    We're victorious,
        Hurrah !
    We've won the day,
    Wine-skin and all !
        Hurrah !

---

* Drinking without deglutition; still practised in Catalonia—the Thracian
Amystis.

THE KNIGHTS.

THE KNIGHTS.

THE following translation not being calculated for general circulation, it is not likely that it should fall into the hands of any reader whose knowledge of antiquity would not enable him to dispense with the fatigue of perusing a prefatory history. Such prefaces are already before the public, accompanying the translations of Mr. Mitchell and Mr. Walsh, and will be found satisfactory to those who may be desirous of preliminary information.

It may not, however, be altogether superfluous to prefix a brief summary of preceding circumstances. We have already seen, that the poet, in his comedy of "The Babylonians," had made an attack upon the leading demagogues and peculators of his time. In return for this aggression, Cleon (as described in "The Acharnians"),

> "Had dragged him to the Senate House,
> And trodden him down and bellowed over him,
> And mauled him till he scarce escaped alive."

The poet, however, recovered himself, and in the Parabasis of the same play had defied and insulted the demagogue in the most unsparing terms. In the course, however, of the following summer, Cleon, by a singular concurrence of circumstances, had been raised to the highest pitch of favour and popularity. A body of 400 Spartans having been cut off, and blockaded in an island of the Bay of Pylos, now Navarino, this disaster, in which many of the first families of Sparta were involved, induced that republic to sue for peace; which Cleon, who considered his power and influence as dependent on the continuance of the war, was determined to oppose. Insisting, therefore, that the blockaded troop could be considered in no other light than as actual prisoners, he finally pledged himself, with a given additional force, to reduce the Spartans to surrender within a limited time; this he had the good fortune and dexterity to effect, and to secure the whole credit of the result for himself; having in virtue of his appointment superseded the blockading general, Demosthenes; while at the same time he secured the benefit of his experience and ability by retaining him as a colleague. The reader, if he has the work at hand, will do well to refer to Mr. Mitford's History, c. xv. sec. x., for a detailed account of this most singular incident, strikingly illustrative of the distinct character of the two rival republics. It was then, imme. diately after this event, when his adversary's power and popularity were at their height, that the poet, undeterred by these apparent disadvantages, produced this memorable and extraordinary drama.

For those readers to whom any further introduction may be necessary, a list of the dramatis personæ, with some accompanying explanations, will perhaps be sufficient.

DRAMATIS PERSONÆ.

DEMUS.—A personification of the Athenian people, the John Bull of Athens, a testy, selfish, suspicious old man, a tyrant to his slaves, with the exception of one (a new acquisition), the Paphlagonian—Cleon, by whom he is cajoled and governed.

NICIAS and DEMOSTHENES.—The two most fortunate and able generals of the republic, of very opposite characters; the one cautious and superstitious in the extreme; the other a blunt, hearty, resolute, jolly fellow, a very decided lover of good wine. These two, *the servants of the public*, are naturally introduced as *the slaves of Demus*. After complaining of the ill-treatment to which they are subject in consequence of their master's partiality to his newly purchased slave the Paphlagonian, they determine to supplant him, which they effect in conformity to the directions of a secret Oracle, in which they find it predicted that the Tanner (*i.e.*, Cleon the Paphlagonian) shall be superseded by a person of meaner occupation and lower character.

CLEON.—The Tanner (as he is called from his property consisting in a leather manufactory), or the Paphlagonian (a nickname applied in ridicule of his mode of speaking from the word *paphlazo*, to foam), has been already described. He is represented as a fawning obsequious slave, insolent and arrogant to all except his master, the terror of his fellow-servants.

A SAUSAGE-SELLER, whose name Agoracritus, "so called from the Agora where I got my living," is not declared till towards the conclusion of the play, is the person announced by the Oracle, as ordained by fate, to baffle the Paphlagonian, and to supersede him in the favour of his master. His breeding and education are described as having been similar to that of the younger Mr. Weller, in that admirable and most unvulgar exhibition of vulgar life, " The Pickwick Papers."

Finally, after a long struggle, his undaunted vulgarity of superior dexterity are crowned with deserved success. He supplants the Paphlagonian, and is installed in the supreme direction of the old gentleman's affairs.

It appears that the poet must have been subjected to some particular disadvantages and embarrassments in the production of this play. We have seen, that in the preceding comedy of "The Acharnians," Lamachus, a rising military character, had been personated on the stage, and had been addressed by name, without disguise or equivocation, throughout the whole of that play. This is no longer the case in the play now before us; Nicias, Demosthenes, and Cleon himself, are in no instance addressed by name. It should seem, therefore, that some enactment must have taken place, restraining the license of comedy in this particular; and here a distinction is to be observed between the choral parts and the dramatic dialogue; for in this very play Cleon is most unsparingly abused by name in the choral songs. The fact seems to have been that the licentious privilege of the "Sacred Chorus," consecrated by immemorial usage, and connected with the rites of Bacchus, could not be abridged by mere human authority; while the dramatic dialogue (originally derived, in all probability, from scenes in dumb show, which had been introduced to relieve the monotony of the Chorus) was regarded as mere recent invention destitute of any divine sanction, and liable to be modified and restrained by the power of the State.

With respect to Nicias and Demosthenes, the poet could have found no difficulty in evading the new law. The masks worn by the actors presenting a caricature-likeness of each of them, would be sufficient to identify them; and it could not be supposed that either of them would be offended at being brought forward in burlesque, when the poet's intention was evidently friendly towards them both; the whole drift of his comedy being directed against their main antagonist and rival. For the caricature in which they themselves were represented, was in no respect calculated to make them unpopular; on the contrary, the blunt heartiness and good-fellowship of the one, and the timid scrupulous piety of the other, were qualities which in different ways recommended them respectively to the favour and goodwill of their fellow-citizens, and which were accordingly exhibited and impressed upon the attention of the audience, through the only medium which was consistent with the essential character of the ancient comedy.

But among the audience themselves there would undoubtedly be some gainsayers, who if they were not silenced at the first outset, might have interrupted the attention of others—"This is too bad," they might have said; "The poet will get himself into a scrape. Here is a manifest infraction of the new law." In order to obviate this, the poet in the first scene, before the proper subject of his comedy is developed, but at the precise point when his individual characters, Nicias and Demosthenes, were sufficiently marked and identified, submits the question to a theatrical vote, appealing to the audience for their sanction and approbation of the course which he has adopted. This appeal, marked as it is with a character of caution and timidity, is, with a humorous propriety, assigned to the part of Nicias; with Cleon, however, the case was different, and there was a difficulty which it required all the courage and ability of the poet to surmount—no actor dared to expose himself to the resentment of the demagogue by personating him upon the stage, and among the artists who worked for the theatre, fearful of being considered as accomplices of the poet in his evasion of the new law, no one could be found who would venture to produce the representation of his countenance in a theatrical mask. The poet, therefore, undertook the part himself, and for want of a mask disguised his own features, according to the rude method of primitive comedy, by smearing them with the lees of wine. It is worthy of remark that in his effort to surmount this difficulty he has contrived to identify the demagogue from the first moment of his appearance, concentrating his essential character and his known peculiarities in a speech of five lines—his habitual boisterous oath and a slangish use of the dual.

———

In order to occupy the vacant space which has been left by the printer, the translator is tempted, for once, to insert a justificatory comment. The speech of Nicias in the opposite page is extended to three lines; in the original it consists of a line and a half, which might be more accurately and concisely translated thus:

> "Yes, let him perish in the worst way possible,
> With all his lies, for a first-rate Paphlagonian."

But there would be one main defect in this accurate translation, namely, that it would not express the intention of the author, nor the effect produced by the actor in repeating the original; for if we consider it in this view, we find that, short as it is, it contains three distinct breaks; one at the end of the second word, another at the end of the third, and a third at the end of the line. These momentary pauses are characteristic of timid resentment, expressing itself by fits and starts,—a character which, to the English reader perusing a printed text, could not be rendered obvious without employing a compass of words much larger than the original).

Again, we see that the courage and anger of Nicias, even with the help
of the beating which he has just received, are barely sufficient to
enable him to follow the example of Demosthenes ; even in wrath
and pain he is contented to "say ditto" to what his comrade had
said before. The poet's intention, in this respect, is made more
distinctly palpable to the English reader by the first line of the translated speech.

And thus much may serve for a commentary on a passage of three lines,
and as a sample of others, which if they were not wearisome and
egotistical might be extended to every page of this and the preceding
play.

> [*After a noise of lashes and screams from behind
> the scenes*, DEMOSTHENES *comes out, and is fol-
> lowed by* NICIAS *the supposed victim of flagella-
> tion (both in the dress of slaves).* DEMOSTHENES
> *breaks out in great wrath; while* NICIAS
> *remains exhibiting various contortions of pain for
> the amusement of the audience.*]

DEM. Out! out alas! what a scandal! what a shame!
May Jove in his utter wrath crush and confound
That rascally new-bought Paphlagonian slave!
For from the very first day that he came—
Brought here for a plague and a mischief amongst us all,
We're beaten and abused continually.

NIC. [*whimpering in a broken voice*]
I say so too, with all my heart I do,
A rascal, with his slanders and lies!
A rascally Paphlagonian! so he is!

DEM. [*roughly and good-humouredly*].
How are you, my poor soul?

NIC. [*pettishly and whining*]. Why poorly enough;
And so are you for that matter.

[NICIAS *continues writhing and m oaning*].

DEM. [*as if speaking to a child that had hurt himself*].
Well, come here then!
Come, and we'll cry together, both of us,
We'll sing it to Olympus's old tune.

BOTH. [DEMOSTHENES *accompanies* NICIAS's *involuntary sobs, so as to make a tune of them.*]
Mo moo momoo—momoo momoo—Momoo momoo.*
DEM. [*suddenly and heartily*].
Come, grief's no use—It's folly to keep crying.
Let's look about us a bit, what's best to be done.
NIC. [*recovering himself*].
Aye, tell me ; what do you think ?
DEM.   No, you tell me—
Lest we should disagree.
NIC.   That's what I won t !
Do you speak boldly first, and I'll speak next.
DEM. [*significantly, as quoting a well-known verse*].
" You first might utter, what I wish to tell." †
NIC. Aye, but I'm so down-hearted, I've not spirit
To bring about the avowal cleverly,
In Euripides's style, by question and answer.
DEM. Well, then, don't talk of Euripides any more,
Or his mother either ; don't stand picking endive ;‡
But think of something in another style,
To the tune of " Trip and away."
NIC.   Yes, I'll contrive it :
Say " Let us " first ; put the first letter to it,
And then the last, and then put E, R, T.
" Let us Az ert."   I say, " Let us Azert."

---

* Our common tune, with a syllable added to it, may be made to suit the trimeter iambic, and may be sung lamentably enough :

  "When War's alarms first tore my Willy from me."
                                              my arms.

A friend who has accidentally taken up this sheet, tells me that he heard this very chant, " Mo moo," &c., on the coast opposite Corfu, in a house where the family were moaning over the dead.

  † From the tragedy of " Phædra : " she is trying to lead her nurse to mention the name of Hippolytus, while she avoids it herself.

  ‡ His mother was said to have been a herb woman.

'Tis now your turn—take the next letter to it.
Put B for A.

DEM.   "Let us Bezert," I say—

NIC. 'Tis now my turn—"Let us Cezert," I say.
'Tis now your turn.

DEM.   "Let us Dezert," I say.

NIC. You've said it!—and I agree to it—now repeat it
Once more !

DEM.   Let us Dezert! Let us Dezert!

NIC. That's well.

DEM.   But somehow it seems unlucky, rather
An awkward omen to meet with in a morning!
"To meet with our deserts !"

NIC.   That's very true ;
Therefore, I think, in the present state of things,
The best thing for us both, would be, to go
Directly to the shrine of one of the gods ;
And pray for mercy, both of us together.

DEM. Shrines! shrines ! Why sure, you don't believe in
   the gods.

NIC. I do.

DEM. But what's your argument ? Where's your proof ?

NIC. Because I feel they persecute me and hate me,
In spite of everything I try to please 'em.

DEM. Well, well. That's true ; you're right enough in that.

NIC. Let's settle something.

DEM.   Come, then—if you like
I'll state our case at once, to the audience here.

NIC. It would not be much amiss ; but first of all,
We must entreat of them ; if the scene and action
Have entertained them hitherto, to declare it,
And encourage us with a little applause beforehand.

DEM. [*to the audience*].
Well, come now ! I'll tell ye about it. Here are we
A couple of servants, with a master at home

Next door to the hustings.   He's a man in years,
A kind of a bean-fed* husky testy character,
Choleric and brutal at times, and partly deaf.
It's near about a month now, that he went
And bought a slave out of a tanner's yard,
A Paphlagonian born, and brought him home,
As wicked a slanderous wretch as ever lived.
This fellow, the Paphlagonian, has found out
The blind side of our master's understanding,
With fawning and wheedling in this kind of way :
" Would not you please to go to the bath, Sir ? surely
It's not worth while to attend the courts to-day." †
And, " Would not you please to take a little refreshment ?
And there's that nice hot broth—And here's the threepence
You left behind you—And would not you order supper ? "
    Moreover, when we get things out of compliment
As a present for our master, he contrives
To snatch 'em and serve 'em up before our faces.
I'd made a Spartan cake at Pylos lately,
And mixed and kneaded it well, and watched the baking ;
But he stole round before me and served it up :
And he never allows us to come near our master
To speak a word ; but stands behind his back
At meal times, with a monstrous leathern fly-flap,
Slapping and whisking it round and rapping us off.
    Sometimes the old man falls into moods and fancies,
Searching the prophecies till he gets bewildered ;
And then the Paphlagonian plies him up,
Driving him mad with oracles and predictions.
And that's his harvest.   Then he slanders us,
And gets us beaten and lashed, and goes his rounds

' * In allusion to the beans used in balloting.
    † Sacrifices, with distribution of meat, and largesses to the people on
holidays.

Bullying in this way, to squeeze presents from us :
" You saw what a lashing Hylas got just now ;
You'd best make friends with me, if you love your lives.
Why then, we give him a trifle, or if we don't,
We pay for it ; for the old fellow knocks us down,
And kicks us on the ground, and stamps and rages,
And tramples out the very guts of us—
    [*turning to* NICIAS]
So now, my worthy fellow; we must take
A fixed determination ;—now's the time,
Which way to turn ourselves and what to do.
    NIC. Our last determination was the best :
That which we settled to A' Be Cè *De-zert.*
    DEM. Aye, but we could not escape the Paphlagonian,
He overlooks us all ; he keeps one foot
In Pylos, and another in the Assembly ;
And stands with such a stature, stride and grasp ;
That while his mouth is open in Eatolia,*
One hand is firmly clenched upon the Lucrians,
And the other stretching forth to the Peribribèans.
    NIC.† Let's die then, once for all ; that's the best way,
Only we must contrive to manage it,
Nobly and manfully in a proper manner.
    DEM. Aye, aye. Let's do things manfully ! that's my
      maxim !
    NIC.‡ Well, there's the example of Themistocles—
To drink bull's blood : that seems a manly death.
    DEM. Bull's blood ! The blood of the grape, I say ! good
      wine !
Who knows ? it might inspire some plan, some project,
Some notion or other, a good draught of it !

---

* Etolia, Locrians, Perrhebians.
† In utter despondency, but with a sort of quiet quakerish composure.
‡ As before.

Nic. Wine truly! wine!—still hankering after liquor!
Can wine do anything for us? Will your drink
Enable you to arrange a plan to save us?
Can wisdom ever arise from wine, do ye think?

Dem. Do ye say so? You're a poor spring-water pitcher!
A silly chilly soul.   I'll tell ye what :
*It's a very presumptuous thing to speak of liquor,
As an obstacle to people's understanding ;
It's the only thing for business and dispatch.
D'ye observe how individuals thrive and flourish
By dint of drink : they prosper in proportion ;
They improve their properties; they get promotion ;
Make speeches, and make interest, and make friends.
Come, quick now—bring me a lusty stoup of wine,
To moisten my understanding and inspire me.

Nic. Oh dear! your drink will be the ruin of us!

Dem. It will be the making of ye! Bring it here.

[*Exit* Nicias.

I'll rest me a bit; but when I've got my fill,
I'll overflow them all, with a flood of rhetoric,
With metaphors and phrases and what not.

[Nicias *returns in a sneaking way with a pot of wine.*]

Nic. [*in a sheepish silly tone of triumph*].
How lucky for me it was, that I escaped
With the wine that I took !

Dem. [*carelessly and bluntly*]. Well, where's the Paphlagonian ?

Nic. [*as before*]. He's fast asleep—within there, on his
back,
On a heap of hides—the rascal! with his belly full,
With a hash of confiscations half-digested.

---

* Though Dem. has not been drinking, his speech has the tone of a
drunken man.

DEM. That's well! Now fill me a hearty lusty draught.

NIC. [*formally and precisely*].

Make the libation first, and drink this cup

To the good Genius.

DEM. [*respiring after a long draught*]. O most worthy
    Genius !   ·

Good Genius! 'tis your genius that inspires me !

> [DEMOSTHENES *remains in a sort of drunken bur-
> lesque ecstasy.*]

NIC. Why, what's the matter?

DEM.   I'm inspired to tell you,

That you must steal the Paphlagonian's oracles

Whilst he's asleep.*

NIC.   Oh dear then, I'm afraid,

This Genius will turn out my evil Genius.   [*Exit* NICIAS.

DEM. Come, I must meditate, and consult my pitcher;

And moisten my understanding a little more.

> [*The interval of* NICIAS'S *absence is occupied by action
> in dumb show:* DEMOSTHENES *is enjoying him-
> self and getting drunk in private.*]

NIC. [*re-entering with a packet*].

How fast asleep the Paphlagonian was :

Lord bless me, how mortally he snored and stank.

However, I've contrived to carry it off,

The sacred oracle that he kept so secret—

I've stolen it from him.

DEM. [*very drunk*]. That's my clever fellow !

Here give us hold; I must read 'em. Fill me a bumper.

In the meanwhile—make haste now. Let me see now—

---

* A general feature of human nature, nowhere more observable than
among boys at school ; where the poor timid soul is always dispatched
upon the most perilous expeditions. Nicias is the fag—Demosthenes the
big boy.

What have we got?—What are they,—these same papers?
Oh! oracles! . . . . o—ra—cles!—Fill me a stoup of wine.

> [*In this part of the scene a contrast is kept up
> between the subordinate nervous eagerness of poor
> NICIAS, and the predominant drunken phlegmatic
> indifference of DEMOSTHENES; who is supposed
> to amuse himself with irritating the impatience of
> his companion; while he details to him by driblets
> the contents of his own packet.*]

NIC. [*fidgeting and impatient after giving him the wine*].
Come! come! what says the Oracle?

DEM. Fill it again!

NIC. Does the Oracle say, that I must fill it again?

DEM. [*after tumbling over the papers with a hiccup*].
O Bakis! *

NIC. What?

DEM. Fill me the stoup this instant.

NIC. [*with a sort of puzzled acquiescence*].
Well, Bakis, I've been told, was given to drink;
He prophesied in his liquor people say.

DEM. [*with the papers in his hand*].
Aye, there it is—you rascally Paphlagonian!
This was the prophecy that you kept so secret.

NIC. What's there?

DEM. Why there's a thing to ruin him,
With the manner of his destruction, all foretold.

NIC. As how?

DEM. [*very drunk*]. Why the Oracle tells you how—
distinctly—
And all about it—in a perspicuous manner—
That a jobber † in hemp and flax is first ordained
To hold the administration of affairs.

---

* Dem.'s articulation of this word is assisted by a hiccup.

† After the death of Pericles, Eucrates and Lysicles had each taken the lead for a short time.

NIC. Well, there's one jobber. Who's the next? Read
on!

DEM. A cattle jobber* must succeed to him.

NIC. More jobbers! well—then what becomes of him?

DEM. He too shall prosper, till a viler rascal
Shall be raised up, and shall prevail against him,
In the person of a Paphlagonian tanner,
A loud rapacious leather-selling ruffian.

NIC. Is it foretold then, that the cattle jobber
Must be destroyed by the seller of leather?

DEM.   Yes.

NIC. Oh dear, our sellers and jobbers are at an end.

DEM. Not yet; there's still another to succeed him,
Of a most uncommon notable occupation.

NIC. Who's that? Do tell me!

DEM.   Must I?

NIC.   To be sure.

DEM. A sausage-seller it is, that supersedes him.

NIC.† A sausage-seller! marvellous indeed,
Most wonderful! But where can he be found?

DEM. We must seek him out.

> [DEMOSTHENES *rises and bustles up, with the action
> of a person who, having been drunk, is rousing
> and recollecting himself for a sudden important
> occasion. His following speeches are all perfectly
> sober.*]

NIC.   But see there, where he comes!
Sent hither providentially as it were!

DEM. O happy man! celestial sausage-seller!
Friend, guardian and protector of us all!
Come forward; save your friends, and save the country.

---

* See note † on preceding page.
† In the tone of Domine Sampson.

S. S. Do you call me ?

DEM.   Yes, we called to you, to announce
The high and happy destiny that awaits you.

NIC. Come, now you should set him free from the in-
cumbrance *
Of his table and basket ; and explain to him
The tenor and the purport of the Oracle,
While I go back to watch the Paphlagonian. [*Exit* NICIAS.

DEM. [*to the* SAUSAGE-SELLER *gravely*].
Set these poor wares aside ; and now—bow down
To the ground ; and adore the powers of earth and heaven.

S. S. Heigh-day ! Why, what do you mean ?

DEM.   O happy man !
Unconscious of your glorious destiny,
Now mean and unregarded ; but to-morrow,
The mightiest of the mighty, Lord of Athens.

S. S. Come, master, what's the use of making game ?
Why can't ye let me wash the guts and tripe,
And sell my sausages in peace and quiet ?

DEM. O simple mortal, cast those thoughts aside !   •
Bid guts and tripe farewell ! Look there ! Behold
                                [*pointing to the audience*]
The mighty assembled multitude before ye !

S. S. [*with a grumble of indifference*].
I see 'em.

DEM.   You shall be their lord and master,
The sovereign and the ruler of them all,
Of the assemblies and tribunals, fleets and armies ;
You shall trample down the Senate under foot,
Confound and crush the generals and commanders,

---

* This speech is intended to express the sudden impression of reverence
with which Nicias is affected in the presence of the predestined supreme
Sausage-seller. He does not presume to address him ; but obliquely
manifests his respect, by pointing out to Demosthenes (in his hearing) the
marks of attention to which he is entitled.

Arrest, imprison, and confine in irons,
And feast and fornicate in the Council House.*

 S. S. What, I?

Dem.   Yes, you yourself: there's more to come.
Mount here; and from the trestles of your stall
Survey the subject islands circling round.

 S. S. I see 'em.

Dem.   And all their ports and merchant vessels?

 S. S. Yes, all.

Dem.   Then an't you a fortunate happy man?
An't you content? Come then for a further prospect—
Turn your right eye to Caria, and your left
To Carthage! †—and contemplate both together.

 S. S. Will it do me good, d'ye think, to learn to squint?

 Dem. Not so; but everything you see before you
Must be disposed of at your high discretion,
By sale or otherwise; for the Oracle
Predestines you to sovereign power and greatness.

 S. S. Are there any means of making a great man
Of a sausage-selling fellow such as I?

 Dem. The very means you have, must make ye so,
Low breeding, vulgar birth, and impudence,
These, these must make ye, what you're meant to be.

 S. S. I can't imagine that I'm good for much.

 Dem. Alas! But why do ye say so? What's the
  meaning
Of these misgivings? I discern within ye
A promise and an inward consciousness

---

* The Prytaneum, see "Acharnians," v. 126: the honour of a seat at the public table was sometimes conferred on persons of extraordinary merit in advanced years. See the Parabasis of this play; see also the Apology of Socrates. Cleon had obtained this privilege for himself, and abused it insolently as appears elsewhere.

† "Carthage" must be the true reading, the right eye to Caria and the left to "Chalcedon" would not constitute a squint.

Of greatness.   Tell me truly : are ye allied
To the families of gentry ?
    S. S.   Naugh, not I ;
I'm come from a common ordinary kindred,
Of the lower order.
    Dem.   What a happiness !
What a footing will it give ye ! What a groundwork
For confidence and favour at your outset !
    S. S. But bless ye ! only consider my education !
I can but barely read . . . . in a kind of a way.
    Dem. That makes against ye !—the only thing against
      ye—
The being able to read, in any way :
For now; no lead nor influence is allowed
To liberal arts or learned education,
But to the brutal, base, and under-bred.
Embrace then and hold fast the promises
Which the oracles of the gods announce to you.
    S. S. But what does the Oracle say ?
    Dem.   Why thus it says,
In a figurative language, but withal
Most singularly intelligible and distinct,
Neatly expressed i'faith, concisely and tersely.*

" Moreover, when the eagle in his pride,
With crooked talons and a leathern hide,
Shall seize the black and blood-devouring snake ;
Then shall the woeful tanpits quail and quake ;
And mighty Jove shall give command and place,
To mortals of the sausage-selling race ;
Unless they choose, continuing as before,
To sell their sausages for evermore."

---

* This is perfectly in character. Demosthenes (as we have seen) does
not profess to believe in the gods ; yet we see that upon occasion he can
discuss the merit of the "sacred classics ;" like other critics therefore, of
the same description, he does it with a sort of patronizing tone.

S. S. But how does this concern me? Explain it, will ye?

DEM. The leathern eagle is the Paphlagonian.

S. S. What are his talons?

DEM.   That explains itself—
Talons for peculation and rapacity.

S. S. But what's the snake?

DEM.   The snake is clear and obvious:
The snake is long and black, like a black-pudding;
The snake is filled with blood, like a black-pudding.
Our Oracle foretells then, that the snake
Shall baffle and overpower the leathern eagle.

S. S. These oracles hit my fancy! Notwithstanding . . . .
I'm partly doubtful, how I could contrive . . . .
To manage an administration altogether . . . .

DEM. The easiest thing in nature!—nothing easier!
Stick to your present practice: follow it up
In your new calling.   Mangle, mince and mash,
Confound and hack, and jumble things together!
And interlard your rhetoric with lumps
Of mawkish sweet, and greasy flattery.
Be fulsome, coarse, and bloody!   For the rest,
All qualities combine, all circumstances,
To entitle and equip you for command;
A filthy voice, a villainous countenance,
A vulgar birth, and parentage, and breeding.
Nothing is wanting, absolutely nothing.
And the oracles and responses of the gods,
And prophecies, all conspire in your behalf.
Place then this chaplet on your brows!—and worship
The anarchic powers; and rouse your spirits up
To encounter him.

S. S.   But who do ye think will help me?
For all our wealthier people are alarmed,

And terrified at him ; and the meaner sort
In a manner stupefied, grown dull and dumb.
  DEM. Why there's a thousand lusty cavaliers,
Ready to back you, that detest and scorn him ;
And every worthy well-born citizen ;
And every candid critical spectator ;
And I myself; and the help of heaven to boot.
And never fear ; his face will not be seen,
For all the manufacturers of masks,
From cowardice, refused to model it.
It matters not ; his person will be known :
Our audience is a shrewd one—they can guess—
  NIC. [*in alarm from behind the scenes*].
Oh dear ! oh dear ! the Paphlagonian's coming.

    Enter CLEON *with a furious look and voice.*

  CLEON. By heaven and earth ! you shall abide it
    dearly,
With your conspiracies and daily plots
Against the sovereign people ! Hah ! what's this ?
What's this Chalcidian goblet doing here ?
Are ye tempting the Chalcidians to revolt ? *
Dogs ! villains ! every soul of ye shall die.
            [*The* SAUSAGE-SELLER *runs off in a fright.*
  DEM. Where are ye going ? Where are ye running ?
    Stop !
Stand firm, my noble valiant Sausage-seller !
Never betray the cause. Your friends are nigh.
            [*to the* CHORUS]
Cavaliers and noble captains ! now's the time ! advance in
    sight !
March in order—make the movement, and out-flank him on
    the right !

---

  * The Chalcidians did in fact revolt in the following year ; their intentions
were probably suspected at the time.

[*to the* SAUSAGE-SELLER]

There I see them bustling, hasting !—only turn and make a
stand,

Stop but only for a moment, your allies are hard at hand.

It is necessary to repair an omission which the reader may have already
noticed. Among the dramatis personæ enumerated in page 84, no
mention has been made of the Chorus, from which, as usual, the
comedy derived its title—" The Knights." This body composing
the middle order of the State were, as it appears, decidedly hostile
to Cleon. In the first lines of the preceding play, the merit of having
procured his conviction and punishment on a charge of bribery is
ascribed to them ; and again, in the same play, the Chorus express
their detestation of the demagogue by threatening to sacrifice him
to the vengeance of the knights,* and we have just seen that Demosthenes encourages the Sausage-seller by promising him the assistance
of a thousand of these " lusty cavaliers," who " scorn and detest"
his antagonist.

[*During the last lines the* CHORUS OF CAVALIERS
*with their hobby-horses have entered and occupied
their position in the orchestra. They begin their
attack upon* CLEON.]

CHOR. Close around him, and confound him, the con-
founder of us all.

Pelt him, pummel him and maul him ; rummage, ransack,
overhaul him,

Overbear him and out-bawl him ; bear him down and bring
him under.

Bellow' like a burst of thunder, robber ! harpy ! sink of
plunder !

Rogue and villain ! rogue and cheat ! rogue and villain, I
repeat !

Oftener than I can repeat it, has the rogue and villain
cheated.

---

* See "Acharnians," p. 28.

A.

Close around him left and right; spit upon him; spurn and
smite :
Spit upon him as you see; spurn and spit at him like
me.
But beware, or he'll evade ye, for he knows the private
track,
Where Eucrates * was seen escaping with the mill dust on
his back.

CLEON. Worthy veterans of the jury, you that either right
or wrong,
With my threepenny provision,† I've maintained and
cherished long,
Come to my aid ! I'm here waylaid—assassinated and
betrayed !

CHOR. Rightly served ! we serve you rightly, for your
hungry love of pelf,
For your gross and greedy rapine, gormandizing by
yourself;
You that ere the figs are gathered, pilfer with a privy
twitch
Fat delinquents and defaulters, pulpy, luscious, plump, and
rich ;
Pinching, fingering, and pulling—tampering, selecting, cull-
ing,
With a nice survey discerning, which are green and which
are turning,
Which are ripe for accusation, forfeiture, and confiscation.
Him besides, the wealthy man, retired upon an easy
rent,
Hating and avoiding party, noble-minded, indolent,

---

* See note to p. 94.—He was also an owner of mills, as appears by the
Scholiast.
† The juryman's fee, a means of subsistence to poor old men driven from
their homes by the war.

Fearful of official snares, intrigues and intricate affairs ;
Him you mark ; you fix and hook him, whilst he's gaping unawares ;
At a fling, at once you bring him hither from the Chersonese,*
Down you cast him, roast and baste him, and devour him at your ease.

    CLEON. Yes ! assault, insult, abuse me ! this is the return, I find,
For the noble testimony, the memorial I designed :
Meaning to propose proposals, for a monument of stone,
On the which, your late achievements,† should be carved and neatly done.

    CHOR. Out, away with him ! the slave ! the pompous empty fawning knave !
Does he think with idle speeches to delude and cheat us all ?
As he does the doting elders, that attend his daily call.‡
Pelt him here, and bang him there ; and here and there and everywhere.

    CLEON. Save me, neighbours ! O the monsters ! O my side, my back, my breast !

    CHOR. What, you're forced to call for help ? You brutal overbearing pest.

    S. S. [*returning to* CLEON].
I'll astound you with my voice ; with my bawling looks and noise.

    CHOR. If in bawling you surpass him, you'll achieve a victor's crown ;
If again you overmatch him, in impudence, the day's our own.

---

  * Of Thrace. Many Athenians possessed estates, and resided there for a quiet life.
  † In the expedition to Corinth.
  ‡ The veterans of the jury. See note, p. 102.

CLEON. I denounce this traitor here, for sailing on clandestine trips,
With supplies of tripe and stuffing, to careen the Spartan
ships.
S. S. I denounce then and accuse him, for a greater worse
abuse :
That he steers his empty paunch, and anchors at the public
board :
Running in without a lading, to return completely stored !
    CHOR. Yes ! and smuggles out, moreover, loaves and
luncheons not a few,
More than ever Pericles, in all his pride, presumed to do.
    CLEON. [*in a thundering tone*]. Dogs and villains, you
shall die !
    S. S. [*in a louder, shriller tone*].
                Aye ! I can scream ten times as high.
    CLEON. I'll overbear ye, and out-bawl ye.
    S. S.   But I'll out-scream ye, and out-squall ye.
    CLEON. I'll impeach you, whilst aboard,
                Commanding on a foreign station.
    S. S.*   I'll have you sliced, and slashed, and scored.
    CLEON. Your lion's skin of reputation,
                Shall be flayed off your back and tanned.
    S. S.   I'll take those guts of yours in hand.
    CLEON. Come, bring your eyes and mine to meet !
                And stare at me without a wink !
    S. S.   Yes ! in the market-place and street,
                I had my birth and breeding too ;
                And from a boy, to blush or blink,
                I scorn the thing as much as you.
    CLEON. I'll denounce you if you mutter.
    S. S.   I'll douse ye the first word you utter.

---

* The threats of each party are in the terms of their respective trades.

CLEON. My thefts are open and avowed ;
And I confess them, which you dare not.
S. S.   But I can take false oaths aloud,
And in the presence of a crowd ;
And if they know the fact I care not.
CLEON. What ! do you venture to invade
My proper calling and my trade ?
But I denounce here, on the spot,
The sacrificial tripe you've got ;
The tithe it owes was never paid :
It owes a tithe, I say, to Jove ;
You've wronged and robbed the powers above

CHORUS.—*Cretic Metre.**

Dark and unsearchably profound abyss,
Gulf of unfathomable
Baseness and iniquity !
Miracle of immense,
Intense impudence !
Every court, every hall,
Juries and assemblies, all
Are stunned to death, deafened all,
Whilst you bawl.
The bench and bar
Ring and jar.
Each decree
Smells of thee,
Land and sea
Stink of thee.
Whilst we
Scorn and hate, execrate, abominate,
Thee the brawler and embroiler, of the nation and the State.
You that on the rocky seat of our assembly raise a din,

---

* See note to "Acharnians," p. 24.

Deafening all our ears with uproar, as you rave and howl
  and grin ;
Watching all the while the vessels with revenue sailing in.
Like the tunny-fishers perched aloft, to look about and
  bawl,
When the shoals are seen arriving, ready to secure a
  haul.

CLEON. I was aware of this affair, and every stitch of it
  I know,
Where the plot was cobbled up and patched together, long
  ago.

S. S. Cobbling is your own profession, tripe and sausages
  are mine :
But the country folks complain,* that in a fraudulent
  design,
You retailed them skins of treaties, that appeared like trusty
  leather,
Of a peace secure and lasting ; but the wear-and-tear and
  weather
Proved it all decayed and rotten, only fit for sale and
  show.

DEM. Yes ! a pretty trick he served me ; there was I
  despatched to go,
Trudged away to Pergasæ,* but found upon arriving there,
That myself and my commission, both were out at heels and
  bare.

In a review of Mr. Mitchell's Aristophanes, a passage in his translation
of one of the choruses is noted with particular commendation. It
is said, "Mr. Mitchell has hit upon the very key-note of Aristophanes, whose choruses are so contrived throughout this play as to
afford a relief and contrast to the vulgar acrimony of the dialogue ;

---

* The allusions in these lines relate to some incidents not recorded in
history, some artifice by which Cleon had succeeded in deluding and
disappointing the party ; the country people in particular (long excluded
from the enjoyment of their property) who were anxious for peace.

not in their logical and grammatical sense, but in their form and rhythm, and in the selection of the words, which if heard imperfectly, would appear to belong to a grave or tender or beautiful subject." If the occasion had admitted of it, this observation might have been applied more particularly to the first lines of each chorus ; for we may remark instances in which the contrast of grave or graceful lines at the commencement was intended to give additional force to the vehemence of invective immediately following in the chorus itself. Thus, in the original of the chorus which is given above, an expression of wonder and awe* is conveyed to the ear by the mere rhythm of the first line, independent of, and in fact contradictory to, the sense of the words themselves, a kind of contrast which appeared unattainable in the English language. What could not, therefore, be accomplished by "form and rhythm " has in this instance been attempted by "the selection of words." But justificatory criticism has already been renounced, as absurd and tiresome. This note had been begun solely for the purpose of bringing under the notice of the reader, with due modification, the observation, somewhat too largely expressed, in the review above mentioned.

CHORUS.

Even in your tender years,
    And your early disposition,
You betrayed an inward sense
Of the conscious impudence,
    Which constitutes a politician.
Hence you squeeze and drain alone the rich milch kine of
    our allies ;
Whilst the son of Hippodamus licks his lips with longing
    eyes.
        But now, with eager rapture we behold
        A mighty miscreant of baser mould !
        A more consummate ruffian !
        An energetic ardent ragamuffin !
        Behold him there ! He stands before your
        eyes,

---

* O altitudo !

To bear you down, with a superior frown,
   A fiercer stare,
And more incessant and exhaustless lies.

The metre of the lines which follow, namely, the tetrameter-iambic, is
so essentially base and vulgar that no English song afforded a specimen fit to be quoted, and the songs themselves were not proper to
be mentioned ; at last, Mr. Cornewall Lewis, whose kind importunities had extorted the publication of the preceding play of " The
Acharnians," suggested as a produceable specimen the first line of a
sufficiently vulgar but otherwise inoffensive song—

   " A captain bold of Halifax, who lived in country quarters."

It would not be right that Mr. Lewis's name should be mentioned here
without an acknowledgment of the obligations due to him, for his
friendly zeal in forwarding that play through the press, and correct-
ing some inaccuracies incidental to the work of a very unsystematic
scholar.

The metre, of which so derogatory a character has been given, is always
appropriated in the comedies of Aristophanes, to those scenes of
argumentative altercation in which the ascendency is given t> the
more ignoble character ; in this respect it stands in decided contrast
with the anapæstic measure.

IAMBIC TETRAMETER.

CHOR. [*to the* SAUSAGE-SELLER].
Now then do you, that boast a birth, from whence you
   might inherit,
And from your breeding have derived a manhood and a
   spirit,
Unbroken by the rules of art, untamed by education,
Show forth the native impudence and vigour of the nation !
   S. S   Well ; if you like, then, I'll describe the nature of
   him clearly,
The kind of rogue I've known him for.
   CLEON.   My friend, you're somewhat early.
First give *me* leave to speak.
   S. S.   I won't, by Jove ! Aye. You may bellow !
I'll make you know, before I go, that I'm the baser fellow.

CHOR. Aye! stand to that! Stick to the point; and
  for a further glory,
Say that your family were base, time out mind before ye.
  CLEON. Let me speak first!
  S. S.   I won't.
  CLEON.   You shall, by Jove!
  S. S.   I won't, by Jove, though!
  CLEON. By Jupiter, I shall burst with rage!
  S. S.   No matter, I'll prevent you.
  CHOR. No; don't prevent, for Heaven's sake! Don't
  hinder him from bursting.
  CLEON. What means—what ground of hope have you
  —to dare to speak against me?
  S. S. What! I can speak! and I can chop—garlic and
  lard and logic.
  CLEON. Aye! You're a speaker, I suppose! I should
  enjoy to see you,
Like a pert scullion set to cook—to see your talents fairly
Put to the test, with hot blood-raw disjointed news arriving,*
Obliged to hash and season it, and dish it in an instant.
  You're like the rest of 'em—the swarm of paltry weak
  pretenders.
You've made your pretty speech perhaps, and gained a little
  lawsuit
Against a merchant foreigner, by dint of water-drinking,
And lying long awake o' nights, composing and repeating,
And studying as you walked the streets, and wearing out
  the patience
Of all your friends and intimates, with practising before-
  hand:
And now you wonder at yourself, elated and delighted
At your own talent for debate—you silly saucy coxcomb.

---

* When the character of the debate is suddenly changed by the receipt
of unexpected intelligence.

S. S. What's your own diet? How do you contrive to keep the city

Passive and hushed—What kind of drink drives ye to that presumption?

CLEON. Why mention any man besides, that's capable to match me;

That after a sound hearty meal of tunny-fish and cutlets,

Can quaff my gallon; and at once, without premeditation,

With slang and jabber overpower the generals at Pylos.*

S. S. But I can eat my paunch of pork, my liver and my haslets,

And scoop the sauce with both my hands; and with my dirty fingers

I'll seize old Nicias by the throat, and choke the grand debaters.

CHOR. We like your scheme in some respects; but still that style of feeding,

Keeping the sauce all to yourself, appears a gross proceeding.

CLEON. But I can domineer and dine on mullets at Miletus.

S. S. And I can eat my shins of beef, and farm the mines of silver.

CLEON. I'll burst into the Council House, and storm and blow and bluster.

S. S. I'll blow the wind into your tail, and kick you like a bladder.

CLEON. I'll tie you neck and heels at once, and kick ye to the kennel.

CHOR. Begin with us then! Try your skill!—kicking us all together!

CLEON. I'll have ye pilloried in a trice.

S. S. I'll have you tried for cowardice.

---

* See Mitford, ch. xv., sect. 10, p. 293.

CLEON. I'll tan your hide to cover seats.

S. S.   Yours shall be made a purse for cheats.
The luckiest skin* that could be found.

CLEON. Dog I'll pin you to the ground
     With ten thousand tenter-hooks.

S. S.   I'll equip you for the cooks,
     Neatly prepared, with skewers and lard.

CLEON. I'll pluck your eyebrows off, I will.

S. S.   I'll cut your collops out, I will.

It is evident that a scuffle or wrestling match takes place here between the two rivals. It continues during the verses of Demosthenes and those of the Chorus, the last of which mark that the Sausage-seller has the advantage; and the Sausage-seller's speech of four lines which follows, implies that he is at the same time exhibiting his adversary in a helpless posture.

It is to be observed that the palæstra was not a mere school of wrestling or boxing. The attention of the masters of the palæstra, like the dancing-masters of former times in France and England, was directed to form their pupils to a general dignity and elegance of carriage.

Hence all awkward or indecent effort was disallowed in the palæstra of the better educated class. But, as wrestling was a universal national exercise, it would of course be practised vulgarly amongst the vulgar, and there would be many tricks and casts retained and practised by the lowest class which were rejected by the more dignified palæstra. The Sausage-seller was represented as foiling his opponent by some unbecoming unsightly effort which was characteristic of a town blackguard. Thus the scuffle between them formed a kind of dumb show, analogous to, and illustrative of the dialogue; exhibiting in the triumph of the Sausage-seller the peculiar advantages reserved for superior impudence and vulgarity both in word and deed.

DEMOSTHENES.

Yes, by Jove! and like a swine,
Dangling at the butcher's door,

---

* It is well known that purses made from the skins of different animals are more or less lucky. Among ourselves the skin of a weasel, or of a *black* cat, is esteemed the most universally lucky.

Dress him cleanly, neat and fine,
  Washed and scalded o'er and o'er;
Strutting out in all his pride,
With his carcase open wide,
And a skewer in either side ;
While the cook, with keen intent,
  By the steady rules of art,
  Scrutinizes every part,
The tongue, the throat, the maw, the vent.

Chorus.

Some element may prove more fierce than fire !
  Some viler scoundrel may be seen,
  Than ever yet has been !
And many a speech hereafter, many a word,
  More villainous, than ever yet was heard.
We marvel at thy prowess and admire !
  Therefore proceed!
  In word and deed,
  Be firm and bold,
  Keep steadfast hold !
Only keep your hold upon him .   Persevere as you began ;
He'll be daunted and subdued ; I know the nature of the
  man.
  S. S. Such as here you now behold him, all his life has
  he been known.
Till he reaped a reputation, in a harvest not his own ;
Now he shows the sheaves* at home, that he clandestinely
  conveyed,
Tied and bound and heaped together, till his bargain can
  be made.

---

* The Spartan prisoners taken at Pylos, and kept in the most severe
confinement.

CLEON. [*released and recovering himself*].
I'm at ease, I need not fear ye, with the Senate on my side,
And the Commons all dejected, humble, poor, and stupefied.

CHORUS.

Mark his visage ! and behold,
   How brazen, unabashed, and bold !
How the colour keeps its place
   In his face !
CLEON. Let me be the vilest thing, the mattress that
   Cratinus* stains;
Or be forced to learn to sing, Morsimus's † tragic strains;
If I don't despise and loath, scorn and execrate ye both.

CHORUS.

Active, eager, airy thing !
   Ever hovering on the wing,
      Ever hovering and discovering
Golden sweet secreted honey,
Nature's mintage and her money.
May thy maw be purged and scoured,
   From the gobbets it devoured ;
      By the emetic drench of law !
With the cheerful ancient saw,
Then we shall rejoice and sing,
   Chanting out with hearty glee,
   " Fill a bumper merrily,
   For the merry news I bring ! "
But he, the shrewd and venerable
Manciple‡ of the public table,

---

* The famous comic poet, now grown old ; and infirm, as it appears.
† Ridiculed elsewhere as a bad writer of tragedy. See "The Peace," v. 803.
‡ The old butler and steward of the Prytaneum, who had hitherto been
used to well-bred company and civil treatment, would be overjoyed at his
deliverance from such a guest as Cleon.

Will chant and chuckle and rejoice,
　　With heart and voice.
CLEON. May I never eat a slice, at any public sacrifice,
If your effrontery and pretence, shall daunt my steadfast
　　impudence.
S. S. Then, by the memory which I value, of all the
　　bastings in our alley,
When from the dog butcher's tray I stole the lumps of meat
　　away.
I trust to match you with a feat, and do credit to my meat,
Credit to my meat and feeding, and my bringing up and
　　breeding.
　　CLEON. Dog's meat! What a dog art thou! But I shall
　　dog thee fast enow.
　　　　[CLEON *pays no attention to the short dialogue which
　　　　follows between the* SAUSAGE-SELLER *and the*
　　　　CHORUS. *The actor's part was in dumb show,
　　　　exhibiting a mimicry of the Demagogue's usual
　　　　gesture and deportment, when exciting himself in
　　　　preparation for a vehement burst of oratory.*]
S. S. Then, there were other petty tricks, I practised as a
　　child ;
Haunting about the butchers' shops, the weather being
　　mild.
"See, boys," says I, "the swallow there! Why summer's
　　come I say,"
And when they turned to gape and stare, I snatched a steak
　　away.
　　CHOR. A clever lad you must have been, you managed
　　matters rarely,
To steal at such an early day, so seasonably and fairly.
　　S. S. But if by chance they spied it, I contrived to hide
　　it handily ;
Clapping it in between my hams, tight and close and even ;
Calling on all the powers above, and all the gods in heaven ;

And there I stood, and made it good, with staring and for-
swearing.

So that a statesman of the time, a speaker shrewd and
witty,

Was heard to say, " That boy one day will surely rule the
city."

CHOR. 'Twas fairly guessed, by the true test, by your
address and daring,

First in stealing, then concealing, and again in swearing.

CLEON. I'll settle ye ! Yes, both of ye ! the storm of
elocution

Is rising here within my breast, to drive you to confusion,

And with a wild commotion, overwhelm the land and
ocean.

S. S. Then I shall hand my sausages, and reef 'em close
and tight,

And steer away before the wind, and run you out of
sight.

DEM. And I shall go, to the hold below, to see that all
is right.   [*Exit.*

CLEON. By the holy goddess I declare,
.Rogue and robber as you are,
I'll not brook it, or overlook it ;
The public treasure that you stole,
I'll force you to refund the whole . . . .

CHOR. (Keep near and by—the gale grows high.)

CLEON. [*in continuation*]
. . . . Ten talents, I could prove it here,
Were sent to you from Potidea.

S. S.   Well, will you take a single one
To stop your bawling and have done ?

CHOR. Yes, I'll be bound—he'll compound,
And take a share—the wind grows fair.
This hurricane will overblow,
Fill the sails and let her go !

CLEON. I'll indict ye, I'll impeach,
        I'll denounce ye in a speech ;
        With four several accusations,
        For your former peculations,
            Of a hundred talents each.
S. S.   But I'll denounce ye,
        And I'll trounce ye,
            With accusations half a score ;
        Half a score, for having left
        Your rank in the army ; and for theft
            I'll charge ye with a thousand more.
CLEON. I'll rummage out your pedigree,
        And prove that all your ancestry
            Were sacrilegious and accurst.*
S. S.   I'll prove the same of yours ; and first
        The foulest treasons and the worst—
        Their deep contrivance to conceal
        Plots against the common weal ;
        Which I shall publish and declare—
        Publish, and depose, and swear.
CLEON. Plots, concealed and hidden !   Where ?
S. S.   Where ?   Where plots have always tried
        To hide themselves—beneath a hide !
CLEON. Go for a paltry vulgar slave.
S. S.   Get out for a designing knave.
CHOR.   Give him back the cuff you got !
CLEON. Murder ! help ! a plot ! a plot !
            I'm assaulted and beset !
CHOR.   Strike him harder ! harder yet !
        Pelt him,—rap him,
        Slash him,—slap him,
        Across the chops there, with a wipe

---

* Many of the first families were involved in the guilt of a sacrilegious massacre, committed nearly 200 years before. See Mr. Clinton's "Fasti Olymp." 40.

Of your entrails and your tripe !*
Keep him down—the day's your own.
O cleverest of human kind ! the stoutest and the boldest,
The saviour of the State, and us, the friends that thou
  beholdest;
No words can speak our gratitude ; all praise appears too
  little.
You've fairly done the rascal up, you've nicked him to a
  tittle.
CLEON. By the holy goddess, it's not new to me
This scheme of yours.   I've known the job long since,
The measurement and the scantling of it all,
And where it was shaped out and tacked together.
  CHOR. Aye ! There it is ! You must exert yourself ; †
Come, try to match him again with a carpenter's phrase.
  S. S. Does he think I have not tracked him in his intrigues
At Argos?—his pretence to make a treaty
With the people there?—and all his private parley
With the Spartans?—There he works and blows the coals ;
And has plenty of other irons in the fire.
  CHOR. Well done, the blacksmith beats the carpenter.†
  S. S. [*in continuation*]
And the envoys that come here, are all in a tale ;
All beating time to the same tune.   I tell ye,
It's neither gold nor silver, nor the promises,
Nor the messages you send me by your friends,
That will ever serve your turn ; or hinder me
From bringing all these facts before the public.
  CLEON. Then I'll set off this instant to the Senate ;
To inform them of your conspiracies and treasons,
Your secret nightly assemblies and cabals,

---

* A slap on the face of this kind is proverbial, in Spain, as the most
outrageous of all insults.

† In these passages, the poet marks the degradation of public oratory,
infected with vulgar jargon and low metaphors,

Your private treaty with the king of Persia,
Your correspondence with Bœotia,
And the business that you keep there in the cheese-press,
Close packed you think, and ripening out of sight.

S. S. Ah! cheese? Is cheese any cheaper there, d'ye
hear?

CLEON. By Hercules! I'll have ye crucified!

[*Exit* CLEON.

CHORUS *to the* S. S.

Well, how do you feel your heart and spirits now?
Rouse up your powers! If ever in your youth
You swindled and forswore as you profess;
The time is come to show it. Now this instant
He's hurrying headlong to the Senate House;
To tumble amongst them like a thunderbolt;
To accuse us all, to rage, and storm, and rave.

S. S. Well, I'll be off then. But these guts and pudding,
I must put them by the while, and the chopping knife.

CHOR. Here take this lump of lard, to 'noint your neck
with;
The grease will give him the less hold upon you,
With the gripe of his accusations.

S. S.   That's well thought of.

CHOR. And here's the garlic. Swallow it down!

S. S.   What for?

CHOR. It will prime you up,* and make you fight the
better.
Make haste!

S. S.   Why, so I do.

CHOR.   Remember now—
Show blood and game. Drive at him and denounce him!
Dash at his comb, his coxcomb, cuff it soundly!

---

* Game-cocks are dieted with garlic, see "Acharnians," p. 21, Theorus's
warning to Dicæopolis, where a similar note should have been given.

Peck, scratch, and tear, conculcate, clapperclaw !
Bite both his wattles off, and gobble 'em up !
And then return in glory to your friends.

[*Exit* S. S.

CHORUS.

Well may you speed
In word and deed.
May all the powers of the market-place
Grant ye protection, and help, and grace,
With strength of lungs and front and brain ;
With a crown of renown, to return again.
[*turning to the audience*]
But you that have heard and applauded us here,
In every style and in every way,
Grant us an ear, and attend for a while,
To the usual old anapæstic essay.

The following Parabasis has been already noticed (p. 44 of "The Acharnians ") in the long preliminary notice prefixed to the Parabasis of
that play ; but the inference which is there so concisely assumed in
the foot-note, will be better and more conveniently estimated,
when placed in juxtaposition with the composition itself. It has
been said, in brief and strong terms, that the poet had become the
poetical serf of the community. Our knowledge of antiquity is too
scanty, to enable us to define precisely the mode and degree of this
vassalage, to which he thus voluntarily subjected himself ; but it is
evident, that by demanding (as the text has it) *a chorus for himself,*
he was in effect doing that which is expressed in the translation,
namely, *embracing a profession,* from which he could not retreat.
The whole tenor of the following Parabasis turns upon the decisive
and irretrievable step, which the poet (after long hesitation, and
resisting the importunity of his friends) had at length determined to
take, undeterred by the discouraging example of his predecessors in
the same line, whom he enumerates and describes, devoting himself
irrevocably and exclusively to the composition of comedy.
Yet the poet was already publicly known as the author of three
comedies; "The Daitaleis," in which he had exhibited the contrast of
two young men, brothers : the one, steady and manly, according to
the old fashion, instructed in the old music and poetry, addicted to

gymnastic exercises, living with his father in the country, a lover of hunting and rural sports ; the other, a thoroughly depraved town rake—a scamp of that new school, of which Alcibiades was the patron and the model ; aspiring to distinguish himself by foppery, litigation, and speechifying. That excellent comedy of Gresset's, " Le Méchant," may be considered as somewhat analogous to this— produced with the same intention, and in a state of society and manners not altogether dissimilar.

His second play, "The Babylonians," has been already mentioned (see " Acharnians," p. 44) ; of this he was avowedly the author, and had been held responsible for it, as we have already seen.

" The Acharnians," his third play, is generally speaking a comic pleading in favour of peace ; but it includes a justification of the poet as the author of the preceding play (distinctly and palpably in the Para- basis, and in a burlesque form in other parts) ; for Dicæopolis in his defence before the Chorus is the representative of the poet himself ; and that portion of the Chorus, which continues inveterate and un- appeased, bring an accusation against him, which has no reference to anything which has occurred in the preceding scenes of the same play ; but which is distinctly applicable to the main purport and argument of " The Babylonians " *—(see " Acharnians," p. 40)—

" Inveighing against informers."

The original, more scrupulously translated, would stand thus— *abusing any man that happened to be an informer,* an offence, of which the Dicæopolis of " The Acharnians " (for the informer Nicar- chus has not yet appeared) had been, up to this point at least, entirely guiltless. Dicæopolis then, in this instance, is a burlesque represen- tative of the poet himself, put upon his trial for misdemeanours perpetrated in a former play. His adversaries attack him, for having stigmatized individuals as informers. The party who are become favourable to him, justify him, by affirming the truth and correct- ness of all his imputations. The reply to this is, that though they might be true, he had no right to give publicity to scandalous and offensive truths ; and that he deserves to be punished for it. There is nothing in this altercation, which can in any way be made to bear the slightest reference to anything that had occurred in the preceding scenes of the play itself.

We have made a wide digression in our way to a very unsatisfactory conclusion. It may be said: we see very clearly, from what has

---

* It is noticed as having contained attacks upon a great number of persons.

been already stated, that Aristophanes was already an avowed writer for the comic theatre ; regarded as responsible for his productions, when they were deemed objectionable ; justifying them himself in person in the first instance, and afterwards under a feigned character, in a subsequent drama. What then was the change in his condition and prospects which was produced by *demanding a chorus for himself?* a term as it appears of great import ; implying a devotion of himself exclusively to the task of writing for the stage. What were the emoluments and privileges attached to this profession of a comic author, thus authentically assumed ? What, on the other hand, were the disadvantages and disabilities, by which those privileges and emoluments were counterbalanced ? This is a question, of which the learning and industry of continental scholars may perhaps procure a solution, if they have not already afforded it, to those who are conversant in the language and literature of Germany. But something in the meanwhile may be deduced from the testimony of the poet himself. It appears from the scene of Euripides in "The Acharnians," that the author must have been entitled to the dresses of the actors ; and his perquisites probably extended to the other properties (as they are called) of the stage : with the exception of those which were permanent and immovable. We find the poet thus speaking of himself in the Parabasis of "The Peace," contrasting his own conduct with that of other cotemporary comic authors—he says (v. 763) :

> "On former occasions he never made use
> Of the credit he gained, to corrupt and seduce ;
> *But packed up his alls,* after gaining the day,
> Contented and joyous, and so went away."

We find, moreover, that the comic poets received a salary from the State ; for in the play of "The Frogs," exhibited almost at the close of the war, at a time of great pecuniary difficulty, it seems that their pay was reduced. And the poet introduces his Chorus of happy spirits in the Elysian fields, excommunicating the economists—in company with other reprobates and profane persons who are warned to withdraw from the sacred rites :—they include, in their interdict,

> "All *statesmen* retrenching the *fees and the salaries*
> Of *theatrical bards* in revenge for the railleries
> And jests and lampoons of this holy solemnity."

This appears evidently not to have been serious ; or if serious, would have been very unreasonable ; for the retrenchment at that period was universal, extending even to the omnipotent jurymen, who were reduced from a daily pay of three oboli, to two. Whatever the

retrenchment may have been, it seems, as is suggested above, not to
have been one which was seriously complained of; and we may
safely infer, from the general munificence of the Athenians in all
matters of art, and from their peculiar passion for the theatre, that
in better and more prosperous times the allowances made to the
comic poets must have been sufficiently liberal—at least to the three
successful competitors; for there were three dramatic prizes, assigned
to the first, second, and third best play; a circumstance, which of
itself implies a considerable pecuniary recompense ; for the third,
the least of all, must have been worth having in a pecuniary view;
otherwise, to be ranked as a third-rate poet would have been felt as
an unqualified mortification. Supposing the prizes to have been
merely honorary, no third prize could have existed; for it could
never have been considered as an honour.

From the question of emoluments we may turn to that of privileges
and immunities : and here, in the absence of positive authority, we
may be contented for the present with general inferences and
analogy. According to the notions of heathen antiquity, a professed
comic poet would have been considered as a person devoted to the
service of Bacchus ; a certain character of inviolability must therefore have been attached to him, in common with other persons
separated and set apart from the common concerns of the State, and
dedicated for life to the service of any other deity. Though modified no doubt in later times, this principle was essentially inherent
in the Grecian mind. The slaughter of a poet, "a servant of the
Muses," was condemned as an act of sacrilege ; and it was in these
terms, that the assassin of Archilochus was excommunicated by the
Oracle, and expelled from the temple, which he had presumed to
enter. It is not conceivable, that these feelings, however modified,
could have been altogether extinct, in the times of which we are now
treating ; and it is a singular fact, considering the enormous outrages
and attacks upon private character, perpetrated by the comic poets,
that (with the exception of the exploded fable of the death of
Eupolis) there is no trace to be met with of any personal vengeance
directed against any of them. The comic poets have been spoken
of above, as persons separate and set apart from the ordinary concerns of the State ; and so they must have been, either by positive
law, or by established and authoritative custom ; for it is not to be
supposed, that to any man standing in all other respects upon an
equal footing with his fellow-citizens, the privilege should have been
allowed of assailing them with unlimited ribaldry and abuse. Whatever may be thought of such a privilege in modern times, it was
certainly not consonant to the spirit of antiquity, to allow it to

be enjoyed by any individual, unaccompanied with corresponding disabilities. The office of a comic poet, during the reign of the Athenian democracy, has not been unaptly compared to that of the court jester during the Middle Ages. They were both of them authorized to take the most extraordinary liberties, in reflections on the sovereign, and the highest persons in the State ; but theirs was a situation obviously incompatible with the exercise of any other office or privilege. The parallel may be carried further ; for it would appear, from many recorded instances, that of these royal jesters many must have been men, not only of a lively fancy and imagination, but of just feelings and a sound judgment, whose privileged sallies occasionally directed the attention of the sovereign to truths which could not have been conveyed to him by any other channel. Aristophanes was certainly a most judicious though ineffectual adviser to the multitudinous sovereign, whom it was his office to amuse ; and Charles of Burgundy might have lived and died in prosperity, if his counsels had been moderated by the sarcasms of his jester.

But to return to our subject : thus far, in the absence of direct and positive information, an attempt has been made, by conjecture and inference, to define the new position in which the poet was placing himself, as a member of the community to which he belonged ; whether in this respect he had any reason to repent of his resolution, it would be idle and superfluous to risk any conjecture ; but in regard to his success as an author, the forebodings expressed in the Parabasis appear to have been verified. Up to this time, while unengaged and at liberty, he had been courted by the public, and indulged with applause and success ; for the strong feeling excited in the public by his play of "The Babylonians," at first hostile, and gradually (like their representatives the Chorus of Acharnians) subsiding into acquiescence and approbation, must have been felt as more than an equivalent to the highest theatrical success. But he was now irrevocably engaged in the service of the public : the first prize, as a kind of premium for enlisting, was awarded to the present play, the first which he exhibited as a regular writer for the stage ; but from this time he was destined, like his predecessors, to experience the rigours and caprices of theatrical discipline. His next play was "The Clouds," in which, following up the design of "The Daitaleis," he had traced to its source that sudden change in morality and manners, of which the outward manifestations had been exhibited in the former play. This play of "The Clouds," which he affirms (adjuring Bacchus as the patron deity of theatrical poets) to have been the best that ever was written, was rejected. The play of

"The Wasps," in which he thus asserted the merit of "The Clouds," was acted in the following year, and obtained the first prize. But we find that another mortification had in the meanwhile befallen him, in the diminished zeal and ardour of his friends—he had been, as the phrase is, *"had up"* by Cleon before the Senate, and subjected to the infliction of a severe invective; during which time, he complains, that his friends and partizans who were in attendance, and upon whose countenance be depended, "had shown themselves indifferent and even amused." They imagined, no doubt, that being once engaged, he must go on. But he tells them, that he does not mean to compromise himself to the same extent in future; and reminds them of the fable of the vine, which being left unsupported, ceased to produce fruit (v. 1291):

"So (the story says) the stake deserted and betrayed the vine."

Here then we trace a turn in the poet's mind; he became less of a public personage: and though his fancy and wit remained the same, and his principles continued unchanged; and though his courage and spirit occasionally broke forth in public emergencies, yet having adopted the stage as his occupation, he approached more nearly to the common standard of theatrical writers; and he might have made the same complaint, which was uttered by Shakespeare:

"So that almost my nature is subdued
To what it deals in, like the dyer's hand."

But the text is already too much clogged with this long interpolation of prose. We will not stop, therefore, to lament over the loss of "The Daitaleis" and "The Babylonians," composed at an' earlier period, and with an unbroken spirit.

But the money-loving spirit of our age manifests itself even in our literary researches, and we cannot refrain, even with respect to an ancient poet who lived 2300 years ago, from the invariable inquiry —*What was he worth?* It may be inferred then, from grounds of presumption too long to be detailed here, that he must have belonged to the class of the knights. Now the knights were rated (according to the modus fixed by Solon) at an amount of 300 bushels of corn. But how rated? As for the sum total of their income? Or as being that portion of it, which in cases of emergency was exigible for the service of the State? Those students of antiquity, who are not endowed with the faculty of digesting gross absurdities, are under great obligations to Mr. Boeck, for having relieved them from the cruel necessity of being constrained to believe, that a man with £75 a year (taking corn at five shillings a bushel) was bound to keep a war-horse, and to serve in the cavalry at his own expense; or that

another with an income of £225 (estimated according to the same permanent standard of value) could have been charged with the expenses of a ship of war—a proposition, we conceive, wholly contradictory to the experience of the members of the Yacht Club. Mr. Boeck has shown, that these sums were the extreme rates of taxation to which the individuals of these classes were subject ; a rate which was not always exacted in full; and which we may suppose, at the utmost, to have been a double tithe, or four shillings in the pound, a rate of taxation to which, in difficult times, our own country was contented to submit. The elucidation of this point is by far the greatest service which Mr. Boeck has rendered to ancient literature, in the whole of his accurate and learned work. To have dissipated these misapprehensions, which, as long as they were implicitly adopted, diffused an air of utter incredibility and unreality over the whole system of antiquity, is a result far more important than the development of details hitherto unknown and unexamined.
This discussion, already too long, has been prolonged thus far for the sake of restating Mr. Boeck's discovery ; which has been unaccountably overlooked in a recent publication.
With respect to the poet, we may safely conclude, that he was in tolerably easy circumstances ; and we find accordingly that he was able to give away some of his plays with their contingent emoluments : among the rest the very play ("The Frogs") in which he complained of the new retrenchment, and denounced an anathema against the economists.

PARABASIS.

If a veteran author had wished to engage
Our assistance to-day, for a speech from the stage ;
We scarce should have granted so bold a request ;
But this author of ours, as the bravest and best,
Deserves an indulgence denied to the rest.
For the courage and vigour, the scorn and the hate,
With which he encounters the pests of the State ;
A thorough-bred seaman, intrepid and warm,
Steering outright, in the face of the storm.
   But now for the gentle reproaches he bore
On the part of his friends, for refraining before
To embrace the profession, embarking for life
In theatrical storms and poetical strife.

He begs us to state, that for reasons of weight,
He has lingered so long, and determined so late.
For he deemed the achievements of comedy hard,
The boldest attempt of a desperate bard !
The Muse he perceived was capricious and coy,
Though many were courting her few could enjoy.
And he saw without reason, from season to season,
Your humour would shift, and turn poets adrift,
Requiting old friends with unkindness and treason,
Discarded in scorn as exhausted and worn.
    Seeing Magnes's fate, who was reckoned of late
For the conduct of comedy captain and head;
That so oft on the stage, in the flower of his age,
Had defeated the Chorus his rivals had led ;
With his sounds of all sort, that were uttered in sport,
With whims and vagaries unheard of before,
With feathers and wings, and a thousand gay things,
That in frolicsome fancies his Choruses wore—
When his humour was spent, did your temper relent,
To requite the delight that he gave you before?
We beheld him displaced, and expelled and disgraced,
When his hair and his wit were grown aged and hoar.
    Then he saw, for a sample, the dismal example
Of noble Cratinus so splendid and ample,
Full of spirit and blood, and enlarged like a flood ;
Whose copious current tore down with its torrent,
Oaks, ashes and yew, with the ground where they grew,
And his rivals to boot, wrenched up by the root ;
And his personal foes, who presumed to oppose,
All drowned and abolished, dispersed and demolished,
And drifted headlong, with a deluge of song.
    And his airs and his tunes, and his songs and lampoons,
Were recited and sung, by the old and the young—
At our feasts and carousals what poet but he ?
And " The fair Amphibribe " and " The Sycophant Tree,"

" Masters and masons and builders of verse ! "—
Those were the tunes that all tongues could rehearse;
But since in decay, you have cast him away,
Stript of his stops and his musical strings,
Battered and shattered, a broken old instrument,
Shoved out of sight among rubbishy things.

His garlands are faded, and what he deems worst,
His tongue and his palate are parching with thirst ;

And now you may meet him alone in the street,
Wearied and worn, tattered and torn,
All decayed and forlorn, in his person and dress ;

Whom his former success should exempt from distress.
With subsistence at large, at the general charge,
And a seat with the great, at the table of state,*
There to feast every day, and preside at the play
In splendid apparel, triumphant and gay.

Seeing Crates the next, always teased and perplexed,
With your tyrannous temper tormented and vexed ;
That with taste and good sense, without waste or expense,
From his snug little hoard, provided your board,
With a delicate treat, economic and neat.

Thus hitting or missing, with crowns or with hissing,
Year after year, he pursued his career,
For better or worse, till he finished his course.

These precedents held him in long hesitation ;
He replied to his friends, with a just observation,
" That a seaman in regular order is bred,
To the oar, to the helm, and to look out ahead ;
With diligent practice has fixed in his mind
The signs of the weather, and changes of wind.
And when every point of the service is known,
Undertakes the command of a ship of his own."

---

* The Prytaneum.

For reasons like these,
If your judgment agrees,
That he did not embark,
Like an ignorant spark,
Or a troublesome lout,
To puzzle and bother, and blunder about,
Give him a shout,
At his first setting out !
And all pull away
With a hearty huzza
For success to the play !
Send him away,
Smiling and gay,
Shining and florid,
With his bald forehead !

The text contains nearly all that is known of two of the three poets here
mentioned, Magnes and Crates ; the last is recorded, as having become distinguished in the second year of the 82 Olymp., thirty-six
years before the exhibition of "The Knights ": Magnes must have
been older. Of Cratinus some few fragments are still in existence : he
lived to vindicate himself from the offensive commiseration here bestowed him, by gaining the first prize in the next year, when the
comedy of "The Clouds" was rejected.

STROPHE.

Neptune, lord of land and deep,
From the lofty Sunian steep,
   With delight surveying
The fiery-footed steeds,
   Frolicking and neighing
As their humour leads—
   And rapid cars contending
   Venturous and forward,
     Where splendid youths are spending
The money that they borrowed.
    Thence downward to the ocean,

And the calmer show
Of the dolphin's motion
In the depths below ;
And the glittering galleys
Gallantly that steer,
When the squadron sallies,
With wages in arrear.
List, O list !
Listen and assist,
Thy Chorus here !
Mighty Saturn's son !
The support of Phormion,*
In his victories of late ;
To the fair Athenian State
More propitious far,
Than all the gods that are,
In the present war.

EPIRREMA.

Let us praise our famous fathers, let their glory be recorded
On Minerva's mighty mantle† consecrated and embroidered.
That with many a naval action and with infantry by
  land,
Still contending, never ending, strove for empire and
  command.
When they met the foe, disdaining to compute a poor
  account
Of the number of their armies, of their muster and amount :

---

* A most able and successful naval commander.

† This mantle was an enormous piece of tapestry adorned with the
actions and figures of the naval heroes and protecting deities. It was re-
newed every year ; and was carried to the temple, at the Panathenaic
procession, suspended and displayed from a tall mast fixed on a movable
carriage See Mr. Wordsworth's "Attica," p. 184.

But whene'er at wrestling matches * they were worsted in
the fray ;
Wiped their shoulders from the dust, denied the fall, and
fought away.
Then the generals † never claimed precedence, or a
separate seat,
Like the present mighty captains ; or the public wine or
meat.
As for us, the sole pretension suited to our birth and years,
Is with resolute intention, as determined volunteers,
To defend our fields and altars, as our fathers did before ;
Claiming as a recompense this easy boon, and nothing
more :
When our trials with peace are ended, not to view us with
malignity ;
When we're curried, sleek and pampered, prancing in our
pride and dignity.

ANTISTROPHE.

It will be seen that there is a want of correspondence and proportion
between the strophe and antistrophe ; the first has been enlarged, to
give scope for the development of the poetic imagery, tinged with
burlesque, which appears in the original. In atonement for this
irregularity, the antistrophe, which offered no such temptation, is
given as an exact *metrical facsimile* of the orignal. In this respect,
it may at least have some merit as a curiosity. The only variation
consists in a triple, instead of a double, rhyme.

Mighty Minerva ! thy command
Rules and upholds this happy land ;
Attica, famed in every part,
With a renown for arms and art,

---

* Thirty-two years before this time, the Athenians, after being foiled in a
great battle at Tanagra, risked another general action at Oinophuta, in
which they were victorious, only sixty-two days after the first !—" Fasti
Hellenici," OL 81.

† Tolmides and Myronides, who commanded in the battles here
alluded to.

Noted among the nations.
Victory bring—the bard's delight;
She that in faction or in fight,
Aids us on all occasions.
Goddess, list to the song ! Bring her away with thee,
Haste and bring her along ! Here to the play with thee.
Bring fair Victory down for us !
Bring her here with a crown for us !
Come with speed, as a friend indeed,
Now or never at our need !

ANTEPIRREMA.

It is observable, that the antepirrema is generally in a lower and less serious tone than its preceding epirrema ; as if the poet were, or thought it right to appear, apprehensive of having been over-earnest in his first address. In the present instance, as the poetical advocate of his party, he had already stated their claims to public confidence and favour ; and, in the concluding lines, had deprecated the jealousy and envy to which they were exposed. He now wishes to give a striking instance of their spirit and alacrity in the service of the country ; and it is given accordingly, in the most uninvidious manner, in a tone of extravagant burlesque humour.

Let us sing the mighty deeds of our illustrious noble steeds.
They deserve a celebration for their service heretofore,
Charges and attacks, exploits enacted in the days of yore :
These, however, strike me less, as having been performed
  ashore.
But the wonder was to see them, when they fairly went
  aboard,
With canteens and bread and onions, victualled and com-
  pletely stored,
Then they fixed and dipped their oars beginning all to shout
  and neigh,
Just the same as human creatures, " Pull away, boys ! Pull
  away ! "

" Bear a hand there, Roan and Sorrel ! Have a care there,
    Black and Bay !
Then they leapt ashore at Corinth ; and the lustier younger
    sort
Strolled about to pick up litter,* for their solace and
    disport :
And devoured the crabs of Corinth, as a substitute for
    clover.
So that a poetic Crabbe,† exclaimed in anguish " All is
    over !
What awaits us, mighty Neptune, if we cannot hope to
    keep
From pursuit and persecution in the land or in the deep."

The poet Carkinus (Crab) had produced a tragedy, on the subject of the
    daughter of a king of Corinth ; who merely, from bathing in the sea,
    had become unconsciously pregnant by Neptune. The lines here
    quoted from it were a complaint of the impossibility of preserving
    the honour of illustrious families from the licentious aggressions of
    the gods.

CHOR. [to the SAUSAGE-SELLER].
O best of men ! thou tightest heartiest fellow !
What a terror and alarm had you created
In the hearts of all your friends by this delay.
But since at length in safety you return,
Say what was the result of your attempt.
    S. S. The result is ; you may call me Nickoboulus ;
For I've nicked the Boule there, the Senate, capitally.

CHORUS.

    Then we may chant amain   ?
    In an exulting strain,

* The usual licentious excesses of an invading army.
† The poet Carkinus.

With ecstasy triumphant bold and high,
O thou!
That not in words alone, or subtle thought,
But more in manly deed,
Hast merited, and to fair achievement brought!
Relate at length and tell
The event as it befell:
So would I gladly pass a weary way;
Nor weary would it seem,
Attending to the theme,
Of all the glories of this happy day.

[*In a familiar tone, as if clapping him on the shoulder.*]
*Come, my jolly worthy fellow, never fear!
We're all delighted with you—let us hear!
S. S. Aye, aye—It's well worth hearing, I can tell ye:
I followed after him to the Senate House;
And there was he, storming, and roaring, driving
His thunderbolts about him, bowling down
His biggest words, to crush the cavaliers,
Like stones from a hill-top; calling them traitors,
Conspirators—what not? There sat the Senate
With their arms folded, and their eyebrows bent,
And their lips puckered, with the grave aspect
Of persons utterly humbugged and bamboozled.
Seeing the state of things, I paused awhile,
Praying in secret with an under voice:
" Ye influential impudential powers
Of sauciness and jabber, slang a d jaw!
Ye spirits of the market-place and street,
Where I was reared and bred—befriend me now!
Grant me a voluble utterance, and a vast
Unbounded voice, and steadfast impudence!"

---

* The encouragement which the poet administers, *to himself* in fact, is
not out of place ; he is preparing to attack the Senate, with the most contemptuous ridicule.

Whilst I thus thought and prayed, on the right hand,
I heard a sound of wind distinctly broken !
I seized the omen at once ; and bouncing up,
I burst among the crowd, and bustled through,
And bolted in at the wicket, and bawled out :
"News ! news ! I've brought you news ! the best of
    news !
Yes, Senators, since first the war began,
There never has been known, till now this morning,
Such a haul of pilchards." Then they smiled and seemed
All tranquillized and placid at the prospect
Of pilchards being likely to be cheap.
I then proceeded and proposed a vote
To meet the emergence secretly and suddenly :
To seize at once the trays of all the workmen,
And go with them to market to buy pilchards,
Before the price was raised. Immediately
They applauded, and sat gaping all together,
Attentive and admiring. He perceived it ;
And framed a motion, suited as he thought
To the temper of the Assembly. "I move," says he,
"That on occasion of this happy news,
We should proclaim a general thanksgiving ;
With a festival moreover, and a sacrifice
Of a hundred head of oxen ; to the goddess."
    Then seeing he meant to drive me to the wall
With his hundred oxen, I overbid him at once ;
And said " two hundred," and proposed a vow,
For a thousand goats to be offered to Diana,
Whenever sprats should fall to forty a penny.
With that the Senate smiled upon me again ;
And he grew stupefied and lost, and stammering ;
And attempting to interrupt the current business,
Was called to order, and silenced and put down.
    Then they were breaking up to buy their pilchards :

But he must needs persist, and beg for a hearing—
" For a single moment—for a messenger—
For a herald that was come from Lacedæmon,
With an offer of peace—for an audience to be given him."
But they broke out in an uproar all together :
" Peace truly !   Peace forsooth !   Yes, now's their time ;
I warrant 'em ; when pilchards are so plenty.
They've heard of it ; and now they come for peace !
No ! No ! No peace !   The war must take its course."
Then they called out to the Presidents to adjourn ;
And scrambled over the railing and dispersed ;
And I dashed down to the market-place headlong ;
Aud bought up all the fennel, and bestowed it
As donative, for garnish to their pilchards,
Among the poorer class of Senators ;
And they so thanked and praised me, that in short,
For twenty-pence, I've purchased and secured them.

CHORUS.

With fair event your first essay began,
Betokening a predestined happy man.
The villain now shall meet
In equal war,
A more accomplished cheat,
A viler far;
With turns and tricks more various,
More artful and nefarious.
But thou !
Bethink thee now ;
Rouse up thy spirit to the next endeavour !
Our hands and hearts and will,
Both heretofore and ever,
Are with thee still.
S. S. The Paphlagonian !   Here he's coming, foaming
And swelling like a breaker in the surf !

With his hobgoblin countenance and look ;
For all the world as if he'd swallow me up.

Enter CLEON.

CLEON. May I perish and rot, but I'll consume and
ruin ye ;
I'll leave no trick, no scheme untried to do it.
S. S. It makes me laugh, it amuses one, to see him
Bluster and storm ! I whistle and snap my fingers.
CLEON. By the powers of earth and heaven! and as I
live !
You villain, I'll annihilate and devour ye.
S. S. Devour me ! and as I live, I'll swallow ye ;
And gulp ye down at a mouthful, without salt.
CLEON. I swear by the precedence, and the seat
Which I achieved at Pylos, I'll destroy ye.
S. S. Seat, precedence truly ! I hope to see you,
The last amongst us in the lowest place.
CLEON. I'll clap you in jail, in the stocks—By heaven !
I will.
S. S. To see it how it takes on ! Barking and tearing !
What ails the creature ?   Does it want a sop ?
CLEON. I'll claw your guts out, with these nails of
mine.
S. S. I'll pare those nails of yours, from clawing victuals
At the public table.
CLEON.   I'll drag you to the Assembly
This instant, and accuse ye, and have you punished.
S. S. And I'll bring accusations there against you,
Twenty for one, and worse than yours tenfold.
CLEON. Aye—my poor soul ! but they won't mind ye or
hear ye,
Whilst I can manage 'em and make fools of 'em.
S. S. You reckon they belong to ye, I suppose ?
CLEON. Why should not they, if I feed and diet 'em ?

S. S. Aye, aye, and like the liquorish greedy nurses,
You swallow ten for one yourself at least,
For every morsel the poor creatures get.

CLEON. Moreover, in doing business in the Assembly,
I have such a superior influence and command,
That I can make them close and hard and dry,
Or pass a matter easily, as I please.

S. S. Moreover, in doing business—my band,
Has the same sort of influence and command;
And plays at fast and loose, just as it pleases.

CLEON. You sha'n't insult as you did before the Senate.
Come, come, before the Assembly.

S. S. [*coolly and drily*]. Aye—yes—why not?
With all my heart! Let's go there—What should hinder us?
[*The scene is supposed to be in front of* DEMUS'S *house.*]

CLEON. My dear good Demus, do step out a moment!

S. S. My dearest little Demus, do step out!

DEM. Who's there? Keep off! What a racket are you
    making;
Bawling and caterwauling about the door;
To affront the house, and scandalize the neighbours.

CLEON. Come out, do see yourself, how I'm insulted.

DEM. Oh, my poor Paphlagonian! What's the matter?
Who has affronted ye?

CLEON.   I'm waylaid and beaten,
By that rogue there, and the rake-helly young fellows,
All for your sake.

DEM.   How so?

CLEON.   Because I love you,
And court you, and wait on you, to win your favour.

DEM. And you there, sirrah! tell me what are you?

S. S.* A lover of yours, and a rival of his, this long
    time;

---

* Very rapidly and eagerly.

That have wished to oblige ye and serve ye in every way :
And many there are besides, good gentlefolks,
That adore ye, and wish to pay their court to ye ;
But he contrives to baffle and drive them off,
In short, you're like the silly spendthrift heirs,
That keep away from civil well-bred company,
To pass their time with grooms and low companions,
Cobblers, and curriers, tanners and such like.
    CLEON. And have not I merited that preference,
By my service ?
    S. S.   In what way ?
    CLEON.   By bringing back
The Spartan captives tied and bound from Pylos.
    S. S. And would not I bring back from the cook's shop
A mess of meat that belonged to another man ?
    CLEON. Well, Demus, call an Assembly then directly,
To decide between us, which is your best friend ;
And when you've settled it, fix and keep to him.
                                        [*Exit* CLEON.
    S. S. Ah, do ! pray do decide !—but not in the Pnyx—
    DEM. It must be there ; it can't be anywhere else ;
It's quite impossible : you must go to the Pnyx.
    S. S. Oh dear! I'm lost and ruined then ! the old fellow
Is sharp and clever enough in his own home ;
But planted with his rump upon that rock,
He grows completely stupefied and bothered.

CHORUS.

Now you must get your words and wit, and all your tackle
    ready,
To make a dash, but don't be rash, be watchful, bold and
    steady.
You've a nimble adversary, shifting, and alert, and wary.
        [*The scene changes and discovers the Pnyx with*
        CLEON *on the Bema, in an orational attitude.*]

*Look out! have a care! behold him there!
He's bearing upon you—be ready, prepare.
Out with the dolphin! Haul it hard!
Away with it up to the peak of the yard!
And out with the pinnace† to serve for a guard.

Cleon's exordium appears to be marked in the original by a trait of
humour which it is impossible to translate or to represent by an
equivalent. The true version is as follows :—"I pray to the goddess
Minerva, my own patroness, and the protecting deity of the city;
that if I stand as a meritorious statesman, in the next rank to
Lysicles,‡ Cynna and Salabaccha ;§ I may be allowed to continue
dining in the Prytaneum, &c. &c.

It should seem that the three discreditable names are substituted for
those of Pericles, Cymon, and Themistocles, with whom it appears
that Cleon was in the habit of comparing himself; for we shall see
that in the present scene he is attacked for having presumed to
place himself in parallel with Themistocles.

---

* Observe that the change of the scene is accompanied by the idea of
naval manœuvre. The ancient theatres being open at top, the machinery
was worked from below ; so that with the help of a little imagination the
stage might at such a moment be thought to resemble the deck of a ship.
Observe too, that as by the change of scene and its transfer to the Pnyx
(which had been deprecated by the Sausage-seller) the advantage is supposed to be transferred to the less ignoble character, the metre changes
from the tetrameter iambic to the anapæst, as in the scenes of altercation
in the other comedies, where the ascendency of the noble or ignoble
personage or argument, is marked by a change of the metre ; though the
scenes which follow may perhaps be considered as an exception; for the
Sausage-seller has the better even in the anapæst ; but his complete triumph
is reserved for the tetrameter.

† The image is that of a merchant vessel defending itself against the
attack of a ship of war: the pinnace was interposed to break the shock of
the enemy's prow ; and the dolphin, a huge mass of lead, was raised to a
great height, at the end of the yard of the enormous lateen sail (still to be
seen in some large old-fashioned craft in the Mediterranean). It was then
dropped suddenly at the moment of contact, to sink the enemy's vessel by
bursting a hole through it.

‡ A statesman of very low repute, who had come forward after the
death of Pericles, but speedily sunk into discredit.

§ Two eminent prostitutes.

It is natural therefore to conclude, that with respect to the two other illustrious, but less extraordinary characters, he must have felt still less scrupulous.

The phrase therefore stands as a contemptuous caricature of Cleon's arrogance. He had spoken of himself as the most meritorious public character:

μετα Περικλεα καὶ Κιμωνα καὶ Θεμιστοκλεα.

The taunting parody of the poet says:

μετα Λυσικλεα καὶ Κυνναν καὶ Σαλαβακχαν.

We see that the two first names have a similarity in sound to those for which they were substituted (Pericles, Lysicles—Cymon, Cynna). And we may be sure that an exact mimicry of Cleon's manner, and tone of voice, would not have been wanting to make the caricature as manifest as possible.

To those who have formed a just estimate of the merits of Aristophanes, this explanation of the passage will not appear unnecessary. It occurs in the most striking part of the play, at the very point to which the attention of the audience had been directed; but surely the most implicit admiration for everything ancient cannot prevent us from perceiving, that, unexplained as it has been hitherto, it appears vapid and senseless in the extreme. We might safely defy the dullest individual to make a poorer attempt at a joke in his own person.

If, on the contrary, we suppose the passage in question to have contained a verbal burlesque heightened by personal mimicry, the audience would hardly have felt a deficiency of amusement at this particular point of the representation.

CLEON. To Minerva the sovereign goddess I call,
Our guide and defender, the hope of us all;
With a prayer and a vow, that, even as now,
If I'm truly your friend, unto my life's end,
I may dine in the hall, doing nothing at all!
But, if I despise you, or ever advise you,
Against what is best, for your comfort and rest;
Or neglect to attend you, defend you, befriend you,
May I perish and pine; may this carcase of mine
Be withered and dried, and curried beside;
And straps for your harness cut out from the hide.

S. S. Then, Demus—if I, tell a word of a lie ;
If any man more can dote or adore,
With so tender a care, I make it my prayer,
My prayer and my wish, to be stewed in a dish ;
To be sliced and slashed, minced and hashed ;
And the offal remains that are left by the cook,
Dragged out to the grave, with my own flesh-hook.

    CLEON. O Demus! has any man shown such a
    zeal,
Such a passion as I for the general weal ?
Racking and screwing offenders to ruin ;
With torture and threats extorting your debts ;
Exhausting all means for enhancing your fortune,
Terror and force and intreaties importune,
With a popular, pure, patriotical aim ;
Unmoved by compassion, or friendship, or shame.

    S. S. All this I can do ; more handily too ;
With ease and despatch ; I can pilfer and snatch,
And supply ye with loaves from another man's batch.

    But now, to detect his saucy neglect ;
(In spite of the boast, of his loyalty due,
Is the boiled and the roast, to your table and you.)
You—that in combat at Marathon sped,
And hewed down your enemies hand over head,
The Mede and the Persian, achieving a treasure
Of infinite honour and profit and pleasure,
Rhetorical praises and tragical phrases ;
Of rich panegyric a capital stock—
He leaves you to rest on a seat of the rock,
Naked and bare, without comfort or care.
Whilst I—look ye there !—have quilted and wadded,
And tufted and padded this cushion so neat
To serve for your seat ! Rise now, let me slip
It there under your hip, that on board of the ship,
With the toil of the oar, was blistered and sore,

Enduring the burthen and heat of the day,
At the battle of Salamis working away.
DEM. Whence was it you came! Oh, tell me your
     name—
Your name and your birth ; for your kindness and worth
Bespeak you indeed of a patriot breed ;
Of the race of Harmodius* sure you must be,
So popular, gracious and friendly to me.
     CLEON. Can he win you with ease, with such trifles as
     these ?
     S. S. With easier trifles you manage to please.
     CLEON. I vow notwithstanding, that never a man
Has acted since first the republic began,
On a more patriotical popular plan :
And if any man else can as truly be said
The friend of the people, I'll forfeit my head ;
I'll make it a wager, and stand to the pledge.
     S. S. And what is the token you mean to allege
Of that friendship of yours, or the good it ensures?
Eight seasons are past that he shelters his head
In a barrack, an outhouse, a hovel, a shed,
In nests of the rock where the vultures are bred,
In tubs, and in huts and the towers of the wall :
His friend and protector, you witness it all !
But where is thy pity, thou friend of the city ;
To smoke him alive, to plunder his hive ?
And when Archeptolemus† came on a mission,
With peace in his hand, with a fair proposition :
So drive them before you with kicks on the rump,
Peace, treaties and embassies, all in a lump !
     CLEON. I did wisely and well ; for the prophecies tell,
That if he perseveres, for a period of years ;

---

* The assassin of Hipparchus, canonized by the democratic fanaticism of
the Athenians.
† After the surrender of the Spartans at Pylos.

He shall sit in Arcadia, judging away
In splendour and honour, at five-pence a day :
Meantime I can feed and provide for his need ;
Maintaining him wholly, fairly and foully,
With jurymen's pay, three-pence a day.

   S. S. No vision or fancy prophetic have you,
Nor dreams of Arcadian empire in view ;
A safer concealment is all that you seek :
In the hubbub of war, in the darkness and reek,
To plunder at large ; to keep him confined,
Passive, astounded, humbled, blind,
Pining in penury, looking to thee,
For his daily provision a juryman's fee.
But if he returns to his country concerns,
His grapes and his figs, and his furmity kettle,
You'll find him a man of a different mettle.
When he feels that your fees had debarred him from
   these;
He'll trudge up to town, looking eagerly down,
And pick a choice pebble, and keep it in view,
As a token of spite,* for a vote against you.
Peace sinks you for ever, you feel it and know,
As your shifts and your tricks and your prophecies show.

   CLEON. 'Tis a scandal, a shame ! to throw slander and
   blame
On the friend of the people ! a patriot name,
A kinder protector, I venture to say,

---

* "As a token of spite : " that is, as a memorandum of anticipated
vengeance. It is recorded of some old Frenchman, in the early times of
the last century, that having suffered in his fortune by the depreciation of
the coinage, he set apart a gold piece of the old stamp ; and used to show
it to his friends, saying "that he kept it for the hire of a balcony looking
into the Place de Greve, against the time when the minister should be
brought out there for execution." With a similar feeling the Athenian
countryman is described as selecting his pebble for a future vindictive vote
against Cleon.

Than ever Themistocles was in his day,
Better and kinder in every way.

S. S. Witness, ye deities ! witness his blasphemies !
You to compare with Themistocles ! you !
That found us exhausted, and filled us anew
With a bumper of opulence ; carving and sharing
Rich slices of empire ; and kindly preparing,
While his guests were at dinner, a capital supper,
With a dainty remove, both under and upper,
The fort and the harbour, and many a dish
Of colonies, islands, and such kind of fish.
But now we are stunted, our spirit is blunted,
With paltry defences, and walls of partition ;
With silly pretences of poor superstition ;
And yet you can dare, with him to compare !
But he lost the command, and was banished the land,
While you rule over all, and carouse in the hall !

CLEON. This is horrible quite, and his slanderous spite,
Has no motive in view but my friendship for you,
My zeal—

DEM.   There have done with your slang and your
stuff,
You've cheated and choused and cajoled me enough.

S. S. My dear little Demus ! you'll find it is true.
He behaves like a wretch and a villain to you.
He haunts your garden and there he plies,
Cropping the sprouts of the young supplies,
Munching and scrunching enormous rations
Of public sales and confiscations.

CLEON. Don't exult before your time,
Before you've answered for your crime—
A notable theft that I mean to prove
Of a hundred talents and above.

S. S. Why do ye plounce and flounce in vain ?
Splashing and dashing and splashing again,

Like a silly recruit, just clapped on board?
Your crimes and acts are on record:
The Mitylenian bribe alone
Was forty minæ proved and shown.

CHORUS.*

O thou, the saviour of the State, with joy and admiration!
We contemplate your happy fate and future exaltation,
Doomed with the trident in your hand to reign in power
    and glory,
In full career to domineer, to drive the world before ye;
To raise with ease and calm the seas, and also raise a
    fortune,
While distant tribes, with gifts and bribes, to thee will be
    resorting.
Keep your advantage, persevere, attack him, work him,
    bait him,
You'll over-bawl him, never fear, and out-vociferate him.

CLEON. You'll not advance; you've not a chance, good
    people, of prevailing;
Recorded facts, my warlike acts, will muzzle you from
    railing;
As long as there remains a shield, of all the trophy taken
At Pylos, I can keep the field, unterrified, unshaken.

S. S. Stop there a bit, don't triumph yet—those shields
    afford a handle
For shrewd surmise; and it implies a treasonable scandal;
That there they're placed, all strapped and braced, ready
    prepared for action;
A plot it is! a scheme of his! a project of the faction!
Dear Demus, he, most wickedly, with villanous advise-
    ment,

---

* The metre now passes from the anapæst to the tetrameter iambic. See
p. 139, note.

Prepares a force, as his resource, against your just chastise-
ment :

The curriers and the tanners all, with sundry crafts of
leather,

Young lusty fellows stout and tall, you see them leagued
together ;

And there beside them, there abide cheesemongers bold
and hearty,

Who with the grocers are allied, to join the tanner's party.

Then if you turn your oyster eye, with ostracizing look,

Those his allies, will from the pegs, those very shields
unhook :

Rushing outright, at dark midnight, with insurrection
sudden,

To seize perforce the public stores, with all your meal and
pudden.

    DEM. Well I declare! the straps are there! O what a
deep, surprising,

Uncommon rascal! What a plot the wretch has been
devising.

    CLEON. Hear and attend, my worthy friend, and don't
directly credit

A tale for truth, because forsooth—"The man that told me,
said it."

You'll never see a friend like me, that well or ill
rewarded,

Has uniformly done his best, to keep you safely guarded ;

Watching and working night and day, with infinite detec-
tions

Of treasons and conspiracies, and plots in all directions.

    S. S. Yes, that's your course, your sole resource, the same
device for ever.

As country fellows fishing eels, that in the quiet river,

Or the clear lake, have failed to take, begin to poke and
muddle,

And rouse and rout it all about and work it to a puddle
To catch their game—you do the same in the hubbub and
    confusion,
Which you create to blind the State, with unobserved collu-
    sion,
Grasping at ease your bribes and fees. But answer! Tell
    me whether
You, that pretend yourself his friend, with all your wealth
    in leather,
Ever supplied a single hide, to mend his reverend battered
Old buskins?

    DEM.   No, not he, by Jove! Look at them, burst
    and tattered!
    S. S. That shows the man! now spick and span, behold,
    my noble largess!
A lovely pair, bought for your wear, at my own cost and
    charges.
    DEM. I see your mind is well inclined, with views and
    temper suiting,
To place the state of things and toes, upon a proper
    footing.
    CLEON. What an abuse! a pair of shoes to purchase
    your affection!
Whilst all my worth is blott ed forth, raised from your recol-
    lection;
That was your guide, so proved and tried, that showed
    myself so zealous,
And so severe this very year, and of your honour jealous,
Noting betimes all filthy crimes, without respect or pity.
    S. S. He that's inclined to filth, may find enough
    throughout the city:
A different view determined you; those infamous
    offenders
Seemed in your eyes, likely to rise, aspirants and pre-
    tenders;

In bold debate, and ready prate, undaunted rhetoricians;
In impudence and influence, your rival politicians.
   But there now, see ! this winter he might pass without his
      clothing ;
The season's cold, he's chilly and old; but still you think
   of nothing !
Whilst I, to show my love, bestow this waistcoat, as a
   present
Comely and new, with sleeves thereto, of flannel warm and
   pleasant.
   DEM. How strange it is ! Themistocles was reckoned
      mighty clever !
With all his wit, he could not hit on such a project ever,
Such a device, so warm, so nice; in short, it equals
   fairly
His famous wall, the port and all, that he contrived so
   rarely.
   CLEON. To what a pass you drive me, alas ! to what a
      vulgar level !
   S. S. 'Tis your own plan ; 'twas you began. As topers
      at a revel,
Pressed on a sudden, rise at once, and seize without
   regarding,
Their neighbours' slippers for the nonce, to turn into the
   garden.
   I stand, in short, upon your shoes—I copy your
      behaviour,
And take and use, for my own views, your flattery and
   palaver.
   CLEON. I shall outvie your flatteries, I !—see here this
      costly favour !
This mantle ! take it for my sake—
   DEM.   Faugh ! what a filthy flavour !
Off with it quick ! it makes me sick, it stinks of hides and
   leather.

S. S. 'Twas by design : if you'll combine and put the facts together,
Like his device of Silphium spice—pretending to bedizen
You with a dress ! 'Twas nothing less, than an attempt to poison.
He sunk the price of that same spice, and with the same intention—
You recollect ?

DEM.   I recollect the circumstance you mention.

S. S. Then recollect the sad effect !—that instance of the jury
All flushed and hot, fixed to the spot, exploding in a fury.
To see them was a scene of woe, in that infectious smother,
Winking and blinking in a row, and poisoning one another.

CLEON. Varlet and knave ! thou dirty slave ! what trash* have you collected ?

S. S. 'Tis your own cue—I copy you. So the Oracle directed.

CLEON. I'll match you still, for I can fill his pint-pot of appointment,
For holidays and working-days.†

S. S.   But here's a box of ointment—
A salve prescribed for heels when kibed, given with my humble duty.

CLEON. I'll pick your white hairs out of sight, and make you quite a beauty.

S. S. But here's a prize, for your dear eyes !—a rabbit-scut ! See there now !

---

* A reprimand which in this, and one or two other instances, the translator is tempted to transfer to himself !

† Donatives on festival days, when the courts were closed and the jury-men's pay suspended.

CLEON. Wipe 'em, and then, wipe it again, dear Demus,
on my hair now.

S. S. On mine, I say! On mine, do, pray!

> [DEMUS *bestows, in a careless manner, his dirty
> preference upon the* S. S. *He pays no attention
> to the altercation which follows, but remains in
> the attitude of a solid old juryman, sitting upon
> a difficult cause concocting the decision which he at
> last pronounces.*]

CLEON. I shall fit you with a ship,
To provide for and equip,
One that has been long forgotten,
Leaky, worm-eaten, and rotten,
On it you shall waste and spend
Time and money without end.
Furthermore, if I prevail,
It shall have a rotten sail.

CHOR. There he's foaming, boiling over:
See the froth above the cover.
This combustion to allay,
We must take some sticks away.

CLEON. I shall bring you down to ruin,
With my summoning and suing
For arrear of taxes due,
And charges and assessments new,
In the census you shall pass
Rated in the richest class.

S. S. I reply with nothing worse
Than this just and righteous curse.
May you stand beside the stove,*
With the fishes that you love,
Fizzling in the tempting pan,
A distracted anxious man;

---

* It is to be presumed that Cleon is indulging himself in the Prytaneum.

The Milesian question * pending,
Which you then should be defending,
With a talent for your hire
If you gain what they desire.
Then their agent, in a sweat,
Comes to say the Assembly 's met ;
All in haste you snatch and follow,
And in vain attempt to swallow ;
Running with your gullet filled,
Till we see you choked and killed.

  Chorus. So be it, mighty Jove ! so be it !
And holy Ceres, may I live to see it !

Dem. [*rousing himself gradually from his meditation*].
. . . In truth and he seems to me, by far the best—
The worthiest that has been long since—the kindest,
And best disposed, to the honest sober class
Of simple humble three-penny citizens.
You, Paphlagonian, on the contrary
Have offended and incensed me.　Therefore now
Give back your seal of office !　You must be
No more my steward !

 Cleon.　　　　　　　Take it ! and withal
Bear this in mind !　That he, my successor,
Whoever he may be, will prove a rascal
More artful and nefarious than myself—
A bigger rogue be sure, and baser far !

 Dem. This seal is none of mine, or my eyes deceive me
The figure's not the same !　I'm sure !

 S. S.　　　　　　　　　　Let's see—
What was the proper emblem upon your seal ?

 Dem. A sirloin of roast beef—

 S. S.　　　　　　　　It is not that

---

 * The Scholiast affords us no light as to the allusion to the Milesian
question.

DEM. Not the roast beef! What is it?

S. S.   A cormorant
Haranguing open-mouthed upon a rock—*

DEM. Oh mercy!

S. S.   What's the matter?

DEM.   Away with it!
That was Cleonymus's seal, not mine—†
But here take this, act with it as my steward.

CLEON. Not yet, Sir! I beseech you. First permit me
To communicate some oracles I possess.

S. S. And me too, some of mine.

CLEON.   Beware of them!
His oracles are most dangerous and infectious!
They strike ye with the leprosy and the jaundice.

S. S. And his will give you the itch, and a scald head;
And the glanders and mad-staggers! take my word for it!

CLEON. My oracles foretell, that you shall rule
Over all Greece, and wear a crown of roses.

S. S. And mine foretell, that you shall wear a robe
With golden spangles, and a crown of gold,
And ride in a golden chariot over Thrace;
In triumph with king Smicythes and his queen.

CLEON [*to the* S. S.].‡
Well, go for 'em! and bring 'em! and let him hear 'em!

S. S. Yes, sure—and you too—go fetch yours!

CLEON.   Heigh-day!

S. S. Heigh-day! Why should not ye? What should
    hinder ye?   [*Exeunt* CLEON *and* S. S.

The following Chorus has no merit whatever in the translation; and not
    much in the original. The first six lines are composed on the prin-
    ciple of contrast pointed out in p. 106.

---

   * The Pnyx, the place of assembly, was called the Rock.
   † Cleonymus's emblem is a bird, to mark his cowardice. See "Achar-
nians," p. 18. The bird is also one of voracious habits.
   ‡ Cleon affects to give orders which the S. S. retorts.

Chorus.

Joyful will it be and pleasant
To the future times and present,
The benignant happy day,
   Which will shine on us at last,
Announcing with his genial ray,
   That Cleon is condemned and cast!
Notwithstanding we have heard
   From the seniors of the city,*
Jurymen revered and feared,
   An opinion deep and pithy :
That the State for household use
   Wants a pestle and a mortar ;
That Cleon serves to pound and bruise,
   Or else our income would run shorter.
But I was told, the boys at school
Observed it as a kind of rule,
   That he never could be made
      By any means to play the lyre,
   Till he was well and truly *paid*—
      I mean with lashes for his hire.
At length his master all at once
Expelled him as an utter dunce ;
   As by nature ill inclined,
   And wanting *gifts* of every kind.

[*Re-enter* CLEON *and the* SAUSAGE-SELLER—CLEON
   with a large packet and the SAUSAGE-SELLER
   staggering under a porter's load.]

CLEON [*to* DEMUS].
Well, there's a bundle you see, I've brought of 'em ;
But that's not all ; there's more of them to come—

---

* There was a portion of the lower class of citizens who conceived that
the State had an interest in supporting the tyrannical exactions of Cleon.

S. S. I grunt and sweat, you see, with the load of 'em ;
But that's not all ; there's more of 'em to come.

DEM. But what are these?—all ?

CLEON.   Oracles.

DEM.   · What, all ?

CLEON. Ah, you're surprised, it seems, at the quantity !
That's nothing ; I've a trunk full of 'em at home.

S. S. And I've a garret and out-house both brimful.

DEM. Let's give 'em a look.   Whose oracles are these ?

CLEON. Bakis's mine are.

DEM. [_to the_ S. S.].   Well, and whose are yours ?

S. S. Mine are from Glanis, Bakis's elder brother.

DEM. And what are they all about ?

CLEON.   About the Athenians,
About the Island of Pylos,—about myself,—
About yourself,—about all kinds of things.

DEM. And what are yours about ?

S. S.   About the Athenians,—
About pease-pudding and porridge,—about the Spartans,—
About the war,—about the pilchard fishery,—
About the state of things in general,—
About short weights and measures in the market,—
About all things and persons whatsoever,—
About yourself and me.   Bid him go whistle.

DEM. Come, read them out then ! that one in particular,
My favourite one of all, about the eagle ;
About my being an eagle in the clouds.

CLEON. Listen then !   Give your attention to the Oracle !
" Son of Erechtheus, mark and ponder well,
This holy warning from Apollo's cell.
It bids thee cherish, him the sacred whelp ;
Who for thy sake doth bite and. bark and yelp.
Guard and protect him from the chattering jay ;
So shall thy juries all be kept in pay."

· DEM. That's quite above me !   Erechtheus and a whelp !

What should Erechtheus do with a whelp or a jay?
What does it mean?*

CLEON.   The meaning of it is this:
I am presignified as a dog, who barks
And watches for you.   Apollo therefore bids you
Cherish the sacred whelp—meaning myself.

S. S. I tell ye, the Oracle means no such thing:
This whelp has gnawed the corner off; but here,
I've a true perfect copy.

DEM.   Read it out then!
Meanwhile I'll pick a stone up for the nonce,
For fear the dog in the Oracle should bite me.

S. S. "Son of Erechtheus, 'ware the gap-toothed dog,
The crafty mongrel that purloins thy prog;
Fawning at meals, and filching scraps away,
The whilst you gape and stare another way;
He prowls by night, and pilfers many a prize,
Amidst the sculleries and the colonies."

DEM. Well, Glanis has the best of it, I declare.

CLEON. First listen, my good friend, and then decide:
" In sacred Athens shall a woman dwell,
Who shall bring forth a lion fierce and fell;
This lion shall defeat the gnats and flies,
Which are that noble nation's enemies.
Him you must guard and keep for public good,
With iron bulwarks and a wall of wood."

DEM. [*to the* S. S.]
D'ye understand it?

S. S.   No, not I, by Jove!

CLEON. Apollo admonishes you, to guard and keep me;
I am the lion here alluded to.

---

* Discussions on the genuine and corrupt copies of oracles were not
unfrequent; we find an instance in Thucydides.—See also the scene of the
Soothsayer in " The Birds."

Dem. A lion ! Why just now you were a dog !

S. S. Aye, but he stifles the true sense of it,
Designedly—that " wooden and iron wall,"
In which Apollo tells ye he should be kept.

Dem. What did the deity mean by it ? What d'ye think ?

S. S. To have him kept in the pillory and the stocks.

Dem. That prophecy seems likely to be verified.

Cleon. "Heed not their strain ; for crows and daws abound,
But love your faithful hawk, victorious found,
Who brought the Spartan magpies tied and bound."

S. S. " The Paphlagonian, impudent and rash,
Risked that adventure in a drunken dash.
O simple son of Cecrops, ill advised !
I see desert in arms unfairly prized :
Men only can secure and kill the game ;
A woman's deed it is to cook the same."

Cleon. Do listen at least to the Oracle about Pylos :
" Pylos there is behind, and eke before,*
The bloody Pylos."

Dem.   Let me hear no more !
Those Pylos's are my torment evermore.

S. S. But here's an Oracle which you must attend to ;
About the navy—a very particular one.

Dem. Yes, I'll attend—I wish it would tell me how
To pay my seamen their arrears of wages.

S. S. " O son of Egeus, ponder and beware
Of the dog-fox, so crafty, lean, and spare,
Subtle and swift." Do ye understand it ?

Dem.   Yes!
Of course the dog-fox † means Philostratus.

---

* There were three places of this name, not very distant from each other.
† The dog was (in a bad sense) the type of impudence—the fox of cunning ; Philostratus, the compound of the two, gained his subsistence by a very infamous trade.

S. S. That's not the meaning—but the Paphlagonian
Is always urging you to send out ships ;
Cruizing about exacting contributions ;
A thing that Apollo positively forbids.

DEM. But why are the ships here called dog-foxes?

S. S.   Why?
Because the ships are swift, and dogs are swift.

DEM. But what has a fox to do with it ? Why dog-
foxes ?

S. S. The fox is a type of the ship's crew ; marauding
And eating up the vineyards.

DEM.   Well, so be it !
But how are my foxes to get paid their wages ?

S. S. I'll settle it all, and make provision for them,
Three days' provision, presently. Only now,
This instant, let me remind you of an Oracle :
"Beware Cullene."

DEM.   What's the meaning of it ?

S. S. Cullene, in the sense I understand,
Implies a kind of a *culling*, asking hand—
The *coiled* hand of an informing bully,
Culling a bribe from his affrighted *cully*,†
A hand like his.

CLEON.   No, no ! you're quite mistaken,
It alludes to Diopithes's lame hand.†
" But here's a glorious prophecy which sings,
How you shall rule on earth, and rank with kings,
And soar aloft in air on eagle's wings."

S. S. " And some of mine foretell that you shall be,
Sovereign of all the world and the Red Sea ;   .

---

* The Scholiast tells us that the common informer at Athens, when
accosting and threatening persons for the purpose of extortion, had an
established token (the hand hollowed and slipped out beneath the cloak),
indicating that they were willing to desist for a piece of money.

† As a soothsayer he ought to have been free from any bodily defect.

And sit on juries in Ecbatana,
Munching sweet buns and biscuit all the day."
CLEON. "But me Minerva loves, and I can tell
Of a portentous vision that befell—
The goddess in my sleep appeared to me,
Holding a flagon, as it seemed to be,
From which she poured upon the old man's crown
Wealth, health, and peace, like ointment running down."
S. S. "And I too dreamt a dream, and it was this:
Minerva came from the Acropolis,
There came likewise, her serpent and her owl;
And in her hand she held a certain bowl;
And poured ambrosia on the old man's head,
And salt-fish pickle upon yours instead."
DEM. Well, Glanis is the cleverest after all.
And therefore I'm resolved, from this time forth,
To put myself into your charge and keeping;
To be tended in my old age and taken care of.
CLEON. No, do pray wait a little; and see how regularly
I'll furnish you with a daily dole of barley.
DEM. Don't tell me of barley! I can't bear to hear of it!
I've been cajoled and choused more than enough,
By Thouphanes* and yourself this long time past.
CLEON. Then I'll provide you delicate wheaten flour.
S. S. And I'll provide you manchets, and roast meat,
And messes piping hot that cry "Come eat me."
DEM. Make haste then, both of ye. Whatever you do—
And whichever of the two befriends me most,
I'll give him up the management of the State.
CLEON. Well, I'll be first then.
S. S.   No, you sha'n't, 'tis I.
[*Both run off; but the* SAUSAGE-SELLER *contrives to get the
start.*]

---

* An adherent of Cleon.

Chorus.

Worthy Demus ! your estate
  Is a glorious thing we own—
The haughtiest of the proud and great
  Watch and tremble at your frown ;
Like a sovereign or a chief,
  But so easy of belief.
Every fawning rogue and thief
Finds you ready to his hand,
Flatterers you cannot withstand.
To them your confidence is lent,
With opinions always bent
To what your last advisers say,
Your noble mind is gone astray.

Demus.

Those brains of yours are weak and green ;
  My wits are sound whate'er ye say :
'Tis nothing but my froward spleen
  That affects this false decay :
  'Tis my fancy, 'tis my way,
  To drawl and drivel through the day.
  But though you see me dote and dream,
  Never think me what I seem !
  For my confidential slave
  I prefer a pilfering knave ;
  And when he's pampered and full-blown ;
  I snatch him up and—dash him down !

Chorus.

We approve of your intent,
If you spoke it as you meant ;
If you keep them like the beasts,
Fattened for your future feasts,

Pampered in the public stall,
Till the next occasion call ;
Then a little easy vote
Knocks them down, and cuts their throat;
And you dish and serve them up,
As you want to dine or sup.

DEMUS.

Mark me !—When I seem to doze,
When my wearied eyelids close ;
Then they think their tricks are hid :
But beneath the drooping lid,
Still I keep a corner left,
Tracing every secret theft.
    I shall match them by-and-by !
All the rogues, you think so sly,
All the deep intriguing set,
Are but dancing in a net,*
Till I purge their stomachs clean
With the hemlock and the bean.

The SAUSAGE-SELLER *and* CLEON *re-enter separately.*

CLEON. Get out there !

S. S.   You, get out yourself ! you rascal !

CLEON. O Demus ! here have I been waiting, ready
To attend upon ye and serve ye, a long, long time.

S. S. And I've been waiting a longer, longer time—
Ever so long—a great long while ago.

---

* Persons subject to an effectual restraint, of which they were themselves
unaware, were said to be *dancing in a net.* The Royalists, in Cromwell's
time, found themselves baffled in all their attempts, without at all suspecting
the system of secret information by which they were circumvented and
restrained. When this came to be known afterwards, it was said that
Cromwell had kept them *dancing in a net—i.e.,* joyous and alert, conspiring
and corresponding in imaginary security, wholly unconscious of the restraint
in which they had been held.

DEM. And I've been waiting here cursing ye both,
A thousand times, a long, long time ago.

S. S. You know what you're to do ?

DEM.   Yes, yes, I know;
But you may tell me, however, notwithstanding.

S. S. Make it a race, and let us start to serve you,
And win your favour without loss of time.

DEM. So be it.   Start now—one ! two ! three !

CLEON.   Heigh-day !

DEM. Why don't you start ?

CLEON.   He's cheated and got before me.
                                        [*Exit.*

DEM. Well truly indeed I shall be feasted rarely ;
My courtiers and admirers will quite spoil me.

CLEON. There, I'm the first you see to bring ye a chair.

S. S. But a table.   Here I've brought it, first and foremost.

CLEON. See here this little half-meal cake from Pylos,
Made from the flour of victory and success.

S. S. But here's a cake ! see here ! which the heavenly
   goddess
Patted and flatted herself, with her ivory hand,
For your own eating.

DEM.   Wonderful, mighty goddess !
What an awfully large hand she must have had !

CLEON. See this pease-pudding, which the warlike virgin
Achieved at Pylos, and bestows upon you.

S. S. The goddess upholds your whole establishment,
And holds this mess of porridge over your head.

DEM. I say the establishment could not subsist
For a single hour, unless the goddess upheld
The porridge of our affairs, most manifestly.*

---

* This refers to a notion very prevalent among the Athenians, and which
is alluded to elsewhere :—

F

CLEON. She, the dread virgin who delights in battle,
And storm and battery, sends this batter-pudding.

S. S. This savoury stew, with comely sippets decked,
Is sent you by the Gorgon-bearing goddess,
Who bids you gorge and gormandize thereon.

CLEON. The daughter of Jove arrayed in panoply
Presents you a pancake to create a panic
Amongst your enemies.

S. S.   And by me she sends
For your behoof this dainty dish of fritters,
Well fried, to strike your foemen with affright;
And here's a cup of wine—taste it and try.

DEM. It's capital, faith!

S. S.   And it ought to be ; for Pallas
Mixed it herself expressly for your palate.

CLEON. This slice of rich sweet-cake, take it from me.

S. S. This whole great rich sweet-cake, take it from me.

CLEON [to the S. S.] Ah, but hare-pie—where will you
get hare-pie?

S. S. [aside]. Hare-pie ! What shall I do !—Come, now's
the time,
Now for a nimble, knowing, dashing trick.

CLEON. [to the S. S., showing the dish which he is going to
present].
            Look there, you poor rapscallion.

S. S.   Pshaw ! no matter.

"Rash and ever in the wrong, a providence protects us ever,
Guiding all your empty plans, assisting every wild endeavour."
                                        "Clouds," v. 586.

It was founded on an anecdote, dating as far back as the time of the
contest between Neptune and Minerva. Neptune, is his chagrin, impre-
cated upon the territory of which he was dispossessed, the curse of being
always governed by "bad councils." This Minerva could not cancel ; but
she subjoined that these bad councils, bad as they might be, should be
successful.

I've people of my own there in attendance.
They're coming here—I see them.

CLEON. Who? What are they?

S. S. Envoys with bags of money.

[CLEON *sets down his hare-pie, and runs off the stage to
intercept the supposed envoys.*]

CLEON. Where? Where are they?
Where? Where?

S. S. What's that to you? Can't ye be civil?
Why don't you let the foreigners alone?
There's a hare-pie, my dear own little Demus,
A nice hare-pie, I've brought ye! See, look there!

CLEON [*returning*]. By Jove, he's stolen it, and served
it up.

S. S. Just as you did the prisoners at Pylos.

DEMUS. Where did ye get it? How did ye steal it? Tell
me.

S. S. The scheme and the suggestion were divine,
The theft and the execution simply mine.

CLEON. I took the trouble.

S. S. But I served it up.

DEMUS. Well, he that brings the thing must get the
thanks.

CLEON [*aside*]. Alas, I'm circumvented and undone
Out-faced and over-impudentified.

S. S. Come, Demus, had not you best decide at once,
Which is your truest friend, and best disposed
To the interest of the State, to your belly and you.

DEMUS. But how can I decide it cleverly?
Which would the audience think is the cleverest way?

S. S. I'll tell ye; take my chest and search it fairly,
Then search the Paphlagonian's and determine.

DEMUS. Let's look; what's here?

S. S. It's empty, don't you see?
My dear old man, I've given you everything.

DEMUS. Well, here's a chest indeed, in strict accordance
With the *judgment* of the public; perfectly *empty!*

S. S. Come now, let's rummage out the Paphlagonian's.
See there!

DEMUS. Oh bless me, what a hoard of dainties!
And what a lump of cake the fellow has kept,
Compared with the little tiny slice he gave me.

S. S. That was his common practice; to pretend
To make you presents, giving up a trifle,
To keep the biggest portion for himself.

DEMUS. O villain, how you've wronged and cheated
    me;
Me that have honoured ye, and have made ye presents.

CLEON. I stole on principle for the public service.

DEMUS. Pull off your garland—give it back to me,
For him to wear!

S. S.   Come, sirrah, give it back!

CLEON. Not so.   There still remains an Oracle,
Which marks the fatal sole antagonist,
Predestined for my final overthrow.

S. S. Yes! And it points to me, my name and person!

CLEON. Yet would I fain inquire and question you;
How far the signs and tokens of the prophecy
Combine in your behalf.   Answer me truly!
What was your early school?   Where did you learn
The rudiments of letters and of music?

S. S. Where hogs are singed and scalded in the shambles,
There was I pummelled to a proper tune.

CLEON. Ha, sayst thou so? this prophecy begins
To bite me to the soul with deep forebodings.
Yet tell me again—What was your course of practice
In feats of strength and skill at the Palæstra?

S. S. Stealing and staring, perjuring and swearing.

CLEON. O mighty Apollo, your decree condemns me!
Say, what was your employment afterwards?

S. S. I practised as a Sausage-seller chiefly,
Occasionally as pimp and errand-boy.

CLEON. Oh misery! lost and gone! totally lost!

[*after a pause*]

One single hope remains, a feeble thread,
I grasp it to the last. Yet answer me:
What was your place of sale for sausages?
Was it the market or the city gate?

S. S. The city gate! Where salted fish are sold!

CLEON. Out! out alas! my destiny is fulfilled:
Hurry me hence within with quick conveyance,
The wreck and ruin of my former self.
Farewell my name and honours! Thou, my garland,
Farewell! my successor must wear you now,
To shine in new pre-eminence—a rogue,
Perhaps less perfect, but more prosperous!

S. S. O Jove! Patron of Greece! the praise be
thine!

DEMOSTHENES.* I wish you joy most heartily; and I
hope,
Now you're promoted, you'll remember me,
For helping you to advancement. All I ask
Is Phanus's place to be under-scrivener to you.

DEM. [*to the* S. S.] You tell me what's your name?

S. S.   Agoracritus;

So called from the Agora where I got my living.

DEM. With you then, Agoracritus, in your hands
I place myself; and furthermore consign
This Paphlagonian here to your disposal.

S. S. Then you shall find me, a most affectionate
And faithful guardian; the best minister
That ever served the sovereign of the Cockneys.

[*Exeunt Omnes.*

---

* In a very civil, submissive tone.

The actors being withdrawn, the Chorus remain again in possession of the theatre. Their first song is a parody from Pindar, which is converted into a lampoon upon Lysistratus, who having reduced himself to poverty had procured (by the assistance of his friends) a lucrative appointment at Delphi. He is mentioned in " The Acharnians,' see the song, p. 60.

To record to future years
The lordly wealthy charioteers,
Steeds, and cars, and crowns victorious,
These are worthy themes and glorious.
   Let the Muse refrain from malice,
Nor molest with idle sallies
Him the poor Lysistratus ;
Taunted for his empty purse,
Every penny gone and spent,
Lately with Thaumantis sent
On a Delphic embassy,
With a tear in either eye,
Clinging to the deity
To bemoan his misery.

EPIRREMA.

An attempt is here made to express what the Scholiast points out ; namely, that the contrast between the two brothers is a piece of dry irony. In other respects the original is hardly capable of translation.

To revile the vile, has ever been accounted just and right,
The business of the comic bard, his proper office, his
   delight.
On the villanous and base, the lashes of invective fall ;
While the virtuous and the good are never touched or
   harmed at all.
Thus, without offence, to mark a profligate and wicked
   brother,
For the sake of explanation, I proceed to name another :

One is wicked and obscure, the brother unimpeached and
    glorious,
Eminent for taste and art, a person famous and notorious.
Arignotus—when I name him, you discern at once, with
    ease,
The viler and obscurer name, the person meant—
    Ariphrades,
If he were a rascal only we should let the wretch alone,
He's a rascal, and he knows it, and desires it to be known.
Still we should not have consented to lampoon him into
    vogue,
As an ordinary rascal, or a villain, or a rogue;
But the wretch is grown inventive, eager to descend and
    try
Undiscovered, unattempted depths of filth and infamy;
With his nastiness and lewdness, going on from bad to
    worse,
With his verses and his music, and his friend Oionychus.
Jolly friends and mates of mine, when with me you quench
    your thirst,
Spit before you taste the wine—spit upon the fellow first.

        Meditating on my bed,
        Strange perplexities are bred
        In my weary, restless head.
        I contemplate and discuss
        The nature of Cleonymus,
        All the modes of his existence,
        His provision and subsistence,
        His necessities and wants,
        And the houses that he haunts,
        Till the master of the table,
        Accosts him like the gods in fable,
        Manifested and adored
        At Baucis' and Philemon's board—

" Mighty sovereign !   Mighty lord !
Leave us in mercy and grace.   Forbear!
Our frugal insufficient fare,
Pardon it ! and in mercy spare !

ANTEPIRREMA.

Our Triremes, I was told, held a conference of late,
One, a bulky dame and old, spoke the first in the debate:
" Ladies, have you heard the news ?   In the town it passed
   for truth,
That a certain low bred upstart, one Hyperbolus forsooth,
Asks a hundred of our number, with a further proposition,
That we should sail with him to Carthage* on a secret
   expedition."
They all were scandalized and shocked to hear so wild a
   project planned,
A virgin vessel newly docked, but which never had been
   manned,
Answered instantly with anger, " If the Fates will not afford
   me
Some more suitable proposal, than that wretch to come
   aboard me,
I would rather rot and perish, and remain from year to
   year,
Till the worms have eat my bottom, lingering in the harbour
   here.
   No, thank heaven, for such a master Nauson's daughter
   is too good ;
And if my name were not Nauphantis, I am made of nails
   and wood.
I propose then to retire in sanctuary to remain
Near the temple of the Furies, or to Theseus and his fane.

---

* Carthage, in this instance, may admit of a doubt. See note to p. 97:
but it was by no means beyond the speculations of Athenian ambition at
that time.

Still the project may proceed ; Hyperbolus can never fail.
He may launch the trays of wood, in which his lamps were
set to *sale.*"

AGORACRITUS (*the* SAUSAGE-SELLER).

Peace be amongst you ! Silence ! Peace !
Close the courts ; let pleadings cease !
All your customary joys,
Juries, accusers, strife and noise !
Be merry, I say ! Let the theatre ring
With a shout of applause for the news that I bring.

CHOR. O thou the protector and hope of the State,
Of the isles and allies of the city, relate
What happy event, do you call us to greet,
With bonfire and sacrifice filling the street.

AG. Old Demus within has moulted his skin ;
I've cooked him, and stewed him, to render him stronger,
Many years younger, and shabby no longer.

CHOR. Oh, what a change ! How sudden and strange !
But where is he now?

AG.   On the citadel's brow,
In the lofty old town of immortal renown,
With the noble Ionian violet crown.

CHOR. What was his vesture, his figure and gesture ?
How did you leave him, and how does he look ?

AG. Joyous and bold, as when feasting of old,
When his battles were ended, triumphant and splendid,
With Miltiades sitting carousing at rest,
Or good Aristides his favourite guest.
You shall see him here strait ; for the citadel gate
Is unbarred ; and the hinges—you hear how they grate !

[*The Scene changes to a view of the Propylæum.*]

Give a shout for the sight of the rocky old height !
And the worthy old wight, that inhabits within !

CHOR. Thou glorious hill! pre-eminent still
For splendour of empire and honour and worth!
Exhibit him here, for the Greeks to revere;
Their patron and master the monarch of earth!
AG. There, see him, behold! with the jewels of gold
Entwined in his hair, in the fashion of old;
Not dreaming of verdicts or dirty decrees;
But lordly, majestic, attired at his ease,
Perfuming all Greece with an odour of peace.
CHOR. We salute you, and greet you, and bid you
    rejoice;
With unanimous heart, with unanimous voice,
Our sovereign lord, in glory restored,
Returning amongst us in royal array,
Worthy the trophies of Marathon's day!

> [DEMUS *comes forward in his splendid old-fashioned
> attire: the features of his mask are changed to
> those of youth, and his carriage throughout this
> scene is marked with the characteristics of youth,
> warmth, eagerness, and occasional bashfulness
> and embarrassment.*]

DEM. My dearest Agoracritus, come here—
I'm so obliged to you for your cookery!
I feel an altered man, you've quite transformed me.
AG. What! I? That's nothing; if you did but know
The state you were in before, you'd worship me.
DEM. What was I doing? How did I behave?
Do tell me—inform against me—let me know.
AG. Why first, then: if an orator in the Assembly
Began with saying, Demus, I'm your friend,
Your faithful zealous friend, your only friend,
You used to chuckle, and smirk, and hold your head up.
DEM. No sure!
AG. So he gained his end, and bilked and choused ye.

DEM. But did not I perceive it? Was not I told?

AG. By Jove, and you wore those ears of yours continually
Wide open or close shut, like an umbrella.

DEM. Is it possible? Was I indeed so mere a driveller
In my old age, so superannuated?

AG. Moreover, if a couple of orators
Were pleading in your presence; one proposing
To equip a fleet, his rival arguing
To get the same supplies distributed
To the jurymen, the patron of the juries
Carried the day. But why do you hang your head so?
What makes you shuffle about? Can't ye stand still?

DEM. I feel ashamed of myself and all my follies.

AG.* 'Twas not your fault—don't think of it. Your advisers
Were most to blame. But for the future—tell me,
If any rascally villanous orator
Should address a jury with such words as these :
" Remember, if you acquit the prisoner
Your daily food and maintenance are at stake,"
How would you treat such a pleader? Answer me.

DEM. I should toss him headlong into the public pit,
With a halter round his gullet, and Hyperbolus
Tied fast to the end of it.

AG.   That's a noble answer !
Wise and judicious, just and glorious !
Now tell me, in other respects, how do you mean
To manage your affairs?

DEM.   Why first of all
I'll have the arrears of seamen's wages paid
To a penny, the instant they return to port.

---

* The tone of the S. S. is that of a considerate, indulgent preceptor to a young man who has been misbehaving.

AG. There's many a worn-out rump will bless ye and
thank ye.

DEM. Moreover, no man that has been enrolled
Upon the list for military service,
Shall have his name erased for fear or favour.

AG. That gives a bang to Cleonymus's buckler.

DEM. I'll not permit those fellows without beards
To harangue in our Assembly ; boys or men.

AG. Then what's to become of Cleisthenes and Strato? *
Where must they speak ?

DEM.   I mean those kind of youths,
The little puny would-be politicians,
Sitting conversing in perfumers' shops,
Lisping and prating in this kind of way :
" Phæax is sharp—he made a good come-off,
And saved his life in a famous knowing style.
I reckon him a first-rate ; quite capital
For energy and compression ; so collected,
And such a choice of language ! Then to see him
Battling against a mob—it's quite delightful !
He's never cowed !   He bothers 'em completely ! "

AG. It's your own fault, in part you've helped to spoil 'em ;
But what do you mean to do with 'em for the future ?

DEM. I shall send them into the country, all the pack of
'em,
To learn to hunt, and leave off making laws.

AG. Then I present you here with a folding chair,
And a stout lad to carry it after you.

DEM. Ah, that reminds one of the good old times.

AG. But what will you say, if I give you a glorious
peace,
A lusty strapping truce of thirty years?
Come forward here, my lass, and show yourself.

---

* See 'Acharnians," p. 1:, where both are mentioned,

DEM. By Jove, what a face and figure ! I should like
To ratify and conclude incontinently.
Where did you find her ?

AG. Oh, the Paphlagonian,
Of course, had huddled her out of sight, within there.
But now you've got her, take her back with you
Into the country.

DEM. But the Paphlagonian,
What shall we do to punish him ? What d'ye think ?

AG. Oh, no great matter. He shall have my trade ;
With an exclusive sausage-selling patent,
To traffic openly at the city gates,
And garble his wares with dogs' and asses' flesh ;
With a privilege, moreover, to get drunk,
And bully among the strumpets of the suburbs,
And the ragamuffin waiters at the baths.

DEM. That's well imagined, it precisely suits him ;
His natural bent, it seems, his proper element
To squabble with poor trulls and low rapscallions.
As for yourself, I give you an invitation
To dine with me in the hall. You'll fill the seat
Which that unhappy villain held before.
Take this new robe ! Wear it and follow me !

And you, the rest of you, conduct that fellow
To his future home and place of occupation,
The gate of the city ; where the allies and foreigners,
That he maltreated, may be sure to find him.

[Exeunt.

THE BIRDS.

Intended to convey some notion of its effect as an acted play, and to illustrate certain points of dramatic humour and character discoverable in the original.

"Terentius Menandrum, Plautus et Cæcilius veteres Comicos interpretati sunt, numquid hærent in verbis, ac non decorem potius et elegantiam in translatione conservant?"—HIERON., Epis. de optimo genere interpretandi.

" Si Graios patrio carmine adire sales
Possumus, optatis plus jam processimus ipsis.
Hoc satis est."—VIRGIL.

THE BIRDS.

DRAMATIS PERSONÆ.

PEISTHETAIRUS.—An Athenian citizen, but disgusted with his own country, starts on his travels proposing to seek his fortune in the kingdom of the Birds. He is represented as the essential man of business and ability, the true political adventurer, the man who directs everything and everybody, who is never in the wrong, never at a loss, never at rest, never satisfied with what has been done by others, uniformly successful in his operations. He maintains a constant ascendency, or if he loses it for a moment, recovers it immediately.

EUELPIDES.—A simple, easy-minied, droll companion, his natural follower and adherent, as the merry-andrew is of the mountebank. It will be seen that, like the merry-andrew, he interposes his buffoonish comments on the grand oration delivered by his master.

EPOPS.—King of the Birds, formerly Tereus king of Thrace, but long ago, according to the records of mythology, transformed into a *Hoopoe*. He appears as the courteous dignified sovereign of a primitive uncivilized race whom he is desirous to improve ; he gives, a gracious reception to strangers arriving from a country more advanced in civilization, and adopts the projects of aggrandizement suggested to him by Peisthetairus.

THE CHORUS OF BIRDS, his subjects, retain, on the contrary, their hereditary hatred and suspicion of the human race ; they are ready to break out into open mutiny against their king, and to massacre his foreign (human) advisers upon the spot. It is with the greatest difficulty that they can be prevailed upon to hear reason, and attend to the luminous exposition of Peisthetairus. His harangue has the effect of conciliating and convincing them : his projects are adopted without a dissentient voice. War is not immediately declared against the gods, but a sort of Mexican blockade is established by proclamation.

PROMETHEUS.—A malcontent deity, the ancient patron of the human race, still retaining a concealed attachment to the deposed dynasty of Saturn. He comes over secretly with intelligence which Peisthetairus avails himself of, and which proves ultimately decisive of the subjugation of the gods.

NEPTUNE, HERCULES, TRIBALLUS, or the TRIBALLIAN.—Joint ambassadors from the gods commissioned to treat with Peisthetairus. Neptune is represented as a formal dignified personage of the old school. Hercules as a passionate, wrong-headed, greedy blockhead; he is cajoled and gained over by Peisthetairus, and in his turn intimidates the Triballian, an ignorant barbarian deity who is hardly able to speak inteliigibly. They join together, Neptune is out-voted, and Peisthetairus concludes a treaty by which his highest pretensions are realized.

The characters above mentioned are the only ones who contribute in any way to the progress of the drama ; the remainder, a very amusing set of persons, are introduced in detached scenes, exemplifying the various interruptions and annoyances incident to the man of business, distracting his attention and embarrassing him in the exercise of his authoritative functions. There are, however, exceptions.

IRIS, who is brought in, having been captured and detained for an infringement of the blockade.

A PRIEST, who comes to sacrifice at the inauguration of the new city.

TWO MESSENGERS, arriving from different quarters with very interesting and satisfactory intelligence.

The rest are a mere series of intruders on the time and attention of the great man.

POET.—A ragged vagabond, who comes begging with an inaugural ode on the foundation of the new city.

A SOOTHSAYER, arriving with Oracles relative to the same important event, and a demand of perquisites due to himself by divine authority.

METON, the Astronomer, proposes to make a plan and survey of the new city.

A COMMISSIONER from Athens, a very authoritative personage.

A VENDOR of copies of decrees, he enters reading them aloud like a hawker to attract purchasers.

PARRICIDE.—A young man, who has beaten his father and proposes to strangle him, offers himself as a desirable acquisition to the new colony.

KINESIAS, the dithyrambic poet, applies for a pair of wings.
INFORMER.—A young man, whose hereditary trade is that of an informer,
and whose practice extends to the islands, comes with the same
application.

SCENE.

*[A wild desolate country with a bare open prospect
on one side, and some upright rocks covered with
shrubs and brushwood in the centre of the stage.
PEISTHETAIRUS and EUELPIDES appear as a
couple of worn-out pedestrian travellers, the one
with a raven and the other with a jackdaw on
his hand. They appear to be seeking for a direction from the motions and signals made to them
by the Birds.]*

EU. *[speaking to his jackdaw].*
Right on, do ye say? to the tree there in the distance?
PEIS. *[speaking first to his raven, and then to his com-
panion].*
Plague take ye! Why this creature calls us back!
EU. What use can it answer tramping up and down?
We're lost, I tell ye : our journey's come to nothing.
PEIS. To think of me travelling a thousand stadia
With a raven for my adviser!
EU. Think of me, too,
Going at the instigation of a jackdaw,
To wear my toes and my toe-nails to pieces!
PEIS. I don't know even the country where we've got to.
EU. And yet you expect to find a country here,
A country for yourself!
PEIS. Truly not I;
Not even Execestides * could do it,
That finds himself a native everywhere.

---

* He is attacked again in this play, as a foreign barbarian arrogating to
himself the privileges of a true-born Athenian.

Eu. Oh dear ! We're come to ruin, utter ruin!

Peis. Then go that way, can't ye : " the Road to Ruin !"

Eu. He has brought us to a fine pass, that crazy fellow,
Philocrates the poulterer ; he pretended
To enable us to find where Tereus lives ;
The king that was, the Hoopoe that is now ;
Persuading us to buy these creatures of him,
That raven there for threepence,—and this other,
This little Tharrelides * of a jackdaw,
He charged a penny for : but neither of 'em
Are fit for anything but to bite and scratch.

[*speaking to his jackdaw*]

Well, what are ye after now ?—gaping and poking !
You've brought us straight to the rock. Where would you
    take us ?
There's no road here !

Peis.   No, none, not even a path.

Eu. Nor don't your raven tell us anything ?

Peis. She's altered somehow—she croaks differently.

Eu. But which way does she point ? What does she say ?

Peis. Say ? Why, she says, she'll bite my fingers off.

Eu. Well, truly it's hard upon us, hard indeed,
To go with our own carcases to the crows,
And not be able to find 'em after all.

[*turning to the audience*] †

For our design, most excellent spectators,

---

* Tharrelides was nicknamed Jackdaw, and Euelpides *in contempt of
his jackdaw* calls it a Tharrelides ! The raven and the jackdaw are
characteristic. Peisthetairus is the bearer of the sagacious bird, his companion is equipped with a jackdaw.

† Peisthetairus, it will be seen, allows his companion to put himself
forward, with the newly discovered natives ; remaining himself in the background as the person of authority, making use of the other as his harbinger ;
he allows him also to address the audience, not choosing to compromise
himself by unnecessary communications.

The full and complete account of their motives and design is, moreover,
much better suited to the careless gossiping character of Euelpides,

(Our passion, our disease, or what you will)
Is the reverse of that which Sacas * feels ;
For he, though not a native, strives perforce
To make himself a citizen : whilst we,
Known and acknowledged as Athenians born,
(Not hustled off, nor otherwise compelled)
Have deemed it fitting to betake ourselves
To these our legs, and make our person scarce.

    Not through disgust or hatred or disdain
Of our illustrious birthplace, which we deem
Glorious and free ; with equal laws ordained
For fine and forfeiture and confiscation,
With taxes universally diffused ;
And suits and pleas abounding in the Courts.

    For grasshoppers sit only for a month
Chirping upon the twigs ; but our Athenians
Sit chirping and discussing all the year,
Perched upon points of evidence and law.

    Therefore we trudge upon our present travels,
With these our sacrificial implements,
To seek some easier unlitigious place ;
Meaning to settle there and colonize.
Our present errand is in search of Tereus,
(The Hoopoe that is now) to learn from him
If in his expeditions, flights, and journeys,
He ever chanced to light on such a spot.

    PEIS. Holloh !
    EU.   What's that?
    PEIS.   My raven here points
    upwards.
Decidedly !

---

* Acestor, a tragical poet, not being a genuine Athenian was called Sakas, from the name of a Thracian tribe.

  We may suppose that Peisthetairus must have accompanied this speech with a grave authoritative gesture indicative of assent and approbation.

Eu.   Ay, and here's my jackdaw too,
Gaping as if she saw something above.
Yes,—I'll be bound for it; this must be the place :
We'll make a noise, and know the truth of it.
Peis. Then "kick against the rock." *
Eu.   Knock you your
    head
Against the rock !—and make it a double knock ! ˙
Peis. Then fling a stone at it !
Eu.   With all my heart,
Holloh there !
Peis.   What do you mean with your Holloh?
You should cry Hoop for a Hoopoe.
Eu.   Well then, Hoop !
Hoop and holloh, there !—Hoopoe, Hoopoe, I say !
Tr. What's here ? Who's bawling there ? Who wants
    my master ?
        [*The door is opened, and both parties start at seeing
        each other.*]
Eu. Oh mercy, mighty Apollo ! what a beak !
Tr. Out ! out upon it ! a brace of bird-catchers !
Eu. No, no ; don't be disturbed ; think better of us.
Tr. You'll both be put to death.
Eu.   But we're not men.
Tr. Not men ! what are ye? what do ye call your-
    selves?
Eu. The fright has turned me into a yellow-hammer.
Tr. Poh ! Stuff and nonsense !
Eu.   I can prove it to·ye.
Search !
    Tr.   But your comrade here ; what bird is he ?
    Peis. I'm changed to a golden pheasant just at
    present.

_____

* "To kick against the rock" was proverbial.

Eu. Now tell me, in heaven's name, what creature
are ye ?

Tr. I'm a·slave bird.

Eu. A slave ? how did it happen?
Were you made prisoner by a fighting cock ?

Tr. No. When my master made himself a Hoopoe,
He begged me to turn bird to attend upon him.

Eu. Do birds then want attendance?

Tr. Yes, of course,
In his case, having been a man before,
He longs occasionally for human diet,
His old Athenian fare : pilchards, for instance.
Then I must fetch the pilchards ; sometimes porridge ;
He calls for porridge, and I mix it for him.

Eu.* Well, you're a dapper waiter, a didapper ;
But didapper, I say, do step within there,
And call your master out.

Tr. But just at present
He's taking a little rest after his luncheon,
Some myrtle berries and a dish of worms.

Eu. No matter, call him here. We wish to speak to
him.

Tr. He'll not be pleased, I'm sure ; but notwithstanding,†
Since you desire it, I'll make bold to call him.

[*Exit.*

Peis. [*looking after him*].
Confound ye, I say, you've frightened me to death.

Eu. He has scared away my jackdaw ; it's flown away.

Peis. You let it go yourself, you coward.

---

* The Trochilus has been unnecessarily communicative, and shown himself a very simple sort of a sewing-man ; Eu. has tact enough to discover
this, and assumes the ascendency accordingly.

† In the tone of Simple, Master Slender's serving man.

Eu.   Tell me,
Have not you let your raven go?
Peis.   Not I.
Eu. Where is it then?
Peis.   Flown off of its own accord.
Eu. You did not let it go ! you're a brave fellow !
[*The* Hoopoe *from within.*]
Hoo. Open the door, I say ; let me go forth.
[*The royal* Hoopoe *appears with a tremendous beak
and crest.*]
Eu. O Hercules, what a creature ! What a plumage !
And a triple tier of crests; what can it be !
Hoo. Who called? who wanted me?
Eu.   May the heavenly powers . . . .
. . . . Confound ye, I say [*aside*].
Hoo.   You mock at me perhaps,
Seeing these plumes.   But, stranger, you must know—
That once I was a man.
Eu.   We did not laugh
At you, Sir.
Hoo.   What, then, were you laughing at?
Eu. Only that beak of yours seemed rather odd.
Hoo. It was your poet Sophocles * that reduced me
To this condition with his tragedies.
Eu. What are you, Tereus?   Are you a bird, or what?
Hoo. A bird.
Eu.   Then where are all your feathers?
Hoo.   Gone.
Eu. In consequence of an illness?
Hoo.   No, the birds
At this time of the year leave off their feathers,
But you ! What are ye? Tell me.

---

* In his tragedy of "'Tereus," Sophocles had represented him as transformed (probably only in the last scenes) with the head and beak of a bird.

Eu.   Mortal men.
Hoo. What countrymen ?
Eu.   Of the country of the Triremes.*
Hoo. Jurymen, I suppose ?
Eu.   Quite the reverse,
We're anti-jurymen.
Hoo.   Does that breed still
Continue amongst you ?
Eu.   Some few specimens †
You'll meet with, here and there, in country places.
Hoo. And what has brought you here ?   What was your
   object ?
Eu. We wished to advise with you.
Hoo.   With me ! For what ?
Eu. Because you were a man : the same as us ;
And found yourself in debt : the same as us ;
And did not like to pay : the same as us ;
And after that, you changed into a bird ;
And ever since have flown and wandered far
Over the lands and seas, and have acquired
All knowledge that a bird or man can learn.
   Therefore we come as suppliants, to beseech
Your favour and advice to point us out
Some comfortable country, close and snug,
A country like a blanket or a rug,
Where we might fairly fold ourselves to rest.
Hoo. Do you wish then for a greater State than
   Athens ?
Eu. Not greater ; but more suitable for us.
Hoo. It's clear you're fond of aristocracy.

---

* Galleys with three banks of oars. The Athenians were at that time
undisputed masters of the sea.

† The love of litigation and the passion for sitting on juries, with the
exception of a few who retained their old agricultural habits, had infected
the whole Athenian community.

Eu. What him, the son of Scellias ! Aristocrates ? *
I abhor him.

Hoo.   Well, what kind of a town would suit ye?

Eu. Why, such a kind of town as this, for instance,
A town where the importunities and troubles
Are of this sort. Suppose a neighbour calls
Betimes in the morning with a sudden summons :
" Now, don't forget," says he, " for heaven's sake,
To come to me to-morrow, bring your friends,
Children and all, we've wedding cheer at home.
Come early, mind ye, and if you fail me now,
Don't let me see your face, when I'm in trouble."

    Hoo. So, you're resolved to encounter all these hard-
    ships !
        [*to* PEISTHETAIRUS]
And what say you ?

PEIS.   My fancy's much the same.

Hoo. How so?

PEIS.   To find a place of the same sort ·
A kind of place, where a good jolly father
Meets and attacks me thus—" What's come to ye
With my young people ? You don't take to 'em.
What ! they're not reckoned ugly ! You might treat 'em,
As an old friend, with a little attention surely,
And take a trifling civil freedom with 'em."

    Hoo. Ay ! You're in love I see with difficulties
And miseries. Well, there's a city in fact
Much of this sort ; one that I think might suit ye,
Near the Red Sea.

Eu.   No, no ! not near the sea ! †

---

* Little or nothing is known of Aristocrates. He lived to the end of the war, and acted in concert with Thrasybulus against Critias. " Dem. in Timoc. '

† A humorous blunder. The Red Sea was in fact as inaccessible to ancient European navigation as the Caspian.

Lest I should have the Salaminian galley *
Arriving some fine morning, with a summons
Sent after me, and a pursuivant to arrest me.
  But could not you tell us of some Grecian city?
  Hoo. Why there's in Elis there, the town of Lepreum.
  Eu. No, no! No Lepreums: nor no lepers neither.
No leprosies for me. Melanthius †
Has given me a disgust for leprosies.
  Hoo. Then there's Opuntius in the land of Locris.
  Eu. Opuntius? Me to be like Opuntius! ‡
With his one eye! Not for a thousand drachmas.
  But tell me among the birds here, how do ye find it?
What kind of an existence?
  Hoo.   Pretty fair;
Not much amiss. Time passes smoothly enough;
And money is out of the question. We don't use it.
  Eu. You've freed yourselves from a great load of dross.
  Hoo. We've our field sports. We spend our idle mornings
With banqueting and collations in the gardens,
With poppy-seeds and myrtle.
  Eu.   So your time
Is passed like a perpetual wedding-day.

[PEISTHETAIRUS, *who has hitherto felt his way by
putting* EUELPIDES *forward, and allowing him to
take the lead, and who has paid no attention to
this trifling inconclusive conversation, breaks out
as from a profound reflective reverie.*]

---

* The Salaminian galley had been sent to arrest Alcibiades, then one of
the joint commanders in Sicily. This was one of the most fatal acts of that
popular insanity which it was the poet's object to mitigate and counteract.

† A tragic poet, said to have been leprous, ridiculed elsewhere by the
author, and by other comic poets, as Plato and Callias.

‡ Nothing is recorded of Opuntius, except that he was reckoned a
poltroon, and was blind of one eye.

PEIS. Ha! What a power is here! What oppor-
tunities!
If I could only advise you. I see it all!
The means for an infinite empire and command!
Hoo. And what would you have us do? What's your
advice?
PEIS. Do? What would I have ye do? Why first of all
Don't flutter and hurry about all open-mouthed,
In that undignified way. With us, for instance,
At home, we should cry out "What creature's that?"
And Teleas would be the first to answer,
"A mere poor creature, a weak restless animal,
A silly bird, that's neither here nor there." *
Hoo. Yes, Teleas might say so. *It would be like him.*
But tell me, what would you have us do?
PEIS. [*emphatically*].　　　　　　　　　　Concentrate !
Bring all your birds together. Build a city.
Hoo. The birds ! How could we build a city? Where?
PEIS. Nonsense. You can't be serious. What a question !
Look down.
Hoo.　　　　I do.
PEIS.　　　　　　　　Look up now.
Hoo.　　　　　　　　　　　　So I do.
PEIS. Now turn your neck round.†
Hoo.　　　　　　　　　　I should sprain it though.
PEIS. Come, what d'ye see?
Hoo.　　　　　　　　　　The clouds and sky; that's all.
PEIS. Well, that we call the pole and the atmosphere ;
And would it not serve you birds for a metropole?

---

* The lines between inverted commas may be understood either as the
words of Teleas or as a description of him ; the ambiguity exists in the
original and is evidently intentional. It is continued in the next line of the
Hoopoe's answer.
† See in "The Knights" a similar instance of ridiculous stage effect,
where the Sausage-seller is mounted on his stool to survey the Athenian
Empire.

Hoo. Pole? Is it called a pole?

PEIS.   Yes, that's the name.

Philosophers of late call it the pole ;

Because it wheels and rolls itself about,

As it were, in a kind of a roly-poly way.*

Well, there then, you may build and fortify,

And call it your Metropolis—your Acropolis.

From that position you'll command mankind,

And keep them in utter, thorough subjugation :

Just as you do the grasshoppers and locusts.

And if the gods offend you, you'll blockade 'em,

And starve 'em to a surrender.

Hoo.   In what way?

PEIS. Why thus. Your atmosphere is placed, you see,

In a middle point, just betwixt earth and heaven.

A case of the same kind occurs with us.

Our people in Athens, if they send to Delphi

With deputations, offerings, or what not,

Are forced to obtain a pass from the Bœotians :

Thus when mankind on earth are sacrificing,

If you should find the gods grown mutinous

And insubordinate, you could intercept

All their supplies of sacrificial smoke.

Hoo. By the earth and all its springs ! springes and
     nooses ! †

Odds, nets and snares ! This is the cleverest notion :

And I could find it in my heart to venture,

If the other birds agree to the proposal.

PEIS. But who must state it to them?

Hoo.   You yourself,

---

* The comic poets ridiculed the new prevailing passion for astronomical
and physical science. See further on the Parabasis and the scene where
Meton the astronomer is introduced.

† The Hoopoe's exclamation and oath are in the original, as they are
here represented, exactly in the style of Bob Acres.

They'll understand ye, I found them mere barbarians,
But living here a length of time amongst them,
I have taught them to converse and speak correctly.*
    PEIS. How will you summon them?
    HOO.   That's easy enough;
I'll just step into the thicket here hard by,
And call my nightingale. She'll summon them.
And when they hear her voice, I promise you
You'll see them all come running here pell-mell.†
    PEIS. My dearest, best of birds! don't lose a moment,
I beg, but go directly into the thicket;
Nay, don't stand here, go call your nightingale.
                                 [*Exit* HOOPOE.

[*Song from behind the scene, supposed to be sung by the*
    HOOPOE]
                  Awake! awake!
        Sleep no more, my gentle mate!
          With your tiny tawny bill,
          Wake the tuneful echo shrill,
             On vale or hill;
          Or in her airy, rocky seat,
          Let her listen and repeat
            The tender ditty that you tell,
              The sad lament,
              The dire event,
          To luckless Itys that befell.
              Thence the strain
              Shall rise again,
              And soar amain,

---

* The characteristic impertinence of a predominant people, considering
their own language as that which ought to be universally spoken.
    † A female performer on the flute, a great favourite of the public and
with the poet, after a long absence from Athens engaged to perform in this
play, which was exhibited with an unusual recklessness of expense.

Up to the lofty palace gate ;
Where mighty Apollo sits in state ;
In Jove's abode, with his ivory lyre,
Hymning aloud to the heavenly choir.
While all the gods shall join with thee
In a celestial symphony.

[*A solo on the flute, supposed to be the nightingale's call.*]

PEIS. O Jupiter ! the dear, delicious bird !
With what a lovely tone she swells and falls,
Sweetening the wilderness with delicate air.
EU. Hist !
PEIS.　　　　What ?
EU.　　　　　　　　Be quiet, can't ye ?
PEIS.　　　　　　　　　　　　What's the matter ?
EU. The Hoopoe is just preparing for a song.
HOO.　　　　Hoop ! hoop !
　　　　Come in a troop,
　　　　Come at a call,
　　　　　One and all,
　　　　Birds of a feather,
　　　　All together.
　　Birds of a humble, gentle bill,
　　　Smooth and shrill,
　Dieted on seeds and grain,
　Rioting on the furrowed plain,
　　　Pecking, hopping,
　　　Picking, popping,
　Among the barley newly sown.
　　　Birds of bolder, louder tone,
　　　Lodging in the shrubs and bushes,
　　　Mavises and thrushes,
　　On the summer berries brousing,
　　On the garden fruits carousing,
　　All the grubs and vermin smousing.

You that in a humbler station,
With an active occupation,
Haunt the lowly watery mead,
Warring against the native breed,
The gnats and flies, your enemies ;
In the level marshy plain
Of Marathon, pursued and slain.

You that in a squadron driving
From the seas are seen arriving,
With the cormorants and mews
Haste to land and hear the news !
All the feathered airy nation,
Birds of every size and station,
Are convened in convocation.
For an envoy, queer and shrewd,
Means to address the multitude,
And submit to their decision
A surprising proposition,
For the welfare of the State
Come in a flurry,
With a hurry-scurry,
Hurry to the meeting and attend to the debate.

The first appearance of the Chorus must have been a critical poirx for the success of a play. The audience had been brought into good-humour by their favourite musical performer, by whom all the pre-ceding songs were probably executed ; for the dialogue on the stage passes solely between Peisthetairus and Euelpides, and the Hoopoe, who is supposed to sing, does not appear. The Chorus now appears, and in the original, forty lines follow, in which Peisthetairus and Euelpides act as showmen to the exhibition of twenty-four figures, dressed in imitation of the plumage of as many different kinds of birds,* which are passed in review with suitable remarks as they

---

* See what is said in p. 184, of the profuse expense bestowed on the exhi-bition of this play.

successively take their places in the orchestra. This passage is here
omitted. Whoever wishes to see how well it can be executed, may
be referred to Mr. Cary's translation.

While the birds are bustling about in their new coop of the orchestra,
Euelpides contemplates them with surprise, which soon changes to
alarm.

The language of the birds consists almost wholly of short syllables, the
effect of which it is impossible to imitate in English. Some accents,
which are added, may serve to mark the attempt: they are added
also to two spondaic lines, of which the imitation is more practicable.

EU. How they thicken, how they muster,
    How they clutter, how they cluster !
    Now they ramble here and thither,
    Now they scramble altogether.
    What a fidgeting and clattering !
    What a twittering and chattering,
    Don't they mean to threaten us ? What think ye ?
PEIS.   Yes, methinks they do.
EU. They're gaping with an angry look against us
    both.
PEIS.   It's very true.
CHOR. Where is he, the mágistrate that assémbled us to
    delíberate.
HOO. Friends and comrádes, here am I, your old associate
    and ally.
CHOR. What have ye to commúnicate for the bénefit of
    the Státe.
HOO. A proposal safe and useful, practicable, profitable,
Two projectors are arrived here, politicians shrewd and
    able.
CHOR. Whee ! Whaw ! Where ? Where ?
    What ? What ? What? What ? What ?
HOO. I repeat it—human envoys are arrived a steady
    pair,
To disclose without reserve a most stupendous, huge affair.

CHOR. Chief, of all that ever were, the worst, the most
unhappy one!
Speak, explain!
Hoo.   Don't be alarmed!
CHOR.   Alas! alas! what have you done?
Hoo. I've received a pair of strangers, who desired to
settle here.
CHOR. Have you risked so rash an act?
Hoo.   I've done it, and I persevere.
CHOR. But, where are they?
Hoo.   Near beside you; near as I am; very near.
CHOR.   Oút alás! oút alás!
          We are betráyed, crúelly betrayed
          To a calámitous end,
          Our cómrade and our friénd,
Our compánion in the fiélds and in the pástures
Is the aúthor of all our míseries and dísasters.
          Our áncient sácred láws and sólemn oáth!
· 　　　　Tránsgréssing bóth!
          Tréasonably delívering us as a prize
          To our hórrible immemórial enemiés,
          To a detéstable ráce
          Exécrably base!
For the bird our chief, hereafter he must answer to the
State;
With respect to these intruders, I propose, without
debate,
On the spot to tear and hack them.
Eu.   There it is, our death and ruin!
Ah, the fault was all your own, you know it; it was all your
doing;
You that brought me here; and why?
PEIS.   Because I wanted an attendant.
Eu. Here, to close my life in tears.
PEIS.   No, thats a foolish fear, depend on't.

Eu. Why a foolish fear?

Peis.　　　　Consider; when you're left without an eye,

It's impossible in nature; how could you contrive to cry?

Chor.　Form in rank, form in rank;

Then move forward and outflank:

Let me see them overpowered,

Hacked, demolished and devoured;

Neither earth, nor sea, nor sky,

Nor woody fastnesses on high,

Shall protect them if they fly?

Where's the Captain? What detains him? What prevents

us to proceed?

On the right there, call the Captain! Let him form his

troop and lead.

Eu. There it is, where can I fly?

Peis.　　　　　　　Sirrah, be quiet, wait a bit.

Eu. What, to be devoured amongst them!

Peis.　　　　　　　Will your legs or will your wit

Serve to escape them?

Eu.　　　　　　I can't tell.

Peis.　　　　　　But I can tell; do as you're bid;

Fight we must; you see the pot, just there before ye; take

the lid,

And present it for a shield; the spit will serve you for a

spear;

With it you may scare them off, or spike them if they venture

near.

Eu. What can I find to guard my eyes?

Peis.　　　　　　Why there's the very thing you wish,

Two vizard helmets ready made, the cullender and skim-

ming dish.

Eu. What a clever, capital, lucky device, sudden and new!

Nicias * with all his tactics, is a simpleton to you.

---

* Nicias was at this time in the chief command of the Sicilian expedition,
Alcibiades having been recalled. See note to p. 187.

Chor. Steady, birds! present your beaks! in double time,
    charge and attack,
Pounce upon them, smash the potlid, clapperclaw them, tear
    and hack.
    Hoo. Tell me, most unworthy creatures, scandal of the
    feathered race;
Must I see my friends and kinsmen massacred before my
    face?
    Chor. What, do you propose to spare them? where will
    your forbearance cease,
Hesitating to destroy destructive creatures such as these?
    Hoo. Enemies they might have been; but here they
    come, with fair design,
With proposals of advice, for your advantage and for mine.
    Chor. Enemies time out of mind! they that have spilt
    our fathers' blood,
How should they be friends of ours, or give us counsel for
    our good?
    Hoo. Friendship is a poor adviser; politicians deep and
    wise
Many times are forced to learn a lesson from their enemies;
Diligent and wary conduct is the method soon or late
Which an adversary teaches; whilst a friend or intimate
Trains us on to sloth and ease, to ready confidence; to
    rest,
In a careless acquiescence; to believe and hope the best.
Look on earth!* behold the nations, all in emulation
    vieing,
Active all, with busy science engineering, fortifying;
To defend their hearths and homes, with patriotic industry,
Fencing every city round with massy walls of masonry:

---

* The vast changes and improvement in the practice and the art of war
which took place about this time were a subject of general speculation and
remark. The concise allusions in the text, are therefore somewhat enlarged
in the translation.

Tactical devices old they modify with new design ;
Arms offensive and defensive to perfection they refine ;
Galleys are equipped and armed, and armies trained to dis-
cipline.
Look to life, in every part; in all they practise, all they know;
Every nation has derived its best instruction from the foe.

CHOR. We're agreed to grant a hearing ; if an enemy can
teach
Anything that's wise or useful, let him prove it in his
speech.

PEIS. [*aside*]. Let's retire a pace or two; you see the change
in their behaviour.

Hoo. Simple justice I require, and I request it as a
favour.

CHOR. Faith and equity require it, and the nation hitherto
Never has refused to take direction and advice from you.

PEIS. [*aside*]. They're relenting by degrees ;
Recover arms and stand at ease.

CHOR.* Back to the rear ! resume your station,
Ground your wrath and indignation !
Sheathe your fury ! stand at ease,
While I proceed to question these :
What design has brought them here ?
Ho, there, Hoopoe ! can't he hear?

Hoo. What's your question ?

CHOR.   Who are these ?

Hoo. Strangers from the land of Greece.

CHOR. What design has brought them thence ?
What's their errand or pretence ?

Hoo. They come here simply with a view
To settle and reside with you ;
Here to remain and here to live.

---

* Thirteen lines, which unaccompanied by the action on the stage would
appear tiresome and unmeaning, are here omitted from 3?7 to 400.

CHOR. What is the reason that they give ?
Hoo. A project marvellous and strange.
CHOR. Will it account for such a change,
       Coming here so vast a distance ?
       Does he look for our assistance
       To serve a friend or harm a foe ?
Hoo. Mighty plans he has to show
       (Hinted and proposed in brief)
       For a power beyond belief ;
       Ocean, earth, he says, and air,
       All creation everywhere,
       Everything that's here or there,
       An empire and supremacy
       Over all beneath the sky,
       Is attainable by you,
       Your just dominion and your due.
CHOR. Tell us, was he fool or mad ?
Hoo. No, believe me ; grave and sad.
CHOR. Did his reasons and replies
       Mark him as discreet and wise ?
Hoo. With a force, a depth, a reach
       Of judgment ; a command of speech ;
       An invention, a facility,
       An address, a volubility,
       More than could be thought believable ;
       'Tis a varlet inconceivable !
CHOR. Let us hear him ! let us hear him !
       Bid him begin ! for raised on high
       Our airy fancy soars ; and I
       Am rapt in hope ; ready to fly.

The King Hoopoe now gives some orders in a pacific spirit, directing
that all warlike weapons be removed and hung up at the back of the
chimney as before.   He then calls upon Peisthetairus to communicate to the assembled commonalty the propositions which had been
before discussed in private conference between themselves.   Peisthe-

tairus, however, sees his advantage and insists upon the previous conclusion of a formal treaty of peace: this is done, and the Chorus swear to it (relapsing for a moment into their real character) " as they hope to win the prize by a unanimous vote." But if they should fail they imprecate upon themselves the penalty of (gaining the prize notwithstanding, but) "gaining it only by a casting vote." Peace is proclaimed, the armament is dissolved by proclamation, and the Chorus recommenced singing.

[*to the* CHORUS]

Hoo. Here you, take these same arms, in the name of heaven,
  And hang them quietly in the chimney corner;
  [*turning to* PEISTHETAIRUS]
  And you communicate your scheme, exhibiting
  Your proofs and calculations—the discourse
  Which they were called to attend to.

PEIS.   No, not I!
  By Jove; unless they agree to an armistice;
  Such as the little poor baboon, our neighbour,
  The sword cutler, concluded with his wife;
  That they sha'n't bite me, or take unfair advantage
  In any way.

CHOR.   We won't.

PEIS.   Well, swear it then!

CHOR. We swear; by our hope of gaining the first prize,
  With the general approval and consent,
  Of the whole audience, and of all the judges—
  And if we fail, may the reproach befall us,
  Of gaining it, only by the casting vote.

It should seem that the success of this play must have been a subject of more than usual anxiety both to the poet himself, and to the Choregus * and his friends : we may conceive it to have been intended as a sedative to the mind of the commonalty, excited as they were at

---

* The wealthy citizen charged with the expense and management of a theatrical entertainment.

the time, almost to madness by the suspicion of a conspiracy against
the religion and laws of the country ; a suspicion originating in a
profane outrage secretly perpetrated, to a great extent, in mere insolence and wantonness, by some young men of family.   In the opinion,
however, of the Athenian people, the offence was viewed in a very
serious light, as the result of an extensive secret combination (on
the part of persons bound and engaged to each other by their common participation in the guilt of sacrilege), preparatory to other
attempts still more criminal and dangerous.   In this state of things,
and while the popular fury and jealousy upon religious subjects was
at its height, the poet ventured to produce this play ; in which it
will be seen, that the burlesque of the national mythology is carried
higher an I continued longer than in any of his other existing plays.
The confident hopes expressed by the Chorus were not realized ; the
first prize was assigned to a play the title of which, the " Comastæ,"
or " Drunken Rioters," seems to imply that its chief interest must
have been derived from direct allusions to the outrage above mentioned, and to the individuals suspected to have been engaged in it.

But we must return to the Herald dismissing the troops.

HER. Hear, ye good people all ! the troop are ordered,
   To take their arms within doors ; and consult
   On the report and entry to be made
   Upon our journal of this day's proceedings.

            CHOR. Since time began
               The race of man
         Has ever been deceitful, faithless ever.
            Yet may our fears be vain !
            Speak therefore and explain :
            If in this realm of ours,
   Your clearer intellect, searching and clever,
            Has noticed means or powers,
            Unknown and undetected,
      In unambitious indolence neglected.
      Guide and assist our ignorant endeavour :
      You for your willing aid, and ready wit,
      Will share with us the common benefit.

Now speak to the business and be not afraid
The birds will adhere to the truce that we made.

The long series of anapæstic lines which follows, holds the place of
the debates which occur in other comedies, and which are conducted
in anapæstic verse. Peisthetairus could not properly have been
matched with an opponent or antagonist ; the uniformity of his speech
is, however, relieved by the interruptions and comments of Euelpides,
who acts an under part to him, much in the same style as a merry-
andrew to a mountebank. Observe that Peisthetairus never vouch-
safes an answer or takes any kind of notice of his companion, but
proceeds continuously, except once or twice in reply to the Chorus
and the Hoopoe.

PEIS. I'm filled with the subject and long to proceed,
My rhetorical leaven is ready to knead.
Boy, bring me a crown * and a basin and ewer.
EU. Why, what does he mean ? Are we banqueting sure ?
PEIS. A rhetorical banquet, I mean ; and I wish
To serve them at first with a sumptuous dish,
To astound and delight them.† " The grief and compas-
sion
That oppresses my mind on beholding a nation
A people of sovereigns . . . ."
CHOR.   Sovereigns we !
PEIS. Of all the creation ! of this man and me,
And of Jupiter too ; for observe that your birth
Was before the old Titans, and Saturn and Earth.
CHOR. And Earth !
PEIS.   I repeat it.
CHOR.   That's wonderful news !
PEIS. Your wonder implies a neglect to peruse,
And examine old Æsop ; from whom you might gather,

---

* A crown was worn by the public orators when haranguing the people,
and also at feasts.
† The inverted commas mark the premeditatedly abrupt exordium of
Peisthetairus's harangue.

That the lark was embarrassed to bury his father;
On account of the then non-existence of Earth;
And how to repair so distressing a dearth,
He adopted a method unheard of and new.

CHOR. If the story you quote, is authentic and true,
No doubt can exist of our clear seniority;
And the gods must acknowledge our right to authority.

EU. Your beaks will be worn with distinction and pride;
The woodpecker's title will scarce be denied;
And Jove the pretender, will surely surrender.

PEIS. . . . . Moreover, most singular facts are combined
In proof, that the birds were adored by mankind:
For instance; the cock was a sovereign of yore
In the empire of Persia, and ruled it before
Darius's time; and you all may have heard,
That his title exists, as the " Persian bird." . . .

EU. And hence you behold him stalk in pride,
Majestic and stout, with a royal stride,
With his turban upright, a privilege known
Reserved to kings and kings alone.

PEIS. . . . . So wide was his empire, so mighty his sway,
That the people of earth to the present day,
Attend to his summons and freely obey:
Tinkers, tanners, cobblers, all,
Are roused from rest at his royal call,
And shuffle their shoes on before it is light,
To trudge to the workshop.

EU.   I warrant you're right;
I know to my cost, by the cloak that I lost;
It was owing to him I was robbed and beguiled.

For a feast had been made for a neighbour's child,
To give it a name; and I went as a guest,
And sat there carousing away with the rest;
But drinking too deep, I fell soundly asleep;
And he began crowing; and I never knowing,

But thinking it morning, went off at the warning,
(With the wine in my pate, to the city gate
And fell in with a footpad was lying in wait,
Just under the town; and was fairly knocked down;
Then I tried to call out ; but before I could shout,
He stripped me at once with a sudden pull,
Of a bran new mantle of Phrygian wool.

PEIS. . . . . Then the kite was the monarch of Greece
heretofore . . . .

Hoo. Of Greece?

PEIS. . . . . and instructed our fathers of yore,
On beholding a kite, to fall down and adore . . . .

EU. Well, a thing that befell me, was comical quite,
I threw myself down on beholding a kite ;
But turning my face up to stare at his flight,
With a coin in my mouth,* forgetting my penny,
I swallowed it down, and went home without any.

PEIS. . . . . In Sidon and Egypt the cuckoo was
king ;
They wait to this hour for the cuckoo to sing;
And when he begins, be it later or early,
They reckon it lawful to gather their barley . . . .

EU. Ah, thence it comes our harvest cry,
Cuckoo, Cuckoo, to the passers-by.

PEIS. . . . . At an era moreover of modern date,
Menelaus the king, Agamemnon the great,
Had a bird as assessor attending in state,
Perched on his sceptre, to watch for a share
Of fees and emoluments, secret or fair.

EU. Ah, there I perceive, I was right in my guess,
For when Priam appeared in his tragical dress,

---

* It was usual with the Greeks to put small pieces of silver coin in their
mouths, a custom which the turnpike men of Great Britain continued to
retain within the recollection of the writer.

The bird on his sceptre, I plainly could see,
Was watching Lysicrates * taking a fee.

PEIS. . . . Nay, Jupiter now that usurps the command,
Appears with an eagle, appointed to stand
As his emblem of empire; a striking example
Of authority once so extended and ample:
And each of the gods had his separate fowl,
Apollo a hawk, and Minerva an owl.

EU.† That's matter of fact and you're right in the main;
But what was the reason I wish you'd explain?

PEIS. The reason was this : that the bird should be there,
To demand as of right a proportional share,
Of the entrails and fat, when an offering was made,
A suitable portion before them was laid :
Moreover you'll find, that the race of mankind
Always swore by a bird; and it never was heard
That they swore by the gods, at the time that I mention.
And Lampon‡ himself, with a subtle intention,
Adheres to the old immemorial use ;
He perjures and cheats us and swears "by the goose."

Thus far forth have I proved and shown
The power and estate that were once your own,
Now totally broken and overthrown :
And need I describe, your present tribe,
Weak, forlorn, exposed to scorn,
Distressed, oppressed, never at rest,
Daily pursued, with outrage rude ;

---

* Of Lysicrates, the Scholiast only informs us that he was a person in office known to be in the habit of taking bribes, a description which in relation to those times is hardly a distinction.

† This speech seems more properly to belong to the Hoopoe.

‡ As a substitute for common swearing, some persons (Socrates among the rest) made use of less offensive expletives, swearing "by the dog or by the goose." Lampon was a soothsayer, and thought it right probably to be scrupulous in using the name of the god. He is mentioned again in this play.

With cries and noise, of men and boys,
Screaming, hooting, pelting, shooting,
The fowler sets his traps and nets,
Twigs of bird-lime, loops, and snares,
To catch you kidnapped unawares;
Even within the temple's pale.
  They set you forth to public sale,
Pawed and handled most severely:
And not content with roasting merely,
In an insolent device,
Sprinkle you with cheese and spice;
With nothing of respect or favour,
Derogating from your flavour.
Or for a further outrage, have ye
Soused in greasy sauce and gravy.

Hoo.   Sad and dismal is the story,
       Human stranger which you tell,
   Of our fathers' ancient glory,
       Ere the fated empire fell,

   From the depth of degradation,
       A benignant happy fate
   Sends you to restore the nation;
       To redeem and save the State.

   I consign to your protection,
       Able to preserve them best,
   All my objects of affection,
       My wife, my children, and my nest.

If the reader should be inclined to pass over the next hundred lines, I
  should feel no wish to detain him. The subject of them has been
  pretty nearly anticipated, and the whole play is in fact too long.

Hoo. Explain then the method you mean to pursue
To recover our empire and freedom anew.

For thus to remain, in dishonour and scorn,
Our life were a burthen no more to be borne.
PEIS. Then I move, that the birds shall in common repair
To a centrical point, and encamp in the air ;
And intrench and enclose it, and fortify there :
And build up a rampart, impregnably strong,
Enormous in thickness, enormously long;
Bigger than Babylon ; solid and tall,
With bricks and bitumen, a wonderful wall.
    EU. Bricks and bitumen ! I'm longing to see
What a daub of a building the city will be !
    PEIS. As soon as the fabric is brought to an end,
A herald or envoy to Jove we shall send,
To require his immediate prompt abdication ;
And if he refuses, or shows hesitation,
Or evades the demand ; we shall further proceed,
With legitimate warfare avowed and decreed :
With a warning and notices, formally given,
To Jove, and all others residing in heaven,
Forbidding them ever to venture again
To trespass on our atmospheric domain,
With scandalous journeys, to visit a list
Of Alcmenas and Semeles; if they persist,
We warn them, that means will be taken moreover
To stop their gallanting and acting the lover.
    Another ambassador also will go
Despatched upon earth, to the people below,
To notify briefly the fact of accession ;
And enforcing our claims upon taking possession:
With orders in future, that every suitor,
Who applies to the gods with an offering made,
Shall begin, with a previous offering paid
To a suitable bird ; of a kind and degree
That accords with the god, whosoever he be.
In Venus's fane, if a victim is slain,

First let a sparrow be feasted with grain.
When gifts and oblations to Neptune are made,
To the drake let a tribute of barley be paid.
Let the cormorant's appetite* first be appeased,
And let'Hercules then have an ox for his feast.
If you offer to Jove, as the sovereign above,
A ram for his own ; let the golden-crown,
As a sovereign bird, be duly preferred,
Feasted and honoured, in right of his reign ;
With a jolly fat pismire offered and slain.

Eu. A pismire, how droll! I shall laugh till I burst!
Let Jupiter thunder, and threaten his worst.

Hoo. But mankind, will they, think ye, respect and
adore,
If they see us all flying the same as before?
They will reckon us merely as magpies and crows.

Peis. Poh ! nonsense, I tell ye—no blockhead but
knows
That Mercury flies ; there is Iris too ;
Homer informs us how she flew :
"Smooth as a dove, she went sailing along."
And pinions of gold, both in picture and song,
To Cupid and Victory fairly belong.

Hoo. But Jove's thunder has wings; if he send but a
volley,
Mankind for a time may abandon us wholly.

Peis. What then ? we shall raise a granivorous troop,
To sweep their whole crops with a ravenous swoop :
If Ceres is able, perhaps she may deign,
To assist their distress, with a largess of grain. . . . .

Eu. No ! no ! she'll be making excuses, I warrant.

Peis. Then the crows will be sent on a different errand,

---

* With the writers of the old comedy extreme voracity was the characteristic attribute of Hercules.

To pounce all at once, with a sudden surprise,
On their oxen and sheep, to peck out their eyes,
And leave them stone blind for Apollo to cure :
He'll try it ; he'll work for his salary sure !
     Eu. Let the cattle alone ; I've two beeves of my own :
Let me part with them first; and then do your worst.
     Peis. But, if men shall acknowledge your merit and
     worth,
As equal to Saturn, to Neptune, and Earth,
And to everything else ; we shall freely bestow
All manner of blessings.
     Hoo.   Explain them and show.
     Peis. For instance : if locusts arrive to consume
All their hopes of a crop, when the vines are in bloom,
A squadron of owls may demolish them all ;
The midges moreover, which canker and gall
The figs and the fruit, if the thrush is employed,
By a single battalion will soon be destroyed.
     Hoo. But wealth is their object; and how can we
     grant it ?
     Peis. We can point them out mines ; and our help will
     be wanted
To inspect, and direct navigation and trade ;
Their voyages all will be easily made,
With a saving of time, and a saving of cost ;
And a seaman in future will never be lost.
     Hoo. How so ?
     Peis.   We shall warn them : "Now hasten to sail,
Now keep within harbour ; your voyage will fail."
     Eu. How readily then will a fortune be made !
I'll purchase a vessel and venture on trade.
     Peis.* And old treasure concealed will again be revealed ;

---

* The want of stability and good faith, both in the Government and
individuals, obliged the Greeks to secure their moneyed capital by conceal-

The birds as they know it, will readily show it.
'Tis a saying of old, " My silver and gold
Are so safely secreted, and closely interred,
No creature can know it, excepting a bird."

Eu. I'll part with my vessel, I'll not go aboard;
I'll purchase a mattock and dig up a hoard.

Hoo. We're clear as to wealth; but the blessing of health,
Is the gift of the gods.

Peis.   It will make so such odds:
If they're going on well, they'll be healthy still,
And none are in health, that are going on ill.

Hoo.* But then for longevity; that is the gift
Of the gods.

Peis.   But the birds can afford them a lift,
And allow them a century, less or more.

Hoo. How so?

Peis.   From their own individual store:
They may reckon it fair, to allot them a share;
For old proverbs affirm, that the final term
Of a raven's life exceeds the space
Of five generations of human race.

Hoo.† What need have we then for Jove as a king?
Surely the birds are a better thing!

Peis. Surely! surely!   First and most,
We shall economize the cost
Of marble domes and gilded gates.

---

ment. Hence the vast collections of ancient coin which appear in the cabinets of antiquarians.

Observe the shallow shatter-brained character of Euelpides.

* The origin of this notion of life being transferable, cannot be accounted for; in the form of a wish, it appears to have been common.

† This speech must belong to the Hoopoe. Aristophanes would not leave the result of the scene to be summed up by such a silly fellow as Euelpides. We see besides that Peisthetairus replies to it. He never replies to Euelpides,

The birds will live at cheaper rates,
Lodging, without shame or scorn,
In a maple or a thorn ;
The most exalted and divine
Will have an olive for his shrine.
  We need not run to foreign lands,
Or Ammon's temple in the sands ;
But perform our easy vows,
Among the neighbouring shrubs and boughs ;
Paying our oblations fairly,
With a pennyworth of barley.
  CHOR.* O best of all envoys, suspected before,
Now known and approved, and respected the more ;
To you we resign the political lead,
Our worthy director in council and deed.

        Elated with your bold design,
          I swear and vow :
        If resolutely you combine
        Your views and interest with mine ;
        In steadfast councils as a trusty friend,
        Without deceit, or guile or fraudful end :
        They that rule in haughty state,
        The gods ere long shall abdicate
          Their high command ;
        And yield the sceptre to my rightful hand.

Then reckon on us for a number and force ;
As on you we rely for a ready resource,
In council and policy, trusting to you,
To direct the design we resolve to pursue.

---

* There can be no doubt that this speech belongs to the Chorus, though it may seem difficult to account for what is said of the sceptre, which it should seem ought rather to belong to the king. The Hoopoe in answer alludes to the inveterate vice of all Choruses—dawdling and inefficiency.

Hoo. That's well, but we've no time, by Jove, to loiter,
And dawdle and postpone like Nicias.*
We should be doing something. First, however,
I must invite you to my roosting place,
This nest of mine, with its poor twigs and leaves.
And tell me what your names are?

Peis.   Certainly ;
My name is Peisthetairus.†

Hoo.   And your friend ?

Eu. Euelpides from Thria.

Hoo.   Well, you're welcome—
Both of ye.

Peis.   We're obliged.

Hoo.   Walk in together.

Peis. Go first then, if you please.

Hoo.   No, pray move forward.

Peis. But bless me — stop, pray — just for a single moment—
Let's see—do tell me—explain—how shall we manage
To live with you—with a person wearing wings ?
Being both of us unfledged ?

Hoo.   Perfectly well !

Peis. Yes, but I must observe, that Æsop's fables
Report a case in point ; the fox and eagle :
The fox repented of his fellowship ;
And with good cause ; you recollect the story.‡

---

* The Athenians were at that time disappointed at Nicias's delay, in not advancing immediately against Syracuse.

† Peisthetairus answers like a man of sense. Euelpides like a simpleton, and we see the effect of it on the king's mind. There is a momentary pause in the invitation, before they are both included in it.

‡ Peisthetairus has shown that he is not deficient in valour upon compulsion. But a character of extreme subtlety is always prone to suspicion, and the recollection of an example derived from ancient documents in Æsop's Fables, intimidates him for a moment, and makes him distrustful of the

Hoo. Oh! don't be alarmed! we'll give you a certain
  root
That immediately promotes the growth of wings.

Peis. Come, let's go in then ; Xanthias, do you mind,
And Manodorus* follow with the bundles.

Chor. Holloh !

Hoo.   What's the matter ?

Chor.   Go in with your party,
And give them a jolly collation and hearty.
But the bird, to the Muses and Graces so dear,
The lovely sweet nightingale, bid her appear,
And leave her amongst us, to sport with us here.

Peis. O yes, by Jove, indeed you must indulge them ; †
Do, do me the favour, call her from the thicket !
For heaven's sake—let me entreat you—bring her here,
And let us have a sight of her ourselves.

Hoo.‡ Since it is your wish and pleasure it must be so;
Come here to the strangers, Procne ! show yourself !

Peis. O Jupiter, what a graceful, charming bird !
What a beautiful creature it is !

Eu.   I'll tell you what ;
I could find in my heart to rumple her feathers.

Peis. And what an attire she wears, all bright with
  gold !

---

frank invitation of the king. He is then very much ashamed of himself,
and, like Bacchus and Master Slender, begins giving orders to his servants,
and is importunate and hurried and absurd.   Thus the poet, who wanted
some lines of strong importunity to mark the entrance of his favourite
musician, has contrived to give them to his principal personage, and at the
same time to mark his character itself more distinctly, by this momentary
failure of his habitual self-possession, originating in the apprehension of
having lowered himself in the estimation of his host.

  * These slaves do not appear elsewhere in the play ; it might be doubted
whether they appear here and whether Peisthetairus does not call for them
in mere nervous absence of mind.

  † With a hurried, nervous eagerness.

  ‡ With grave good breeding, implying a kind of rebuke to the fussy importunity into which Peisthetairus had fallen.

Eu. Well, I should like to kiss her, for my part.

Peis. You blockhead, with that beak, she'd run you
through.

Eu. By Jove, then, one must treat her like an egg;
Just clear away the shell and kiss her—thus.

Hoo.* Let's go!

Peis.   Go first then, and good luck go with us.

[*Exeunt.*

The actors having left the stage, the Parabasis ought to follow. It is
here prefaced in a singular way by a complimentary song from the
Chorus, addressed to the favourite female musician.

Chor. O lovely, sweet companion meet,
From morn to night my sole delight,
My little, happy, gentle mate,
You come, you come, O lucky fate,
Returning here with new delight,†
To charm the sight, to charm the sight,
    And charm the ear.
Come then anew combine
Your notes in harmony with mine,
And with a tone beyond compare
Begin your anapæstic air.

The sudden passion for science among the Athenians, and the ridicule
of it among the comic poets, has been already noticed.
Much might be said on the subject of the most splendid passage of the
Parabasis, and of the philosophic system of which it presents the
traces: but this would lead to considerations very remote from the
imitation of actual life, and manners and character; which, as con-
stituting the most singular excellence of the author, it has been the
object of the translator to illustrate.
Of the Parabasis before us, the merits are well known, and perhaps no
passage in Aristophanes has been oftener quoted with admiration.

---

* Gravely disapproving the liberties which are taken in his presence.

† See what is said in the Preface. She had been engaged for this performance, and was newly arrived.

To bring the most sublime subjects within the verge of Comedy, and
to treat of them with humour and fancy, without falling into vulgarity
or offending the principles of good taste, seems a task which no poet
whom we know of, could have accomplished : though, if we were
possessed of the works of Epicharmus, it is possible that we might
see other specimens of the same style.

Ye Children of Man ! whose life is a span,
Protracted with sorrow from day to day,
Naked and featherless, feeble and querulous,
Sickly, calamitous, creatures of clay !
Attend to the words of the Sovereign Birds,
(Immortal, illustrious, lords of the air)
Who survey from on high, with a merciful eye,
Your struggles of misery, labour, and care.
Whence you may learn and clearly discern
Such truths as attract your inquisitive turn;
Which is busied of late, with a mighty debate,
A profound speculation about the creation,
And organical life, and chaotical strife,
With various notions of heavenly motions,
And rivers and oceans, and valleys and mountains,
And sources of fountains, and meteors on high,
And stars in the sky.   We propose by-and-by
(If you'll listen and hear) to make it all clear.
And Prodicus henceforth shall pass for a dunce,
When his doubts are explained and expounded at once.

Before the creation of Æther and Light,
Chaos and Night together were plight,
In the dungeon of Erebus foully bedight.
Nor Ocean, or Air, or substance was there,
Or solid or rare, or figure or form,
But horrible Tartarus ruled in the storm :
At length, in the dreary chaotical closet
Of Erebus old, was a privy deposit,

By Night the primæval in secrecy laid ;
A Mystical Egg, that in silence and shade
Was brooded and hatched; till time came about:
And Love, the delightful, in glory flew out,
In rapture and light, exulting and bright,
Sparkling and florid, with stars in his forehead,
His forehead and hair, and a flutter and flare,
As he rose in the air, triumphantly furnished
To range his dominions, on glittering pinions,
All golden and azure, and blooming and burnished :
    He soon, in the murky Tartarean recesses,
With a hurricane's might, in his fiery caresses
Impregnated Chaos ; and hastily snatched
To being and life, begotten and hatched,
The primitive Birds : but the Deities all,
The celestial Lights, the terrestrial Ball,
Were later of birth, with the dwellers on earth,
More tamely combined, of a temperate kind;
When chaotical mixture approached to a fixture.
    Our antiquity proved ; it remains to be shown,
That Love is our author, and master alone,
Like him, we can ramble, and gambol and fly
O'er ocean and earth, and aloft to the sky:
And all the world over we're friends to the lover,
And when other means fail, we are found to prevail,
When a peacock or pheasant is sent as a present.
    All lessons of primary daily concern,
You have learnt from the Birds, and continue to learn,
Your best benefactors and early instructors;
We give you the warning of seasons returning.
    When the cranes are arranged, and muster afloat
In the middle air, with a creaking note,
Steering away to the Lybian sands ;
Then careful farmers sow their lands ;
The crazy vessel is hauled ashore,

The sail, the ropes, the rudder and oar
Are all unshipped, and housed in store.
The shepherd is warned, by the kite reappearing,
To muster his flock, and be ready for shearing.
You quit your old cloak, at the swallow's behest,
In assurance of summer, and purchase a vest.
For Delphi, for Ammon, Dodona, in fine,
For every oracular temple and shrine,
The Birds are a substitute equal and fair,
For on us you depend, and to us you repair
For counsel and aid, when a marriage is made,
A purchase, a bargain, a venture in trade:
Unlucky or lucky, whatever has struck ye,
An ox or an ass, that may happen to pass,
A voice in the street, or a slave that you meet,
A name or a word by chance overheard,
If you deem it an omen, you call it a *Bird;*
And if birds are your omens, it clearly will follow,
That birds are a proper prophetic Apollo.

Then take us as gods, and you'll soon find the odds,*
We'll serve for all uses, as Prophets and Muses ;
We'll give ye fine weather, we'll live here together ;
We'll not keep away, scornful and proud, a-top of a
    cloud,
(In Jupiter's way) ; but attend every day,
To prosper and bless, all you possess,
And all your affairs, for yourselves and your heirs.
And as long as you live, we shall give
You wealth and health, and pleasure and treasure,
In ample measure ;

---

* The series of short lines at the end of a Parabasis was to be repeated
with the utmost volubility and rapidity—as if in a single breath. A comic
effect is sometimes produced in this way on our own stage.

And never bilk you of pigeon's milk,
Or potable gold; you shall live to grow old,
In laughter and mirth, on the face of the earth,
Laughing, quaffing, carousing, bousing,
   Your only distress, shall be the excess
Of ease and abundance and happiness.

SEMICHORUS.

We see here a comic imitation of the tragic choruses of Phrynichus, a
poet older than Æschylus, of whom Aristophanes always speaks with
respect, as an improver of music and poetry—arts which in the
judgment of the ancients were deemed inseparable ; or if disjoined,
es·entially defective and imperfect.

   Muse, that in the deep recesses
      Of the forest's dreary shade,
   Vocal with our wild addresses ;
      Or in the lonely lowly glade,
   Attending near, art pleased to hear,
      Our humble bill tuneful and shrill.

When, to the name of omnipotent Pan,
   Our notes we raise, or sing in praise,
Of mighty Cybele, from whom we began ;
   Mother of Nature, and every creature,
Winged or unwinged, of birds or man.
   Aid and attend, and chant with me
The music of Phrynichus, open and plain,
   The first that attempted a loftier strain,
Ever busy like the bee, with the sweets of harmony.

EPIRREMA.

Is there any person present sitting a spectator here,
Who desires to pass his time, freely without restraint or fear?
Should he wish to colonize ; he never need be checked or
   chid,
For the trifling indiscretions, which the testy laws forbid.

Parricides are in esteem : among the birds we deem it
fair,
A combat honourably fought betwixt a game-cock and his
heir !
There the branded runagate, branded and mottled in the
face,
Will be deemed a motley bird ; a motley mark is no dis-
grace.
Spintharus, the Phrygian born, will pass a muster there
with ease,
Counted as a Phrygian fowl ; and even Execestides,*
Once a Carian and a slave, may there be nobly born and
free ;
Plume himself on his descent, and hatch a proper pedigree.

SEMICHORUS.

This second sample of the style of Phrynichus may serve to give us a
more distinct idea of it.   It seems to have been one of essential
grandeur and harmony, but trespassing occasionally into the regions
of nonsense.

Thus the swans in chorus follow,
On the mighty Thracian stream,
Hymning their eternal theme.
Praise to Bacchus and Apollo :
The welkin rings, with sounding wings,
With songs and cries and melodies ;
Up to the thunderous Æther ascending :

Whilst all that breathe, on earth beneath,
The beasts of the wood, the plain and the flood,
In panic amazement are crouching and bending ;

---

* Already noted as a foreigner in the first scene of this play.

With the awful qualm, of a sudden calm,
Ocean and air in silence blending.
The ridge of Olympus is sounding on high,
Appalling with wonder the lords of the sky,
    And the Muses and Graces
    Enthroned in their places,
Join in the solemn symphony.

ANTEPIRREMA.

Nothing can be more delightful than the having wings to
    wear !
A spectator sitting here, accommodated with a pair,
Might for instance (if he found a tragic chorus dull and
    heavy)
Take his flight, and dine at home ; and if he did not choose
    to leave ye,
Might return in better humour, when the weary drawl was
    ended.
Introduce then wings in use—believe me, matters will be
    mended :
Patroclides* would not need to sit there, and befoul his
    seat ;
Flying off he might return, eased in a moment, clean and
    neat.
Trust me wings are all in all ! Diitrephes has mounted
    quicker
Than the rest of our aspirants, soaring on his wings of
    wicker :

---

   * The posthumous celebrity of Patroclides is not confined to this single
event. He survived the accident many years, and was the author of a very
salutary decree upon the principles advocated by the poet in the Epirrema
of "The Frogs," but (as in the instance before us) he was again fatally too
late. The decree was not passed till after the destruction of the navy at
Ægos Potamos.

Basket work, and crates, and hampers, first enabled him to
   fly ; *
First a captain, then promoted to command the cavalry ;
With his fortunes daily rising, office and preferment new,
An illustrious, enterprising, airy, gallant cockatoo.

The exclusive functions of the Chorus being now at an end, the persons
of the drama appear again upon the stage ; Peisthetairus and Euelpides, having been both in the meanwhile equipped with a sumptuous
pair of wings. They are supposed to have been entertained behind
the scenes, with a royal collation in the palace of the Hoopoe.
Peisthetairus is accordingly in extreme good-humour, and being now
in the height of his advancement, recollects that it will be right to
behave to his former comrade with the hearty familiarity of an old
acquaintance ; he accordingly begins, with a ludicrous similet on his
appearance (a species of raillery common among the Athenians, but
which was considered as the lowest species of jocularity). He takes
his friend's retort in perfect good-humour, and Euelpides is admitted
as a third person, to consult, with him and the king, upon some un-
important matters—such as the name of the new city, and the choice
of a patron Deity—upon all which topics, his idle buffoonish humour
is not misplaced : but a more delicate point is afterwards brought
into discussion (nothing less than the choice of a chief commander
for the citadel) which Euelpides treats with the same silly drollery
as before. Peisthetairus is irritated, or pretends to be so, and dismisses him in a tone of authority, which the other resents, and
appears on the point of mutinying ; upon which Peisthetairus smooths
him down again, as briefly as possible, and having accomplished
this point, immediately turns away from him, to call a servant.[1]

PEIS. Well, there it is ! Such a comical set out,
By Jove, I never saw!
   Eu.   Why, what's the matter ?
What are you laughing at ?

---

* His property consisted in a manufactory of this kind, by which he had
grown rich.
† This is the sort of raillery which Bacchus prohibits in the contest
between Euripides and Æschylus, and of which we have a specimen in "The
Wasps," v. 1308. Some modern traveller has told us that abusive similes in
alternate extempore verse, serve for an amusement, at this day, to the
boatmen of the Nile.

PEIS.   At your pen feathers :
I'll tell ye exactly now, the thing you're like ;
You're just the perfect image of a goose,
Drawn with a pen in a writing master's flourish.
Eu. And you're like a plucked blackbird to a tittle.
PEIS. Well then, according to the line in Æschylus,
" It's our own fault, the feathers are our own." *
Eu. Come, what's to be done.
Hoo.   First, we must choose a
   name,
Some grand sonorous name, for our new city :
Then we must sacrifice.
Eu.   I think so too.
PEIS. Let's see—let's think of a name—what shall
   it be ?
What say ye, to the Lacedæmonian name?
Sparta sounds well—suppose we call it Sparta.
Eu. Sparta ! What *Sparto*? †—Rushes !—no, not I,
I'd not put up with *Sparto* for a mattress,
Much less for a city—we're not come to that.
PEIS. Come then, what name shall it be ?
Eu.   Something appropriate,
Something that sounds majestic, striking and grand,
Alluding to the clouds and the upper regions.
PEIS. What think ye of clouds and cuckoos ? Cuckoo-
   cloudlands
Or Nephelococcugia ?
Hoo.   That will do ;
A truly noble and sonorous name
Eu. I wonder, if that Nephelococcugia,
Is the same place I've heard of : people tell me,

---

* Æschylus alludes to a fable in which an eagle complains of being wounded by an arrow feathered from his own wings.

† Sparto still retains its name, and is still used for mattresses and occasionally for cordage.

That all Theagenes's rich possessions
Lie there ; and Æschines's whole estate.

PEIS. Yes ! * and a better country it is by far,
Than all that land in Thrace, the fabulous plain
Of Phlegra ; where those earthborn landed giants
Were bullied and out-vapoured by the gods.

EU. It will be a genteelish, smart concern, I reckon,
This city of ours . . . . Which of the deities
Shall we have for a patron ?   We must weave our mantle,
Our sacred mantle of course . . . . the yearly mantle †
To one or other of 'em.

PEIS.   Well, Minerva ?
Why should not we have Minerva ? she's established,
Let her continue ; she'll do mighty well.

EU. No—there I object ; for a well-ordered city,
The example would be scandalous ; to see
The goddess, a female born, in complete armour
From head to foot ; and Cleisthenes ‡ with a distaff.

PEIS. What warden will ye appoint for the Eagle tower,
Your citadel, the fort upon the rock ?

HOO. That charge will rest with a chief of our own
    choice,
Of Persian race, a chicken of the game,
An eminent warrior.

EU.   Oh my chicky-hiddy—
My little master.   I should like to see him,
Strutting about and roosting on the rock.

----

* Many Athenians (as Miltiades, Alcibiades, and Thucydides the historian) were proprietors of large estates in the Chersonese and along the
coasts of Thrace : Theagenes, it seems, and Æschines, boasting of wealth
which they did not possess, chose to talk of their estates in Thrace.   In the
last century the West Indies was the usual locality assigned to *fabulous*
estates.   Thrace was also mythologically *fabulous*, as the field of battle
between Jupiter and the Titans.

† See "Knights," p. 129, note.

‡ Ridiculed for his effeminacy in various comedies.

PEIS. Come, you now ! please to step to the atmosphere ;
And give a look to the work, and help the workmen ;
And between whiles fetch brick and tiles, and such like ;
Draw water, stamp the mortar—do it barefoot ;
Climb up the ladders ; tumble down again :
Keep constant watch and ward ; conceal your watch lights ;
Then go the rounds, and give the countersign,
Till you fall fast asleep. Send heralds off,
A brace of them—one to the gods above ;
And another, down below there, to mankind.
Bid them, when they return, inquire for me.

EU. For me ! for me ! You may be hanged for me.

PEIS. Come, friend, go where I bid you : never mind ;
The business can't go on without you, anyhow.
It's just a sacrifice to these new deities,
That I must wait for ; and the priest that's coming.
Holloh, you boy there ! bring the basin and ewer !

In the passage which follows the author ridicules the rage for vulgar
realities (a corruption of the theatric art, essentially destructive of all
illusion, as we have witnessed at home, with *real* water, *real* horses,
real elephants). The stage of Athens it should seem had been
degraded by a *real* sacrifice, the paltriness of such a spectacle is
marked by the magnificent exhortation of the Chorus, contrasted with
the meanness of the execution which they anticipate.

CHOR. We urge, we exhort you, and advise,
    To ordain a mighty sacrifice ;
    And before the gods to bring
    A stupendous offering ;
    Either a sheep or some such thing !
    To please the critics of the age,
    Sacrificed upon the stage.
    Sound amain the Pythian strain !
  Let Chœris* be brought here to sing.

---

* Chœris, a bad musician (the constant butt of the comic poets), is called
for, to complete the shabbiness of the performance. His representative, the

PEIS. Have done there with your puffing . . . . heaven
and earth,
What's here! I've seen a many curious things,
But never saw the like of this before,
A crow with a flute and a mouthpiece.   Priest, your office:
Perform it! Sacrifice to the new deities !

PRI. I will — but where's the boy gone with the
basket ?

Let us pray to the holy flame,
And the holy hawk that guards the same;
To the sovereign deities,
All and each, of all degrees,
Female and male !

CHOR. Hail, thou hawk of Sunium, hail!
PRI.   To the Delian and the Pythian swan,
And to the Latonian quail,
All hail !

CHOR. To the bird of awful stature,
Mother of gods, mother of man ;
Great Cybele! nurse of Nature !
Glorious ostrich, hear our cry !
Fearful and enormous creature,
Hugest of all things that fly,
O preserve and prosper us,
Thou mother of Cleocritus ! *
Grant the blessings that we seek,
For us, and for the Chians' eke !

PEIS. That's right, the Chians—don't forget the Chians !
PRI. To the heroes, birds, and heroes' sons,
We call at once, we call and cry,
To the woodpecker, the jay, the pie,

---

crow (who is the Chœris among the birds), sounds some discordant notes
till Peisthetairus stops him.
    * Of Cleocritus nothing is known, except that he was unfortunate in his
figure, which was thought to resemble that of an ostrich.

To the mallard and the wigeon,
To the ringdove and the pigeon,
To the petrel and sea-mew,
To the dottrel and curlew,
To the vultures and the hawks,
To the cormorants and storks,
To the rail, to the quail,
To the peewit, to the tomtit,

Peisthetairus, who can do everything better than everybody else, undertakes to perform the sacrifice. This is sufficiently in character. By
making him the chief operator, a greater comic effect is given to the
series of interruptions which disturb him ; until in despair he deter-
mines to transfer the sacrifice elsewhere. In this way the poet
avoids the vulgar reality which he had before ridiculed.

PEIS. Have done there! call no more of 'em; are you mad?
Inviting all the cormorants and vultures,
For a victim such as this! Why don't you see,
A kite at a single swoop, would carry it off?
Get out of my way there with your crowns and fillets,
I'll do it myself! I'll make the sacrifice !
      PRI. Then must I commence again,
        In a simple, humble strain ;
        And invite the gods anew,
        To visit us—but very few—
        Or only just a single one,
          All alone,
        In a quiet, easy way ;
      Wishing you may find enough,*
        If you dine with us to day.
          Our victim is so poor and thin,
          Merely bones, in fact, and skin.
PEIS. We sacrifice and pray to the winged deities.

---

* Ridicule of the vulgar reality, the poor half-starved sheep being standing
on the stage.

Enter a Poet, very ragged and shabby, with a very mellifluous submissive mendicatory demeanour. Peisthetairus, the essential man of business and activity, entertaining a supreme contempt for his profession and person, is at no great pains to conceal it; but recollecting at the same time, that it is advisable to secure the suffrages of the literary world, and that the character of a patron is creditable to a great man, he patronizes him accordingly, not at his own expense, but by bestowing upon him certain articles of apparel put in requisition for that purpose. This first act of confiscation is directed against the property of the Church; the Scholiast informs us, that he begins by stripping the Priest.

POET. " For the festive, happy day,
        Muse prepare an early lay,
        To Nephelococcugia."
PEIS. What's here to do?   What are you?   Where do
        you come from?
POET. An humble menial of the Muses' train,
As Homer expresses it.
PEIS.   A menial, are you?
With your long hair?*   A menial?
POET.   'Tis not that,
No! but professors of the poetical art,
Are simply styled, the " Menials of the Muses,"
As Homer expresses it.
PEIS.   Aye, the Muse has given you
A ragged livery. Well, but friend, I say—
Friend!—Poet!—What the plague has brought you
        here?
POET. I've made an ode upon your new built city,
And a charming composition for a chorus,
And another, in Simonides's manner.
PEIS.† When were they made?   What time?   How long
        ago?

---

* Slaves were forbidden to wear long hair.
† In a sharp, cross, examining tone.

POET. From early date, I celebrate in song,
The noble Nephelococcugian State.

PEIS. That's strange, when I'm just sacrificing here,
For the first time, to give the town a name.

POET. Intimations, swift as air,
    To the Muses' ear, are carried,
    Swifter than the speed and force,
    Of the fiery-footed horse,
      Hence, the tidings never tarried;
      Father, patron, mighty lord,*
      Founder of the rising State,
    What thy bounty can afford,
      Be it little, be it great,
    With a quick resolve, incline
    To bestow on me and mine.

PEIS. This fellow will breed a bustle, and make mischief,
If we don't give him a trifle, and get rid of him.
You there, you've a spare waistcoat ; pull it off!
And give it this same clever, ingenious poet—
There, take the waistcoat, friend ! Ye seem to want it !

POET. Freely, with a thankful heart,
    What a bounteous hand bestows,
    Is received in friendly part ;
    But amid the Thracian snows,
    Or the chilly Scythian plain,
      He the wanderer, cold and lonely,
      With an under-waistcoat only,
    Must a further wish retain ;
      Which, the Muse averse to mention,
      To your gentle comprehension,
    Trusts her enigmatic strain.

---

* The Scholiast informs us that these lines are in ridicule of certain mendicatory passages in the Odes of Pindar ; one in particular, addressed to Hiero on the foundation of a new city.

PEIS. I comprehend it enough ; you want a jerkin ;
Here, give him yours; one ought to encourage genius.
There, take it, and good-by to ye !

POET.*　　　　　　　　　　　　Well, I'm going ;
And as soon as I get to the town, I'll set to work;
And finish something, in this kind of way.

"Seated on your golden throne,
　Muse, prepare a solemn ditty,
　　To the mighty,
　　To the flighty,
　To the cloudy, quivering, shivering,
　To the lofty-seated city."

PEIS. Well, I should have thought, that jerkin might have
　cured him
Of his " quiverings and shiverings."　How the plague!
Did the fellow find us out ?　I should not have thought it.
　Come, once again, go round with the basin and ewer.
Peace! Silence! Silence!

Enter a Soothsayer with a great air of arrogance and self-importance.
　He comes on the authority of a book of Oracles (which he pretends
　to possess, but which he never produces), in virtue of which he lays
　claim to certain sacrificial perquisites and fees.　Peisthetairus en-
　counters him with a different version composed upon the spot ; in
　virtue of which he dismisses the Soothsayer with a good lashing.

SOOTH.　　　　　　　　　Stop the sacrifice!
PEIS. What are you ?
SOOTH.　　　　　　　　　A Soothsayer, that's what I am.
PEIS. The worse luck for ye.
SOOTH.　　　　　　　　　Friend, are you in your senses ?†
Don't trifle absurdly with religious matters.

---

* The Poet withdraws, gradually turning round and reciting.　Peisth.
does not appear to take notice, but watches till he is fairly gone.
　† See p. 154 of "'The Knights," where there is the same allusion to
disputes on the authentic copies of oracles.

Here's a prophecy of Bakis, which expressly
Alludes to Nephelococcugia.

PEIS. How came it, then, you never prophesied
Your prophecies before the town was built?

SOOTH. The spirit withheld me.

PEIS.   And is it allowable now,
To give us a communication of them?

SOOTH.   Hem!
   " Moreover, when the crows and daws unite,
   To build and settle, in the midway right,
   Between tall Corinth and fair Sicyon's height,
   Then to Pandora, let a milk white goat
   Be slain, and offered, and a comely coat
   Given to the Soothsayer, and shoes a pair;
   When he to you this Oracle shall bear."

PEIS. Are the shoes mentioned?

SOOTH. [*pretending to feel for his papers*]. Look at the
   book, and see!
   "And let him have the entrails for his share."

PEIS. Are the entrails mentioned?

SOOTH. [*as before*]. Look at the book, and see!
   " If you, predestined youth, shall do these things,
   Then you shall soar aloft, on eagle's wings;
   But, if you do not, you shall never be
   An eagle, nor a hawk, nor bird of high degree."

PEIS. Is all this, there?

SOOTH. [*as before*]. Look at the book, and see!

PEIS. This Oracle differs most remarkably,
From that which I transcribed in Apollo's temple.
   " If at the sacrifice . . . . * which you prepare,
   An uninvited vagabond . . . . should dare

---

* The breaks in the text . . . . may serve to indicate what was more
distinctly expressed by the actor—viz., that Peisthetairus's Oracle is an
extempore production.

To interrupt you, and demand a share,
Let cuffs and buffets . . . . be the varlet's lot.
Smite him between the ribs . . . . and spare him
    not."
SOOTH. Nonsense, you're talking !
PEIS. [*with the same action as the* SOOTHSAYER, *as if he were feeling for papers*]. Look at the book, and see !
    " Thou shalt in no wise heed them, or forbear
    To lash and smite those eagles of the air,
    Neither regard their names, for it is written,
    Lampon and Diopithes shall be smitten."
SOOTH. Is all this, there ?
PEIS. [*producing a horsewhip*]. Look at the book, and
    see !
Get out ! with a plague and a vengeance.
SOOTH.   Oh dear ! oh !
PEIS. Go soothsay somewhere else, you rascal, run !
                                    [*Exit* SOOTH.

Meton the Astronomer appears, encumbered with a load of mathematical
    instruments, which are disposed about his person. He advances
    with short steps, a straight back, and his chin in the air, modifying,
    by what he conceives to be a tone of condescending familiarity, a
    manner of habitual self-importance.

MET. I'm come, you see, to join you.
PEIS. [*aside*].   (Another plague !)
For what ?   What's your design ?   Your plan, your notion ?
Your scheme—your apparatus—your equipment—
Your outfit ?   What's the meaning of it all ?
MET. I mean to take a geometrical plan
Of your atmosphere—to allot it, and survey it
In a scientific form.
PEIS.   In the name of heaven !
Who are ye and what ?   What name ?   What manner of
    man ?

MET. Who am I and what! Meton's my name, well
   known
In Greece, and in the village of Colonos.

PEIS. But tell me, pray; these implements, these articles,
What are they meant for?*

MET.   These are—*Instruments!*
An atmospherical geometrical scale.

First, you must understand, that the atmosphere
Is formed—in a manner—altogether—partly,
In the fashion of a furnace, or a funnel;

I take this circular arc, with the movable arm,
And so, by shifting it round, till it coincides
At the angle;—you understand me?

PEIS.   Not in the least.

MET. . . . . I obtain a true division, with the quadrature †
Of the equilateral circle. Here, I trace
Your market-place, in the centre, with the streets—
Converging inwards—! and the roads, diverging—!
From the circular wall, without—! like solar rays
From the circular circumference of the sun.

PEIS. [*in a pretended soliloquy; then calling to him with a
   tone of mystery and alarm*].
Another Thales! absolutely, a Thales!—
Meton!

MET. [*startled*]. Why, what's the matter?

PEIS.   You're aware,
That I've a regard for you. Take my advice;
Don't be seen here—withdraw yourself—abscond!

MET. Is there any alarm or risk?

PEIS.   Why, much the same,
As it might be in Lacedæmon. There's a bustle
Of expelling aliens; people are dragged out

---

* Peist. going up to him and pulling them about.

† Meton with animation and action illustrative of the proposed plan.

From the inns and lodgings, with a deal of uproar,
And blows and abuse in plenty, to be met with
In the public street.
MET.   A popular tumult—heh?
PEIS.* Oh, fie! no, nothing of that kind.
MET.   How do you mean then?
PEIS.† We're carrying into effect a resolution
Adopted lately ; to discard and cudgel . . . .
Coxcombs and mountebanks . . . . of every kind.
MET. Perhaps . . . . I had best withdraw.
PEIS.   Why, yes, *perhaps* . . . .
But yet, I would not answer for it, neither;
Perhaps, you may be too late ; the blows I mentioned
Are coming—close upon you—there they come!
MET. Oh, bless me !
PEIS.   Did not I tell you, and give you warning?
Get out, you coxcomb, find out by your geometry,
The road you came, and measure it back : you'd best.
                                          [*Exit* METON.

A Commissioner from Athens advances with an air of importance and
ascendency ; like other consequential persons sent on a foreign
mission, he wishes it to be understood that he considers it a sort of
banishment.

COM. Is nobody here? None of the proxeni,
To receive and attend upon me?
PEIS.   What's all this?
Sardanapalus‡ in person come amongst us !
COM. I come, appointed as Commissioner
To Nephelococcugia,
PEIS.   A Commissioner !
What brings you here?

---

* Peist. scandalized at the supposition.
† During this speech Peisthetairus keeps his eye quietly fixed upon the
Astronomer.
‡ A name proverbial for pomp and luxury.

Com. A paltry scrap of paper,
A trifling, silly decree, that sent me away
Here to this place of yours.
Peis. Well now I suppose,
To make things easy on both sides—could not you
Just take your salary at once ; and so return,
Without any further trouble ?
Com. Truly, yes,
I've other affairs at home : a speech and a motion,
ThatI meant to have made in the general Assembly,
About a business, that I took in hand,
On the part of my friend Pharnaces, the satrap.
Peis. Agreed then, and farewell. Here, take your salary.
Com. What's here ?

[Peisthetairus *has held out his left hand, as if
with an offer of money ; he grasps the right hand
of the* Commissioner, *and with this advantage
proceeds to buffet him.*]

Peis. A motion on the part of Pharnaces !
Com. Bear witness here ! I'm beaten and abused
In my character of Commissioner ! [*Exit* Com.
Peis. Get out !
With your balloting-box and all. It's quite a shame,
Quite scandalous ! They send Commissioners here *
Before we've finished our first sacrifice.

Enter a Hawker with copies of new laws relating to the colony, which
he has brought out with him for sale. Like all itinerant vendors of
literature, he is trying to attract purchasers by reciting and bawling
out select passages from the papers in his hand. The sale of them is
his only object ; and he is quite unconscious that the specimen which
he recites is applicable to an incident which has just occurred. He

* Peisthetairus, in expectation of the Commissioner's return, is working himself into a proper state of wrath, in order to be ready for him. Mere
gratuitous complaint would not be suitable to his character.,

enters on the opposite side with the monotonous chant of a vendor of a last dying speech, confronting Peisthetairus, who is returning after having driven out the Commissioner.

HAW. " Moreover, if a Nephelococcugian
Should assault or smite an Athenian citizen " . . . .
PEIS. What's this? What's all this trumpery paper here?
HAW. I've brought you the new laws and ordinances,
And copies of the last decrees to sell.
PEIS. [*drily and bitterly*]. Let's hear 'em.
HAW. " It is enacted and ordained
That the Nephelococcugians shall use
Such standard weights and measures " . . . .
PEIS. Friend, you'll find
Hard *measure* here, and a heavy *weight*, I promise you,
Upon your shoulders shortly.
HAW. What's the matter?
What's come to you?
PEIS. Get out, with your decrees !
I've bloody decrees against you, dire decrees.
[*drives him off.*
COM. [*returning*]. I summon Peisthetairus to his answer,
In an action of assault and battery,
For the first day of the month, Munichion.
PEIS. Ha, say you so? You're there again ! Have at you. [*drives him off.*
HAW. [*returning*]. " And in case of any assault or violence,
Against the person of the Magistrate." . . . .
PEIS. Bless me ! What you ! You're there, again.
[*drives him off.*
COM. [*returning again*]. I'll ruin you ;
I'll lay my damages at ten thousand drachmas.
PEIS. In the mean time, I'll smash your balloting-boxes.

Com. Remember, how you effaced the public monu-
ment,*
On the pillar, and defiled it late last night.
Peis. Pah! stuff! There seize him, somebody. What
you're off, too.
Come, let's remove, and get away from hence,
And sacrifice our goat, to the gods within doors.

It is to be feared that, without having it pointed out to him, the reader
will hardly be aware that in some of the following lines an attempt
is made to imitate the effect of the spondaic passages in the
original.

CHORUS.

Henceforth—our worth,
Our right—our might,
Shall be shown,
Acknowledged, known;
Mankind shall raise
Prayers, vows, praise,
To the birds alone.
Our employ, is to destroy
The vermin train,
Ravaging amain,
Your fruits and grain:
We're the wardens
Of your gardens,
To watch and chase
The wicked race,
And cut them shorter,
In hasty slaughter.

The first lines of the Epirrema are descriptive of the cruel madness of
the times, see note to p. 199. Diagoras was a poet, a foreigner resident

---

* The sort of accusations which were current at the time similar to those
of the mutilation of the Hermæ. Peisthetairus does not take any notice or
bestow a whole line upon his accuser; the last words of the verse are
addressed to the Hawker.

at Athens (being suspected of Atheism and consequently of. being
an accomplice in the imaginary plot), he was proscribed and a price
set upon his head ; it seems also that, in other instances which are
alluded to, assassination was encouraged by public rewards.

The history of a similar period. The times of Titus Oates's plot (admirably described by Roger North in his Examen) may serve to illustrate the lines 13 and 14, the community in both instances remaining
subject to a reign of terror under obscure wretches whose sole instrument of dominion was perjury ; as it was necessary for those sovereign witnes-es to extort respectable subsidiary evidence in support
of their main system of perjury, threats and imprisonment were the
means employed in both instances, as appears by the narrative of
Andocides.

EPIRREMA.

At the present urgent crisis, all your efforts and attention
Are directed to secure Diagoras's apprehension:
Handsome bounties have been offered of a talent for his
    head
Likewise, with respect to tyrants (tyrants that are gone
    and dead)
Bounties of a talent each, for all that can be killed or
    caught:
    With a zealous emulation, we, the Birds, have also
    thought
Just and proper, to proclaim, from this time forth, that we
    withdraw
From Philocrates, the fowler, the protection of the law:
Furthermore, we fix a price, for bringing him alive or dead,
Four, if he's secured alive; a single talent for his head:
He, that ortolans and quails to market has presumed to
    bring;
And the sparrows, six a penny, tied together in a string,
With a wicked art retaining, sundry doves in his employ,
Fastened, with their feet in fetters, forced to serve for a
    decoy;
    Farther, we declare and publish our command to men
    below,

All the birds you keep in prison, to release, and let them go.
We shall, else, revenge ourselves, and we shall teach the
    tyrants yet,
How to chirp and dance in fetters, in the tangles of a
    net.

CHORUS.

Blest are they,
The birds alway,
With perfect clothing,
Fearing nothing,
Cold or sleet or summer heat.
As it chances,
As he fancies,
Each his own vagary follows,
Dwelling in the dells and hollows
When, with eager weary strain,
The shrilly grasshoppers complain,
Parched upon the sultry plain;
Maddened with the raging heat,
We secure a cool retreat,
In the shady nooks and coves,
Recesses of the sacred groves,
Many a herb, and many a berry
Serves to feast, and make us merry.

ANTEPIRREMA.

To the judges of the prize, we wish to mention in a
    word,
The return we mean to make, if our performance is pre-
    ferred.
  First then, in your empty coffers, you shall see the sterling
    owl,*
From the mines of Laurium, familiar as a common fowl;

---

* The figure of an owl stamped on the coin of Athens.

Roosting among the bags and pouches, each at ease upon
his nest;
Undisturbed, rearing and hatching little broods of interest:
If you wish to cheat in office, but are inexpert and raw,
You should have a kite for agent, capable to gripe and
claw;
Cranes and cormorants shall help you, to a stomach and a
throat;
When you feast abroad, but, if you give a vile, unfriendly
vote,
Hasten and provide yourselves, each, with a little silver
plate,
Like the statues of the gods, for the protection of his
pate;
Else, when forth abroad you ramble, on a summer holiday,
We shall take a dirty vengeance, and befoul your best
array.

In the following scene a foot messenger arrives at full speed from the
new city, apparently in a state of great exhaustion. He communi-
cates his important intelligence to Peisthetairus in a single gasp of
breath—"Your fortification's finished!" The report which he
makes of the building of a new Babylon by the nation of the Birds, as
it considerably exceeds even that license of assuming impossibilities
which is the privilege of the ancient comedy, may lead us to examine
the mode of humorous contrivance by which the author has
managed in some degree to maintain that balance between truth and
falsehood, which I have (in another place) endeavoured to point out
as essential to the character of all dramatic representations whether
serious or comic.

The interest which we take in the development of moral truth and in
the illustration of human character, is so much stronger than that
which we attach to mere matter of fact, that where the two are combined (that is to say, where a supposed fact is made the foundation
of a new and striking illustration of character), our attention is, generally speaking, wholly directed to the latter, and we are inclined to
take the fact for granted ; as we allow the scrawl, which a mathema-
tician draws, to stand for a circle or square, our whole attention
being absorbed in the acquisition of a general and a permanent truth.
It is, we believe, an established axiom in the art of lying that almost

anything may be made credible of almost any person, provided that
the imaginary facts are accompanied by a just representation of the
behaviour of the person, such as it might be supposed to be under
the alleged circumstances ; and this will be more strikingly the case,
if some trait of his character, not generally observed, but likely to be
immediately recognized, is exhibited for the first time. It has been
observed elsewhere, of the Aristophanic or ancient comedy, that it
is essentially a grave, humorous, impossible "great lie," related
with an accurate mimicry of the language and manners of the
persons introduced. As the humour of a "narrative lie" is more
easily comprehended than that of a dramatic one, we may venture
to examine the drama, such as it would have appeared if it had been
helped out in some degree by a narrative comment ; if, like the explanatory heroic prologue in "Henry the Fifth," the ancient comedy
had made use of a buffoonish prologue, explanatory and preparatory
to the different scenes. We might suppose Aristophanes or his pro-
locutor on this occasion to have said : "Gentlemen, the information, which I apprehend you will shortly receive of the progress of
the new buildings at Nephelococcugia, may perhaps strike you as
extraordinary. I should not be surprised, if, to some amongst you,
it should appear little short of being absolutely incredible ; but I
would not have you rely entirely upon your own judgment. There
is Peisthetairus, who has every means of information, and of whose
abilities you can have no doubt : you will see him as much astonished
as any amongst you ; and you will see him so for the first and only
time. But, will he disbelieve the fact ? Far from it. Like the
judicious amongst yourselves, he will not entertain the least doubt of
it ; on the contrary, unless I am very much mistaken in his character,
you will be able to detect evident symptoms of jealousy and uneasi-
ness at the idea of such an object having been accomplished, inde-
pendently of his direction and superintendence ; and indeed, not
without reason ; for, you will see, that both the Chorus and the
Messenger himself appear to abate something of their accustomed
respect and deference to him. You will observe likewise, that the
Messenger is far from anticipating the slightest incredulity, as to the
general fact of the completion of the work of which he himself has
been a witness ; while he is apparently very anxious in his negative
testimony, as to the total absence of any extraneous aid or assistance
whatever."

PEISTHETAIRUS.

Well, friends and birds ! the sacrifice has succeeded,
Our omens have been good ones : good and fair.

But, what's the meaning of it? We've no news
From the new building yet! No messenger!
Oh! there, at last, I see—there's somebody
Running at speed, and panting like a racer.

[*Enter a Messenger, quite out of breath; and
speaking in short snatches.*]

MESS. Where is he? Where? Where is he? Where?
Where is he?—
The president Peisthetairus?

PEIS. [*coolly*].   Here am I.

MESS. [*in a gasp of breath*]. Your fortification's
finished.

PEIS.   Well! that's well.

MESS. A most amazing, astonishing work it is!
So, that Theagenes and Proxenides *
Might flourish and gasconade and prance away,
Quite at their ease, both of them four-in-hand,
Driving abreast upon the breadth of the wall,
Each in his own new chariot.

PEIS.   You surprise me.

MESS. And the height (for I made the measurement
myself)
Is exactly a hundred fathoms.

PEIS.   Heaven and earth!
How could it be? such a mass! who could have built it?

MESS. The Birds; no creature else, no foreigners,
Egyptian bricklayers,† workmen or masons,
But, they themselves, alone, by their own efforts,
(Even to my surprise, as an eye-witness)—
The Birds, I say, completed everything:

---

* Pretenders to great wealth and affecting extraordinary expense and
display. See note to p. 222.

† Egyptian labourers are mentioned in "The Frogs."   \

There came a body of thirty thousand cranes
(I won't be positive, there might be more)
With stones from Africa, in their craws and gizzards,
Which the stone-curlews and stone-chatterers
Worked into shape and finished. The sand-martens
And mud-larks, too, were busy in their department,
Mixing the mortar, while the water birds,
As fast as it was wanted, brought the water
To temper, and work it.

PEIS. [*in a fidget*].   But, who served the masons?
Who did you get to carry it?

MESS.   To carry it?
Of course, the carrion crows and carrying pigeons.

PEIS. [*in a fuss, which he endeavours to conceal*].
Yes! yes! But after all, to load your hods,
How did you manage that?

MESS.   Oh capitally,
I promise you.   There were the geese, all barefoot
Trampling the mortar, and, when all was ready,
They handed it into the hods, so cleverly,
With their flat feet!

PEIS. [*A bad joke, as a vent for irritation* *].
                    They *footed* it, you mean—
Come; it was handily done though, I confess.

MESS. Indeed, I assure you, it was a sight to see them;
And trains of ducks, there were, clambering the ladders,
With their duck legs, like bricklayer's 'prentices,
All dapper and handy, with their little trowels.

PEIS.† In fact, then, it's no use engaging foreigners,
Mere folly and waste, we've all within ourselves.

---

* Like Falstaff, when he is annoyed and perplexed, joking perforce.
† Peisthetairus is at a loss, unable to think of a new objection, he maintains his importance by a wise observation. As soon as an objection occurs, he states it with great eagerness; but with no better success than before.

Ah, well now, come ! But about the woodwork ? **Heh !**
Who were the carpenters ? Answer me that !
    MESS. The woodpeckers, of course: and there they
    were,
Labouring upon the gates, driving and banging,
With their hard hatchet beaks, and such a din,
Such a clatter, as they made, hammering and hacking,
In a perpetual peal, pelting away
Like shipwrights, hard at work in the arsenal.
    And now their work is finished, gates and all,
Staples and bolts, and bars and everything ;
The sentries at their posts ; patrols appointed ;
The watchmen in the barbican ; the beacons
Ready prepared for lighting ; all their signals
Arranged—but I'll step out, just for a moment,
To wash my hands. You'll settle all the rest.   [*Exit.*

> [PEISTHETAIRUS, *surprised at the rapid conclusion*
> *of the work, feeling from the volubility and*
> *easy manner of the Messenger, the blow which*
> *his authority has received ; seeing that nothing*
> *is left for him to superintend, nothing to direct,*
> *nothing to suggest, or to find fault with, remains*
> *in an attitude of perplexity and astonishment,*
> *with his hands clasped across his forehead.*]

    CHOR. [*to* PEISTHETAIRUS, *in a sort of self-satisfied*
    drawling tone].
Heigh-day ! Why, what's the matter with ye ? Sure I
Ah ! well now, I calculate, you're quite astonished ;
You did not know the nature of our birds :
I guess you thought it an impossible thing,
To finish up your fortification job
Within the time so cleverly.
    PEIS. [*recovering himself and looking round*]. Yes, truly.
Yes, I'm surprised indeed ; I must confess—

I could almost imagine to myself
It was a dream, an illusion, altogether—
 But, there's the watchman of the town, I see !
In alarm and haste, it seems ! He's running here—

   [*The* WATCHMAN *enters, with a shout of alarm*].

—Well, what's the matter ?
W.   A most dreadful business :
One of the gods, just now—Jupiter's gods—
Has bolted through the gates, and driven on
Right into the atmosphere, in spite of us,
And all the jackdaws, that were mounting guard.
 PEIS. [*animated at the prospect of having something to*
  manage].
What an outrage ! what an insult ! Which of 'em ?
Which of the gods ?
 W.   We can't pretend to say ;
We just could ascertain that he wore wings.
We're clear upon that point.
 PEIS.   But a light party
Ought surely to have been sent in such a case ;
A detachment—*
 W.   A detachment has been sent
Already : a squadron of ten thousand hawks,
Besides a corps of twenty thousand hobby hawks,
As a light cavalry, to scour the country :
Vultures and falcons, ospreys, eagles, all
Have sallied forth ; the sound of wings is heard,
Rushing and whizzing round on every side,
In eager search. The fugitive divinity
Is not far off, and soon must be discovered.

---

 * Peisthetairus is exposed to a fresh mortification ; the orders which he
was ready to give have been anticipated ! He contrives, however, to detect
an omission, and upon the strength of it to assume a tone of authority and
command.

PEIS. Did nobody think of slingers ?   Where are they?
Where are the slingers got to?   Give me a sling.
Arrows and slings, I say!—Make haste with 'em.

CHORUS.

The verses which follow belong to a species of songs, which are alluded
to in Aristophanes more than once.   They may properly be called
" Watch-songs," being sung by the Watchmen and Soldiers on
guard, to keep themselves and their comrades awake and alert.

War is at hand,
On air and land,
    Proclaimed and fixt.
War and strife,
Eager and rife,
    Are kindled atwixt
This State of ours,
And the heavenly powers.
    Look with care,
To the circuit of air,
    Watch lest he,
    The deity,
Whatever he be,
    Should unaware
Escape and flee.

But hark ! the rushing sound of hasty wings
Approaches us.   The deity is at hand.

PEIS. Holloh you !   Where are ye flying?   Where are ye
    going?
Hold !   Halt!   Stop there, I tell ye !—Stop this instant !
What are ye?   Where do you come from ?   Speak,
    explain.
    IRIS. Me?   From the gods, to be sure ! the Olympian
    gods.

PEIS. [*pointing to the flaunting appendages of her dress*].*
What are ye? With all your flying trumpery!
A helmet? or a galley? What's your name?

IRIS. Iris, the messenger of the gods.

PEIS.   A messenger!
Oh! you're a naval messenger, I reckon,
The Salaminian galley, or the Paralian? †
You're in full sail, I see.

IRIS.   What's here to do?

PEIS. Are there no birds in waiting? Nobody
To take her into custody?

IRIS.   Me, to custody?
Why, what's all this?

PEIS.   You'll find to your cost, I promise ye.

IRIS. Well, this seems quite unaccountable!

PEIS.   Which of the gates
Did ye enter at, ye jade? How came you here?

IRIS. Gates!—I know nothing about your gates, not I.

PEIS. Fine innocent ignorant airs, she gives herself!
You applied to the pelicans, I suppose?—The captain
Of the cormorants on guard admitted you?

IRIS. Why, what the plague! what's this?

PEIS.   So, you confess!
You come without permission!

IRIS.   Are you mad?

PEIS. Did neither the sitting magistrates nor bird-
masters
Examine and pass you?

IRIS.   Examine me, forsooth!

PEIS. This is the way then!—without thanks or leave

---

* Iris, the rainbow personified, is of course attired in all the colours of
the rainbow, with abundance of lappets and streamers.

† The two sacred galleys of the Athenians. The most splendidly
equipped were despatched upon the most important occasions. See note,
page 187.

You ramble and fly, committing trespasses
In an atmosphere belonging to your neighbours !
   IRIS. And where would you have us fly then?   Us, the
   gods !
   PEIS. I neither know nor care.   But, I know this,
They sha'n't fly here.   And another thing, I know.
I know—that, if there ever was an instance
Of an Iris or a rainbow, such as you,
Detected in the fact, fairly condemned,
And justly put to death—it would be you.
   IRIS. But, I'm immortal.
   PEIS. [*coolly and peremptorily*]. That would make no
   difference :
We should be strangely circumstanced indeed;
With the possession of a sovereign power,
And you, the gods, in no subordination,
No kind of order ! fairly mutinying,
Infringing and disputing our commands.
—Now then, you'll please to tell me—where you're
   going?
Which way you're steering with those wings of yours?
   IRIS. I? . . . . I'm commissioned from my father Jove,*
To summon human mortals to perform
Their rites and offerings and oblations, due
To the powers above.
   PEIS.   And who do you mean? what powers?
   IRIS. What powers?   Ourselves, the Olympian deities !
   PEIS. So then ! you're deities, the rest of ye !
   IRIS. Yes, to be sure.   What others should there be ?
   PEIS. Remember—! once for all—! that we, the Birds,
Are the only deities, from this time forth;
And, not your father Jove.   By Jove ! not he !

---

* Iris, in a great fright, hesitating and hurried, but attempting to assume
a tone of authority.

IRIS. Oh ! rash, presumptuous wretch ! Incense no more
The wrath of the angry gods ! lest ruin drive *
Her ploughshare o'er thy mansion ; and destruction,
With hasty besom sweep thee to the dust ;
Or flaming lightning smite thee with a flash,   .
Left in an instant smouldering and extinct.

PEIS. Do ye hear her?—Quite in tragedy !—quite
sublime !
Come, let me try for a bouncer in return.†
Let's see. Let's recollect. "Me dost thou deem,
Like a base Lydian or a Phrygian slave,
With hyperbolical bombast to scare ?
I tell ye, and you may tell him. Jupiter—
If he provokes me, and pushes things too far—
Will see some eagles of mine, to outnumber his,
With firebrands in their claws about his house.

And, I shall send a flight of my Porphyrions.‡
A hundred covey or more, armed cap-a-pie
To assault him in his sublime celestial towers :
Perhaps, he may remember in old times,
He found enough to do with one Porphyrion.

And for you, Madam Iris, I shall strip
Your rainbow-shanks, if you're impertinent,
Depend upon it, and I myself, in person
Will ruin you, myself—! Old as I am.

IRIS Curse ye, you wretch, and all your filthy words.

PEIS. Come, scuttle away ; convey your person elsewhere ;
Be brisk, and leave a vacancy. Brush off.

---

* A medley from terrific passages in the tragic poets.

† Peisthetairus at last hits upon a tragic passage which he thinks will serve for a suitable reply. A vulgar line which disfigures a very fine scene of Euripides.

‡ The Greek name for a flamingo, also the name of one of the giants who made war against the gods.

IRIS. I shall inform my father. He shall know
Your rudeness and impertinence. He shall,—
He'll settle ye and keep ye in order. You shall see.
PEIS. Oh dear! is it come to that! No, you're mistaken,
Young woman, upon that point, I'm not your man,
I'm an old fellow grown ; I'm thunder-proof,
Proof against flames and darts and female arts :
You'd best look out for a younger customer.

Poor Iris, in her rage, unwittingly makes use of the same sort of phrase
with which a young girl at Athens would repel, or affect to repel,
improper familiarities. Peisthetairus, taking advantage of this,
pretends to consider her indignation as a mere coquettish artifice
intended to inveigle and allure him.

The *Athenian Father*—"I shall inform my father".—may be considered
as equivalent to the *Irish Brother*. The menace in one case would
imply a duel, in the other a lawsuit.

CHORUS.

Notice is hereby given,
To the deities of heaven ;
 Not to trespass here,
 Upon our atmosphere ;
Take notice ; from the present day,
No smoke or incense is allowed
To pass this way.

PEIS. Quite strange it is ! quite unaccountable !
That herald to mankind, that was despatched,
What has become of him ? He's not yet returned.

[*Enter* HERALD.]

HER. O Peisthetairus, happiest, wisest, best,
Cleverest of men ! Oh ! most illustrious !
Oh ! most inordinately fortunate !
Oh ! most . . . . Oh ! do for shame, do, bid me have done.

PEIS. What are you saying ?

HER.   All the people of Earth
Have joined in a complimentary vote, decreeing
A crown of gold to you, for your exertions.

PEIS. I'm much obliged to the people of Earth. But why?
What was their motive ?

HER.   O most noble founder
Of this supereminent celestial city,
You can't conceive the clamour of applause,
The enthusiastic popularity,
That attends upon your name ; the impulse and stir,
That moves among mankind, to colonize
And migrate hither.   In the time before,
There was a Spartan mania, and people went
Stalking about the streets, with Spartan staves,
With their long hair, unwashed and slovenly,
Like so many Socrates's : but, of late,
Birds are the fashion—Birds are all in all—
Their modes of life are grown to be mere copies
Of the birds' habits ; rising with the lark,
Scratching and scrabbling suits and informations;
Picking and pecking upon points of law ;
Brooding and hatching evidence.   In short,
It has grown to such a pitch, that names of birds
Are given to individuals ; Chærephon
Is called an owl, Theagenes, a goose,
Philocles, a cock sparrow, Midias,
A dunghill cock.   And all the songs in vogue,
Have something about birds ; swallows or doves ;
Or about flying, or a wish for wings.

Such is the state of things, and I must warn you,
That you may expect to see some thousands of them
Arriving here, almost immediately,
With a clamorous demand for wings and claws :
I advise you to provide yourself in time.

PEIS. Come, it won't do then, to stand dawdling here;
Go you, fill the hampers and the baskets there
With wings, and bid the loutish porter bring them.
While I stop here, to encounter the new-comers.

It has been already observed in reference to the Chorus of the Acharnæ
(p. 68), that when his Choruses have ceased to contribute to the
progressive action of the drama, the poet has sometimes relieved
himself, from the embarrassment which they created, by turning into
ridicule the essential character and attributes of the Chorus itself.
In that comedy, as in the present, the hostility of the Chorus had given
spirit and animation to some of the earlier scenes, but, from the
moment when their hostility ceased, they had remained a mere
superfluous appendage;—nothing being left for them to be done,
and scarcely anything to be said; they could barely contrive to
make their existence manifest from time to time by interposing with
the expression of their acquiescence and approbation. The poet
then having no further use for them, amuses his audience at their
expense. The character of Choruses (except when they happen to
be in a violent passion) being habitually obsequious and conform-
able—their obsequiousness is represented as connected with the
display of Dicæopolis's good cheer, the sight of which confirms
their favourable opinion of his political principles, and induces them
to pass over his selfish treatment of the poor countryman with an
apologetical observation.
But with respect to the Chorus now before us (that of the *Birds*), there
is another point of the choral character (arising out of the very
condition of their existence as a Chorus) which must not be overlooked. All Choruses are essentially poetic and imaginative, the
votaries of ideal harmony and beauty. Under this point of view,
the following passage places them in amusing contrast with the
practical active bustling spirit of Peisthetairus. The Chorus begin
chanting their namby-pamby anticipations of future splendour and
happiness, Peisthetairus, in the first instance, favouring them with
a sort of gruff acquiescence. But as they proceed he loses all
patience, contriving however to relieve himself, and give a vent to
his ill humour, by scolding the servant. The obsequious character
of the Chorus now displays itself; they affect to sympathize with his
impatience; expressing their own displeasure, in a style suited to
their choral character, that is to say, pedantic and formal. Peisthetairus, utterly disgusted with them, evades their sympathy, by
relapsing into comparative good-humour. The Chorus then betake

themselves to their usual practice of exhorting and advising. This
is more than he can endure—instead of taking any notice of them,
he flies into a pretended rage against his servant ; and is running
off the stage to beat him, when he is encountered by the first
specimen of the new colonists.

This explanation must not be regarded as fanciful or superfluous.
We should in that case be compelled to adopt a conclusion, in
which the admirers of Aristophanes would not readily acquiesce,
namely, that the poet had (in a play already of unusual length)
inserted a passage of twenty-four lines destitute of poetical merit,
without any comic intention and wholly unamusing as a dramatic
exhibition.

Peisthetairus says little in the following scene, but is not the less amusing,
from his restless fidget and ill-disguised impatience and disgust.

CHORUS.

Shortly shall the noble town,
   Populous and gay,
  Shine in honour and renown.
PEIS. [*drily*]. Why, perhaps she may.
CHOR.   The benignant powers of love,
    From their happy sphere,
  From the blest abodes above . . . .
PEIS. [*venting his ill humour on the servant*].
  Curse ye, rascal ! can't ye move !
CHOR.   . . . . Are descending here,
Where in all this earthly range,*
He that wishes for a change
  Can he find a seat,
Joyous and secure as this,
Filled with happiness and bliss,
  Such a fair retreat ?
Here are all the lovely faces,
Gentle Venus and the Graces,
  And the little Cupid ;

---

* The Chorus in their idealizing and poetical character.

Order, ease and harmony,
Peace and affability.
PEIS.   The scoundrel is so stupid,
Quicker, sirrah ! bring it quicker !
CHOR.   Let him bring the woven wicker
With the winged store.
I, myself, in very deed,
With the varlet will proceed,
And smite him more and more ;
Like a sluggish ass he seems,
Or even, as a man that dreams,
Therefore smite him sore.
PEIS.†   He's a lazy rogue, it's true.
CHOR.‡ Now range them forth, displayed in order due,
Feathers of every form and size and hue,
With shrewd intent, adapting every pinion,
To the new residents of your dominion.
PEIS. I vow by the hawks and eagles ! I won't bear it ;
I'll beat ye, I will myself, you lazy rascal !

As a practical comment upon the anticipations of the Chorus, and as a
sample of the kind of population likely to resort to a new colony,
the first arrival is that of a young reprobate, who wishes his father
out of the way ; and who conceives that the laws of the Birds will
permit him to hasten that desirable conclusion.   Peisthetairus
receives and attends to him, without being betrayed into any
expression of moral indignation, which would be inconsistent with
his character, as a perfect politician.   He merely states, as a matter
of fact, some difficulties arising out of a point of law, professes a
wish to serve him, as a hearty partisan, well disposed to the cau-e
of the new colony ; and finally, in an easy way, recalls to his
recollection one of the precepts of his Catechism, and at the same

---

* Chorus in their obsequious character, but with a formal pedantic tone.
† Peisthetairus determined to cross them, relapses into good-humour.
‡ The Chorus assume their admonitory character ; Peisthetairus can bear
it no longer ; he breaks from them, and runs off the stage, as if to beat the
servant.

time points out to him a mode of life suited to his situation and
tastes. The young man, who is more of a wild, desperate, than a
confirmed villain, is struck with the suggestion, expresses a resolution to adopt it, and departs.

Enter a fellow, singing.

"Oh ! for an eagle's force and might,*
　　Loftily to soar
　　Over land and sea, to light
　　On a lonely shore."

PEIS. Well, here's a song that's something to the purpose.

Y. MAN. Ay, ay, there's nothing like it—wings and
　　flying !
Wings are your only sort. I'm a bird-fancier.
In the new fashion quite. I've taken a notion
To settle and live amongst ye. I like your laws.

PEIS.† What laws do you mean? We've many laws
　　amongst us.

Y. MAN. Your laws in general; but particularly
The law that allows of beating one's own father.

PEIS. Why, truly, yes ! we esteem it a point of valour,
In a chicken, if he clapperclaws the old cock.

Y. MAN. That was my view, feeling a wish in fact
To throttle mine, and seize the property.

PEIS.‡ Yes, but you'd find some difficulties here,
An obstacle insurmountable, I conceive ;
An ancient statute standing unrepealed,
Engraved upon our old Ciconian columns.
It says, that when a stork or a ciconia
Has brought his lawful progeny of young storks
To bird's estate, and enabled them to fly :

---

* From a chorus of Sophocles ; dramatic poetry and music was popular,
like opera airs on the Continent. See "Knights," p. 126.
† Peisthetairus very gravely and methodically.
‡ Peisthetairus with great candour and composure simply stating a fact.

The sire shall stand entitled to a maintenance
At the son's cost and charge in his old age.

Y. MAN.* I've managed finely it seems to mend myself!
Forced to maintain my father after all!

PEIS.† No, no ; not quite so bad ; since you're come here,
As a well-wisher to the establishment,
Zealous and friendly, we'll contrive to equip you
With a suit of armour, as a soldier's orphan.‡
And now, young man, let me suggest some notions,
Things that were taught me when a boy. " Your father?"§
"Strike him not,"—rather take this pair of wings ;
And this cockspur ;‖ imagine, you've a coxcomb
Upon your head, to serve you for a helmet ;
Look out for service, and enlist yourself ;
Get into a garrison ; live upon your pay ;
And let your father live. You're fond of fighting,
And fond of flying—take a flight to Thrace ;
There you may please yourself ; and fight your fill.

Y. MAN. By Jove, you're right. The notion's not a bad
one.
I'll follow it up!

PEIS. [*very gravely and quietly*].
You'll find it the best way. [*Exit.* Y. MAN.

Cinesias, a lame dithyrambic poet and musician, arrives in the hopes of
being able to provide himself with wings, which will enable him to
look after his concerns among the clouds, the great emporium for

---

* Y. Man with a start of disappointment, slapping his forehead.
† Peisthetairus in a soothing consolatory tone.
‡ The sons of citizens slain were publicly presented with a suit of
armour.
§ A want of harmony in the original verse appears to indicate the in-
sertion of a formula—but again, if we resolve this formula into its two
component parts, the question and answer, with a consequent pause between
them, the harmony of the verse is very sensibly improved. The formula
was part of a series of moral prohibitions taught to children by question and
answer.
‖ Giving him a sword.

business with all persons who are embarked in the dithyrambic line. Peisthetairus amuses himself with affronting and laughing at him, but he persists in his purpose, and professes his determination to continue worrying and persevering, till it is accomplished.

The reader who refers to the original will perceive that the interrup-tions, with which Peisthetairus breaks in upon Cinesias's recitation or song, are omitted in the translation. To the Athenian audience, the original must have been familiar, and probably sufficiently hackneyed, to make them feel amusement at hearing it accompanied with burlesque interruptions; but as only one other fragment of dithyrambic poetry has been preserved to modern times, and neither of them has appeared in our language, it seemed more advisable to present it to the English reader in an unbroken form.*

Enter CINESIAS, *singing.*

" Fearless, I direct my flight,
To the vast Olympian height;
Thence at random, I repair,
Wafted in the whirling air;
With an eddy, wild and strong,
Over all the fields of song."

PEIS. Ah! well, Cinesias, I'm quite glad to see ye;
But, what has brought ye and all your songs and music,
Hobbling along with your old chromatic joints?

CIN. [*singing*]. " Let me live, and let me sing,
Like a bird upon the wing."

PEIS. No more of that; but tell us plainly in prose,
What are ye come for? what's your scheme, your object?

CIN. I was anxious to procure a pair of wings,
To say the truth; wishing to make a tour
Among the clouds, collecting images
And metaphors, and things of that description.

PEIS. How so! do you procure 'em from the clouds?

CIN. Entirely! Our dithyrambic business absolutely
Depends upon them; our most approved commodities,

---

* It is singular that this other fragment presents the image of flying.

The dusty, misty, murky articles,
With the suitable wings and feathers, are imported
Exclusively from thence.   I'll give you a sample,
A thing of my own composing.   You shall judge.
    PEIS. But, indeed, I'd rather not.
    CIN.   But, indeed, you must ;
It's a summary view of flying, comprehending it
In all its parts, in every point of view.

CINESIAS, *singing.*

" Ye gentle feathered tribes,
    Of every plume and hue,
That, in uninhabited air,
    Are hurrying here and there ;
    Oh ! that I, like you,
Could leave this earthly level,
    For a wild aërial revel :
        O'er the waste of ocean,
    To wander, and to dally
        With the billow's motion ;
    Or, in an eager sally,
        Soaring to the sky,
        To range and rove on high
    With my plumy sails.
Buffeted and baffled, with the gusty gales,
Buffeted and baffled. . . . . ."
    [*While* CINESIAS *is repeating these last lines,* PEIS-
    THETAIRUS *comes behind him, and gives him a
    flap with a huge pair of wings.*]
    CIN. A pretty, civil joke indeed !
    PEIS.   What joke ?
I'm only buffeting you with the plumy sails,
I thought it was what you wanted.
    CIN.   Well, that's fine !

Pretty respect for a master such as me,
A leader of the band, that all the tribes
Are ready to fight for, to bespeak him first.

    PEIS. Well, we've a little unfledged chorus here,
That Leotrophides* hatched, poor puny nestlings,
I'll give 'em you for scholars.

    CIN.   Ah, laugh on !
Laugh on ! but take may word for it, here I stay,
Till you provide me with a pair of wings,
Proper to circumnavigate the skies.   [*Exit* CIN.

Peisthetairus is represented in the following scene, as a perfect master
of his art ; amusing himself in angling and playing with a stupid, impudent young scoundrel ; sometimes twitching him in with a slight
jerk of his hook, and again allowing him to run out to the full length
of his line. If any one passage were to be selected from the remains of
Aristophanes, as particularly illustrative of the manner in which he
delights to exhibit character, perhaps it would be this; it is not a
serious struggle for ascendency, such as he displays elsewhere ; in this
instance, he shows Peisthetairus as a consummate practitioner, re-
linquishing and reassuming it at pleasure. But this is one of those
scenes which, to be thoroughly appreciated, would require to be
developed in dramatic action by a superior comedian. The mere
printed page, unless we suppose the reader to bestow as much
attention on it as an actor would do in studying his part, will be
found to convey a very confused and inadequate notion of it.
The song with which the Sycophant enters, is said by the Scholiast to be
from Alcæus ; it should seem more consonant to his character, to
suppose it to be some modern parody or adaptation from one of the
comedies of the time.

Enter SYCOPHANT, *singing.*

"Tell us who the strangers are,
    Gentle swallow. Birds of air,
    Party-coloured, poor and bare,

---

    * Cinesias was ridiculed for his slight flimsy figure, adapted for flying ;
Leotrophides, the Scholiast tells us, resembled him in this respect.

Tell us who the strangers are.
Gentle swallow, tell me true."
PEIS. Here's a fine plague broke out. See yonder
fellow
Sauntering along this way, swaggering and singing.
SYC. Ho! gentle swallow! I say, my gentle swallow,
My gentle swallow! how often must I call?*
PEIS. Why, there it is ; the prodigal in the fable
Seeking for swallows in a ragged coat.
SYC. [*in an arrogant overbearing tone*].
Who's he, that's set to serve out wings?   Where is he?
PEIS. 'Tis I, but what do you want?   You should explain.
SYC. Wings! Wings! You need not have asked me.
Wings I want.
PEIS. Do you mean to fly for flannel to Pellene?†
SYC. [*a little disconcerted at this allusion to his attire*].
No, no! But I'm employed .... I employ myself,
In fact, among the allies and islanders ;
I'm in the informing line.

PEIS. [*in a tone of very grave irony, which the* SYCOPHANT,
not perceiving, proceeds more fluently than before].
I wish you joy.
SYC. And a mover and manager for prosecutions,
In criminal suits, and so forth, you understand me ;
So I wish to equip myself with a pair of wings,
To whisk about, and trounce the islanders.
PEIS. Would it be doing things in better form,
To serve a summons flying, think ye ?
SYC. [*not knowing very well what to make of him*].   No,
Not that, but just to avoid the risk of pirates,
To return in company with a flight of cranes,

---

* An expression of impatience in the original has been hitherto mistrans-
lated.

† Pellene was famous for woollen stuff. Pieces of it were given as prizes
at their public games

(As they do with the gravel in their gizzards),
With a bellyful of lawsuits for my ballast.

PEIS. [*in a grave, primitive, and somewhat twaddling tone,
intended to reanimate the impertinence of the* SYCOPHANT].

So, this is your employment! A young man
Like you, to be an informer! Is it possible?

SYC. Why shouldn't it? I was never bred to labour.

PEIS. [*as before*]. But sure, there are other lawful occupa-
tions,
In which a brisk young fellow, such as you,
Might èarn an honest, decent livelihood,
In credit and goodwill, without informing.

SYC. [*thoroughly taken in, and thinking he has to deal with
a mere silly well-meaning old man, becomes emphatically
insolent*].

Wings, my good fellow! wings I want—not words.

PEIS. [*drily*]. I'm giving you wings, already.

SYC. [*a little puzzled and taken aback*]. What, with words?
Is that your way?

PEIS. [*in a tone of very grave banter*].
                         Yes, for mankind in general
Are winged as it were, and brought to plume themselves
In different ways by speeches and discourse.

SYC. [*confused and puzzled*].
What, all?

PEIS. [*as before*]. Yes, all. I'll give you a striking instance:
You must have heard, yourself, elderly people
Sitting conversing in the barber's shop.
And one says—"Well, Diitrephes has talked
So much to my young man, he has brought him at last
To plume himself in driving." And another
Says, that his son is quite amongst the clouds,
Grown flighty of late, with studying tragedy.

SYC. [*with a sort of hesitating laugh*].
So, words are wings, you say.

PEIS.   No doubt of it.
I say it, and I repeat it ; human nature
Is marvellously raised and elevated
By words.   I was in hopes, that I might raise you
By words of good advice, to another sphere ;
To live in an honest calling.

 SYC. [*feeling himself bantered and beaten, but restive and angry*].

      But I won't though.

 PEIS. [*coolly*]. Why, what will you do ?

 SYC. [*sulkily at first, but animating as he proceeds*].

      Why, I won't disgrace my family,
My father and my grandfather before him
Served as informers ; and I'll stick to it,
The profession.   So, you'll please to hand 'em me out ;
A pair of your best wings, vulture's or hawk's,
To fly to the Islands, with my summonses,
And home again, to record them in the courts,
And out again, to the Islands.

 PEIS. [*in a tone of interest and sympathy, as if he was himself an amateur desirous of displaying his professional knowledge*].

      Yes, that's well,
I understand ye, I think ; your method is,
To be beforehand with 'em ?   Your defendant,
You get him cast for non-appearance, heh ?
Before he can arrive ; and finish him
In his absence, heh ?

 SYC. [*completely taken in, delighted—rubbing his hands*].

     By Jove, you're up to it !

 PEIS. Then, whilst he's sailing here you get the start,
And fly, to pounce upon the property,
To rummage out the chattels.

 SYC.   That's the trick,
The notion of it !—I see, you're up to it.

A man must whisk about, here and away,
Just like a whipping-top.

PEIS.   Ay, yes, you're right,
I understand you—the instance is a good one.
A whipping-top, you say. Well, by good luck
I've here a capital slashing suit of wings,
To serve ye, made of a cow-hide from Corcyra.

SYC. O heaven! what's there? a horsewhip?

PEIS.   Wings, I tell ye,
To whisk ye about, to flog ye, and make ye fly.

SYC. Oh dear! oh dear!

PEIS.   Scamper away, you scoundrel!
Vanish, you vagabond! whisk yourself off!
I'll pay ye for your practices in the courts,
Your pettifoggico rascalities.

                               [*Exit* SYC.

    [*to the attendants*]
Come bundle up the wings. Let's take 'em back.

                               [*Exeunt.*

Fabulous notions, respecting the unknown portions of the world, seem to have been nearly the same (or at least of the same character) in the time of Aristophanes as in the days of Sir John Mandeville.

The marvels of these regions, known only to the Birds, are naturally expatiated upon by a Chorus of Birds, when released from the business of the stage and placed in immediate communication with the audience. But it will be seen, that by a strange coincidence those wonderful and remote objects have an unaccountable analogy to things and persons at Athens; as in the following instance of the enormous tree, which by the botanists was considered as belonging to the sycophantic genus; but which was vulgarly called a Cleonymus, whereas at Athens there happened to be a person precisely of the same name, " Cleonymus," equally distinguished for his size; and having the same peculiarity of being classed among the Sycophants. And what is more singular, as the Athenian Cleonymus had lost his shield in battle, it so happened that his vegetable counterpart was a deciduous tree, with leaves of a scutiform or shield-like shape, which it was also in the habit of losing.

The antistrophe is a romantic and mysterious description of a junketing public-house, which seems to have been in vogue ; but from which it was not safe to return to town after dusk. Orestes, an heroic name, was also the name or the nickname of a noted robber (see "Acharnians," p. 77). It was reckoned extremely dangerous to meet a demigod after sunset.

CHORUS.—STROPHE.

We have flown, and we have run,
Viewing marvels, many a one ;
In every land beneath the sun.
   But, the strangest sight to see,
Was a huge exotic tree,
Growing, without heart or pith,
Weak and sappy, like a withe ;
But, with leaves and boughs withal,
Comely, flourishing and tall.
   This the learned all ascribe
To the sycophantic tribe ;
But the natives there, like us,
Call it a Cleonymus.
In the spring's delightful hours,
It blossoms with rhetoric flowers ;
I saw it standing in the field,
With leaves, in figure like a shield ;
On the first tempestuous day,
I saw it cast those leaves away.

ANTISTROPHE.

There lies a region out of sight,
Far within the realm of night,
Far from torch and candle light.
There in feasts of meal and wine,
Men and demigods may join,
There they banquet, and they dine,
Whilst the light of day prevails ;

At sunset, their assurance fails.
If any mortal then presumes,
Orestes, sallying from the tombs,
Like a fierce heroic sprite,
Assaults and strips the lonely wight.

The scene which follows may be considered as a short abstract of the mode in which clandestine political information is received, attended to, and dismissed. The informant presents himself with an extraordinary display of precaution and apprehension ; he is received with eagerness and cordiality, attended to with great earnestness, interrupted only by some little ill-humour on the part of the man of business, when, in seeking for information, he is obliged to betray the want of it ; finally, he is dismissed with a sort of indifference, approaching to derision, after having been thoroughly pumped and drained of his intelligence.

PROMETHEUS, PEISTHETAIRUS, CHORUS.

PRO. [*enters muffled up, peeping about him with a look of anxiety and suspicion*].
Oh dear ! If Jupiter should chance to see me !
Where's Peisthetairus? Where?
PEIS.   Why, what's all this ?
This fellow muffled up?
PRO.   Do look behind me ;
Is anybody watching? any gods
Following and spying after me ?
PEIS.   No, none,
None that I can see, there's nobody. But you !
What are ye ?
PRO.   Tell me, what's the time of day ?
PEIS. Why, noon, past noon ; but tell me, who are ye ?
    Speak.
PRO. Much past,—how much ?
PEIS. [*aside*].   Confound the fool, I say
The insufferable blockhead !

Pro.   How's the sky?
Open or overcast?   Are there any clouds?
Peis. [*aloud and angrily*].
Be hanged!
Pro.   Then I'll disguise myself no longer.
Peis. My dear Prometheus!
Pro.   Hold your tongue, I beg;
Don't mention my name!   If Jupiter should see me,
Or overhear ye, I'm ruined and undone.
But now, to give you a full complete account
Of everything that's passing, there in heaven—
The present state of things. . . . . But first I'll trouble
     you
To take the umbrella, and hold it overhead,
Lest they should overlook us.
Peis.   What a thought!
Just like yourself!   A true Promethean thought!
Stand under it, here!   Speak boldly; never fear.
Pro. D'ye mind me?
Peis.   Yes, I mind ye.   Speak away.
Pro. [*emphatically*]. Jupiter's ruined.
Peis.   Ruined!   How?   Since when?
Pro. From the first hour you fortified and planted
Your atmospheric settlements.   Ever since,
There's not a mortal offers anything
In the shape of sacrifice.   No smoke of victims!
No fumes of incense!   Absolutely nothing!
We're keeping a strict fast—fasting perforce,
From day to day—the whole community.
     And the inland barbarous gods in the upper country
Are broken out, quite mutinous and savage,
With hunger and anger; threatening to come down
With all their force; if Jupiter refuses
To open the ports, and allow them a free traffic
For their entrails and intestines, as before.

PEIS. [*a little annoyed at being obliged to ask the question*].
What—are there other barbarous gods, besides,
In the upper country?
PRO.   Barbarous?—to be sure !
They're all of Execestides's kindred.*
PEIS. [*as before hesitating, but with a sort of affected ease*].
Well—but—the name now. The same barbarous deities—
What name do you call 'em?
PRO. [*surprised at* PEISTHETAIRUS'S *ignorance*].
                              Call them ! The Triballi !
PEIS. [*giving vent to his irritation by a forced joke*].
Ah ! well then, that accounts for our old saying:—
Confound the *Tribe* of them !
PRO. [*annoyed and drily*]. Precisely so.
But, now to business. Thus much, I can tell ye;
That envoys will arrive immediately
From Jupiter, and those upland wild Triballi,
To treat for a peace. But, you must not consent
To ratify or conclude, till Jupiter
Acknowledges the sovereignty of the birds;
Surrendering up to you, the sovereign queen,
Whom you must marry.
PEIS.   Why, what queen is that?
PRO. What queen? A most delightful charming girl,
Jove's housekeeper, that manages his matters,
Serves out his thunderbolts, arranges everything;
The constitutional laws and liberties,
Morals and manners, the marine department,
Freedom of speech, and threepence for the juries.
PEIS. Why, that seems all in all.
PRO.   Yes, everything,
I tell ye, in having her, you've everything :

---

* Noted elsewhere in this play as having no just claim to the rights of a
citizen.

I came down hastily, to say thus much;
I'm hearty, ye know; I stick to principle.
Steady to the human interest—always was.*

PEIS. Yes! we're obliged to you for our roast victuals.

PRO. And I hate these present gods, you know, most
thoroughly.
I need not tell you that.

PEIS.† [*with a sort of half sneer*]. No, no, you need not,
You're known of old, for an enemy to the gods.

PRO. Yes, yes, like Timon, I'm a perfect Timon;
Just such another. But I must be going;
Give me the umbrella; if Jupiter should see me,
He'll think that I'm attending a procession.‡

PEIS. That's well, but don't forget the folding chair,
For a part of your disguise. Here, take it with you.

[*Exeunt.*

Under the same form of a description of the wonders of the Terra
Incognita, we have here again one of those pieces of personal satire
peculiar to the ancient comedy. It is directed against Socrates and
his school, including by name his friend Chærephon.

The uncleanly habits imputed to them ("where baths and washing are
forbidden") will have been seen already alluded to in p. 249,
("unwashed and slovenly like so many Socrates's")—but it is
difficult to conceive what is the imputation conveyed, or alluded to,
by describing them as engaged in the evocation of spirits.

It is a question, which might form a curious subject of inquiry for those
who have the means of prosecuting it, and who are better acquainted
' with the history of the Socratic school.

Pisander seems to have been an object of the poet's peculiar aversion;
in his first political comedy, "The Babylonians," he had been

---

* Prometheus had incurred the wrath of Jupiter by his kindness to mankind in having bestowed on them the gift of fire.

† Peisthetairus, who has learned all that he wanted to know, does not
care to lose his time in listening to professions of zeal and attachment. He
contrives, however, to conclude civilly with a piece of obliging attention.

‡ The Canœphoroi were followed by a person bearing an umbrella and a
folding chair.

mentioned in company with two* others, as having given occasion to the origin of the war, by their extortion of compulsory presents from the subject States, an accusation which is repeated in "The Lysistrata," v. 490; again in "The Peace," v. 396, his military pomp and arrogance are mentioned as objects of extreme disgust and contempt, and it seems that he must have been the commander described at length in the Epirrema of the same comedy, most splendidly caparisoned and foremost in running away. He had also been stigmatized by Eupolis as having been guilty of cowardly conduct.

It seems that he is brought in here, by-the-by, not as a follower or disciple of Socrates, but in allusion to his want of military courage, as a person whose *spirit wanted to be raised*, and who therefore naturally resorted to a place where *spirits were raised*.

Chærephon was the most zealous admirer of Socrates; he is recorded to have been a person of most singular aspect.

CHORUS.

Beyond the navigable seas,
Amongst the fierce Antipodes,
There lies a lake, obscure and holy,
Lazy, deep, melancholy,
Solitary, secret, hidden,
Where baths and washing are forbidden.
  Socrates, beside the brink,
Summons from the murky sink
Many a disembodied ghost;
And Pisander reached the coast,
To raise the spirit, that he lost;
With a victim, strange and new,
A gawky camel,† which he slew

---

* "Two;" for by putting the participle in the dual, and transposing the verb and the proper name, the true metre of the fragment (the long anapæst) may be restored.

† A simile by juxtaposition indirectly expressed as when Adam is described *tall and fair beneath* a palm-tree and the gigantic warriors in Homer standing before the *lofty* gates. The indirect simile may be either beautiful or sublime, or, as in the present instance, ludicrous.

Like Ulysses—whereupon,
The grizzly sprite of Chærephon
Flitted round him; and appeared
With his eyebrows and his beard,
Like a strange infernal fowl,
Half a vampire, half an owl.

It is usual with Aristophanes to omit that explanation which a poet of
the new comedy would have put into a soliloquy, or into a confidential conversation between the master and his slave. He gives
his audience credit for being able to comprehend at once the
previous views of the person whom he introduces.
Neptune, the chief of the Embassy, in which Hercules and the barbarous Triballian deity are joined with him, has settled in his own
mind a very satisfactory plan for the management of it. "Hercules
is my nephew, and of course looks up to me. He will be easily
managed, if I can appear to consult and advise exclusively with
him. But I must begin by putting the Triballian wholly out of the
question, as a ragamuffin whom we are both equally ashamed of.
Otherwise, their understandings are so much upon a par, my poor
nephew, I am sorry to say, is such a blockhead, that he and that
beast, the Triballian, from the mere natural sympathy of their
stupidity, will join and act together in spite of me." He accordingly
begins with the Triballian, by settling his dress for him, and as soon
as he has disposed of him, and set him down, as an unproduceable
ruffian, he turns round to consult Hercules, who makes a stupid
answer. Neptune, like a kind uncle, endeavours quietly and calmly
to set him right. Up to this point everything appears promising;
but Neptune, alas! is deficient in presence of mind, he is encumbered
with his dignity; and above all, in the person of Peisthetairus, he
is opposed to a politician, infinitely his superior in resources and
address. They advance within sight of Peisthetairus, who affects
not to notice them, and remains looking down among the dishes,
apparently occupied with his sauces. Neptune, of course, advances
no farther, but remains with a decided attitude and look of dignity,
ready to meet his eye, as soon as it shall be raised to encounter his.
Unfortunately, however, he is so much occupied with his own
attitude, and with the look which seems to say—"well, sir, now
you're at leisure,"—that he omits to restrain Hercules, who, more
impatient and indignant, presses forward with an announcement of
their arrival, calculated, as he thinks, to rouse and astonish Peisthetairus; failing in his attempt to make an impression, and feeling

himself at a loss, he remains exposed to the influence of his natural instincts, which attract him towards the pans and dishes. Hence, a conversation is begun, a recognition takes place, the ice is broken, and the negotiation opened ; while Neptune is left with his dignity in the background.

NEPTUNE, *the* TRIBALLIAN ENVOY, HERCULES.

NEP. There's Nephelococcugia, that's the town,
The point we're bound to, with our embassy.
   [*turning to the* TRIBALLIAN]
But you! What a figure have ye made yourself!
What a way to wear a mantle! slouching off
From the left shoulder! hitch it round, I tell ye,
On the right side. For shame—come—so ; that's better,
These folds, too, bundled up. There, throw them round
Even and easy—so. Why, you're a savage,
A natural born savage. Oh! democracy!
What will it bring us to? When such a ruffian
Is voted into an embassy!
  TRI. [*to* NEPTUNE, *who is pulling his dress about.*]
      Come, hands off!
Hands off!
  NEP.   Keep quiet, I tell ye, and hold your tongue,
For a very beast : in all my life in heaven,
I never saw such another—Hercules,
I say, what shall we do? What should you think?
  HER. What would I do? What do I think? I've told
   you
Already . . . . I think to throttle him—the fellow,
Whoever he is, that's keeping us blockaded.
  NEP. Yes, my good friend ; but we were sent, you
   know,
To treat for a peace. Our embassy is for peace.
  HER. That makes no difference ; or if it does,
It makes me long to throttle him the more.

PEIS. [*very busy, affecting not to see them*].
Give me the Silphium spice.   Where's the cheese-grater?
Bring cheese here, somebody!   Mend the charcoal fire.
HER. Mortal, we greet you and hail you! Three
of us—
Three deities.
PEIS. [*without looking up*].   But I'm engaged at present;
A little busy, you see, mixing my sauce.
HER. Why sure !   How can it be? what dish is
this ?
Birds seemingly!
PEIS. [*without looking up*].   Some individual birds,
Opposed to the popular democratic birds,
Rendered themselves obnoxious.
HER.   So, you've plucked them,
And put them into sauce, provisionally?
PEIS. [*looking up*].   Oh! bless me, Hercules, I'm quite
glad to see you.
What brings you here?
HER.   We're come upon an embassy
From heaven, to put an end to this same war . . . .
SERV. [*to* PEISTHETAIRUS].
The cruet's empty, our oil is out.
PEIS.   No matter,
Fetch more, fetch plenty, I tell ye.   We shall want it.
HER. For, in fact it brings no benefit to us,
The continuance of the war prolonging it ;
And you yourselves, by being on good terms
Of harmony with the gods . . . . why, for the future,
You'd never need to know, the want of rain,
For water in your tanks ; and we could serve ye
With reasonable, seasonable weather,
According as you wished it, wet or dry.
And this is our commission coming here,
As envoys, with authority to treat.

PEIS. Well, the dispute, you know, from the beginning,
Did not originate with us. The war
(If we could hope in any way to bring you
To reasonable terms) might be concluded.
Our wishes, I declare it, are for peace.
If the same wish prevails upon your part,
The arrangement in itself, is obvious.
A retrocession on the part of Jupiter.
The birds, again to be reintegrated
In their estate of sovereignty. This seems
The fair result ; and if we can conclude,
I shall hope to see the ambassadors to supper.

    HER. Well, this seems satisfactory ; I consent.

    NEP. [*to* HERCULES]. What's come to ye ? What do ye
      mean ? Are ye gone mad ?

You glutton ; would you ruin your own father,
Depriving him of his ancient sovereignty ?

PEIS.* [*to* NEPTUNE]. Indeed ! And would not it be a
      better method

For all you deities, and confirm your power,
To leave the birds to manage things below ?
You sit there, muffled in your clouds above,
While all mankind are shifting, skulking, lurking,
And perjuring themselves here out of sight.
Whereas, if you would form a steady strict
Alliance with the Birds, when any man
(Using the common old familiar oath—
" By Jupiter and the crow ") † forswore himself,
The crow would pick his eyes out, for his pains.

    NEP. Well, that seems plausible—that's fairly put.

    HER. I think so, too.

---

  * Peisthetairus with the civil, good-humoured sneer of a superior under-standing.

  † See p. 204 and note.

PEIS. [*to the* TRIBALLIAN]. Well, what say you?

TRIB.   Say true.*

PEIS.† Yes.   He consents, you see!   But I'll explain
now

The services and good offices we could do you.
Suppose a mortal made a vow, for instance,
To any of you; then he delays and shuffles,
And says "the gods are easy creditors."
In such a case, we could assist ye, I say,
To levy a fine.

NEP. [*open to conviction, but anxious to proceed on sure
ground*].

How would you do it?   Tell me.

PEIS. Why, for example, when he's counting money,
Or sitting in the bath, we give the warrant
To a pursuivant of ours, a kite or magpie;
And they pounce down immediately, and distrain
Cash or apparel, money or money's worth,
To twice the amount of your demand upon him.

HER. Well, I'm for giving up the sovereignty,
For my part.

NEP. [*convinced, but wishing to avoid responsibility, by
voting last*].

The Triballian, what says he?

HER. [*aside to the* TRIBALLIAN, *showing his fist*].
You, sir; do you want to be well banged or not?
Mind, how you vote !   Take care how you provoke me.

TRIB. Yaw, yaw.   Goot, goot.

HER.   He's of the same opinion.

NEP. Then, since you're both agreed, I must agree.

---

* It is singular that these two syllables are the last syllables of the word
(or sentence), in his own language, by which the Triballian expresses his
consent.

† Peisthetairus very volubly—quite at his ease.

HER. [*shouting to* PEISTHETAIRUS, *the negotiators having withdrawn to consult at the extremity of the stage*].
Well, you! we've settled this concern, you see,
About the sovereignty; we're all agreed.

PEIS. Oh faith, there's one thing more, I recollect,
Before we part; a point that I must mention.
As for dame Juno, we'll not speak of her;
I've no pretensions, Jupiter may keep her;
But, for that other queen, his manager,
The sovereign goddess, her surrender to me
Is quite an article indispensable.

NEP.* Your views, I find, are not disposed for peace:
We must turn homewards.

PEIS.   As you please, so be it.
Cook, mind what you're about there with the sauce;
Let's have it rich and savoury, thicken it up!

HER. How now, man? Neptune! are you flying off?
Must we remain at war, here, for a woman?

NEP. But, what are we to do?

HER.   Do? Why, make peace.

NEP.† I pity you really! I feel quite ashamed
And sorry to see you; ruining yourself!
If anything should happen to your father,
After surrendering the sovereignty,
What's to become of you? When you yourself
Have voted away your whole inheritance:
At his decease, you must remain a beggar.

PEIS. [*aside to* HERCULES]. Ah there! I thought so; he's
    coming over ye;
Step here a moment! Let me speak to ye!
Your uncle's chousing you, my poor dear friend,

---

* Neptune with gravity and dignity.
† Neptune in great wrath, like a grave uncle scolding a great fool of a nephew.

You've not a farthing's worth of expectation,
From what your father leaves. Ye can't inherit
By law : ye're illegitimate, ye know.
HER. Heigh-day ! Why, what do you mean ?
PEIS. I mean the fact!
Your mother was a foreigner ; Minerva
Is counted an heiress, everybody knows ;
How could that be, supposing her own father
To have had a lawful heir ?
HER. But, if my father
Should choose to leave the property to me,
In his last will.
PEIS. The law would cancel it !
And Neptune, he that's using all his influence
To work upon ye, he'd be the very first
To oppose ye, and oust ye, as the testator's brother.
I'll tell ye what the law says, Solon's law :
    " A foreign heir shall not succeed,*
    Where there are children of the lawful breed :
    But, if no native heir there be,
    The kinsman nearest in degree
    Shall enter on the property."
HER. Does nothing come to me, then ? Nothing at all,
Of all my father leaves ?
PEIS. Nothing at all,
I should conceive. But you perhaps can tell me.
Did he, your father, ever take ye with him,
To get ye enrolled upon the register ?
HER. No, truly I . . . . thought it strange, . . . he . . .
    never did.

---

* Memory must have been in the earliest times the sole repository of
knowledge of every kind. Every means therefore of assistance to the
memory was most carefully cultivated. Amongst other instances, in order
to facilitate the requisite knowledge and recollection of them, the Laws
themselves were composed and recorded in a metrical form. Hence the
same word in Greek signifies both a *Song* and a *Law.*

Peis. Well, but don't think things strange. Don't stand
    there, stammering,
Puzzling and gaping. Trust yourself to me,
'Tis I must make your fortune after all !
    If you'll reside and settle amongst us here,
I'll make you chief commander among the birds,
Captain, and Autocrat and everything.
Here you shall domineer and rule the roast,
With splendour and opulence and pigeon's milk.

    Her. [*in a more audible voice, and in a formal decided
    tone**].
I agreed with you before : I think your argument
Unanswerable. I shall vote for the surrender.

    Peis. [*to* Neptune]. And what say you?

    Nep. [*firmly and vehemently*].   Decidedly I dissent.

    Peis. Then it depends upon our other friend,
It rests with the Triballian, what say you ?

    Tri. Me tell you ; pretty girl, grand beautiful queen,
Give him to birds.

    Her.   Aye, give her up, you mean.

    Nep. Mean! He knows nothing about it. He means
    nothing
But chattering like a magpie.

    Peis.†   Well " the magpies."
He means, the magpies or the birds in general.
The republic of the birds—their government—
That the surrender should be made to them.

    Nep. [*in great wrath*]. Well, settle it yourselves; amongst
    yourselves ;
In your own style : I've nothing more to say.

---

  * They had withdrawn apart, and their previous conversation was supposed not to have been audible to Neptune and the Triballian, whose
by-play might have consisted in Neptune's formal attempts to soothe and
gain the Triballian, who would only shrug up his shoulders.

  † Peisthetairus being sure of his point, amuses himself with arguing non-
sensically to provoke Neptune.

HER. [*to* PEISTHETAIRUS].

Come, we're agreed in fact, to grant your terms ;
But you must come, to accompany us to the sky ;
To take back this same queen, and the other matters.

PEIS. [*very quietly*]. It happens lucky enough, with this
provision
For a marriage feast. It seems prepared on purpose.   ·

HER. Indeed, and it does. Suppose in the meanwhile,
I superintend the cookery, and turn the roast,
While you go back together.

NEP. [*with a start of surprise and disgust*]. Turn the
roast !
A pretty employment! Won't you go with us?

HER. No, thank ye ; I'm mighty comfortable here.

PEIS. Come, give me a marriage robe ; I must be going.

We have here another satyric song, of the same fanciful humour as the
preceding, descriptive of imaginary wonders in an unknown world.
In the last instance, the poet had exhibited a caricature of the
Socratic school of philosophy. The same vein of ridicule is now
directed against another novelty, tending equally, in the opinion
of the poet (more just in this than in the preceding instance)
to produce an undesirable change in the general character of the
nation.

Mercenary professors and teachers of rhetoric, for the most part
foreigners (the Gorgias for instance here mentioned was a Sicilian),
had of late been received and encouraged in Athens. Their public
exhibitions, which were generally resorted to, had operated as an
incentive to the natural propensity of the Athenian people, already
more than enough disposed to divert their attention to the unpro-
ductive pursuits of litigation and speechifying. While at the same
time their private lessons (the course of instruction by which they
engaged to communicate the secrets of their art, and to form young
practitioners) were purchased in some instances at an enormous
price, by young men of wealth aspiring to political eminence and
celebrity.

CHORUS.

Along the Sycophantic shore,
And where the savage tribes adore

The waters of the Clepsydra,*
There dwells a nation, stern and strong,
Armed with an enormous tongue,
    Wherewith they smite and slay : †

With their tongues, they reap and sow,
And gather all the fruits ‡ that grow,
    The vintage and the grain ;
Gorgias is their chief of pride,
And many more there be beside
    Of mickle might and main.

Good they never teach, nor show
But how to work men harm and woe,
    Unrighteousness and wrong ;
And hence the custom doth arise,
When beasts are slain in sacrifice,
    We sever out the tongue.§

It has been already observed, that this play, in the success of which, as
a sedative to the popular insanity, the higher orders of the community were essentially interested, was exhibited with a singular
recklessness of expense.

The concluding scene seems to have been equal in magnificence to those
of the most gorgeous tragedies ; and it is remarkable that in the
passage immediately following, contrary to the invariable custom of
the poet, there is no tinge of burlesque.   The poet has throughout,
as a poet, imitated the style of Sophocles ; while under his direction,
as the manager of a comic drama, the actor who personated Peisthetairus, must have been instructed to reduce the scene to the level
of comedy, by his airs and gestures characteristic of unaccustomed
dignity and authority.   It must have been a very delicate and amusing

---

* The Clepsydra, or water-clock, marked the time allotted to each advocate.   It was a prominent object in the Courts of Justice.   The name also
belonged to certain streams and springs.

† Dangerous as accusers.

‡ Their salaries and profits.

§ This sacrificial form was peculiar to the Athenians.

piece of acting.   An elderly man, a sharp, thorough-going fellow—
to see him

> Assume the god,
> Affect to nod,
> And seem to shake the spheres !

The choral songs which follow are of a peculiar and by no means obvious character, which it is rather difficult to define, and not very
easy to express in imitation.   In the comedy of "The Peace" we
have a rustic Epithalamium, perfectly rustic, and probably not very
different from the rustic extempore poetry of the same race at the
present day.   But in this instance we have a town Epithalamium,
such as we may suppose to have been composed and perpetrated in
honour of the nuptials of the more noble and wealthy families in
Athens.   The vulgar town poet is anxious to exhibit his *education*
by imitating and borrowing passages from the most approved lyrical
poets, but at the same time reduces all their imagery and expressions
to the natural level of his own dulness.   Thus maintaining, in the
verse itself, that balance of the ludicrous and sublime, which in the
first part of the scene had resulted from the contrast of the poetry
and the action.

Some parts of the Epithalamium of Catullus (see v. 100 and the following stanzas) are evidently a humorous imitation of the vulgar
Epithalamia at Rome.   Under cover of this character, he amused
himself at the expense of his new married friends.

HARBINGER *or* HERALD, *announcing the approach
of* PEISTHETAIRUS.

O fortunate ! O triumphant ! O beyond
All power of speech or thought, supremely blest,
Prosperous happy birds ! Behold your king,
Here in his glorious palace ! Mark his entrance,
Dazzling all eyes, resplendent as a star ; .
Outshining all the golden lights, that beam
From the rich roof, even as a summer sun,
Or brighter than the sun, blazing at noon.
    He comes ; and at his side a female form
Of beauty ineffable ; wielding on high,
In his right hand, the winged thunderbolt,
Jove's weapon. While the fumes of incense spread

Circling around, and subtle odours steal
Upon the senses from the wreathed smoke,
Curling and rising in the tranquil air.

See, there he stands ! Now must the sacred Muse
Give with auspicious words her welcome due.

SEMICHORUS.

Stand aside and clear the ground,
Spreading in a circle round
With a worthy welcoming ;
To salute our noble king
In his splendour and his pride,
Coming hither, side by side,
With his happy lovely bride.

O the fair delightful face !
What a figure ! What a grace !
What a presence ! What a carriage !
What a noble worthy marriage.

Let the birds rejoice and sing,
At the wedding of the king :
Happy to congratulate
Such a blessing to the State.
       Hymen, Hymen, Ho !

Jupiter, that god sublime,
When the Fates, in former time,
Matched him with the Queen of Heaven,
At a solemn banquet given,
Such a feast was held above ;
And the charming God of Love,
Being present in command,
As a Bridesman took his stand,
With the golden reins in hand.
       Hymen, Hymen, Ho !

PEIS.* I accept and approve the marks of your love,
Your music and verse I applaud and admire.
But rouse your invention, and raising it higher,
Describe me the terrible engine of Jove,
The thunder of earth and the thunder above.

The reader may have already observed, that in more than one instance
the poet directs the attention of his audience to the lavish expen-
diture of the Choregus. This seems to have been the object of the
following lines, introductory to a new display of theatrical thunder
manufactured upon an improved principle.

CHORUS.

O dreaded bolt of heaven,
The clouds with horror cleaving,
And ye terrestrial thunders deep and low
Closed in the subterranean caves † below,
That even at this instant growl and rage,
Shaking with awful sound this earthly stage;
Our king by you has gained his due;
By your assistance, yours alone,
Everything is made his own,
Jove's dominion and his throne;
And his happiness and pride,
His delightful lovely bride.
                    Hymen, Hymen, Ho!

PEISTHETAIRUS.

Birds of ocean and of air,
Hither in a troop repair,

---

* Peisthetairus puts an end to their nonsense with condescension and
affability.
† Caves of the theatre.

To the royal ceremony,
Our triumphant matrimony !
    Come for us to feast and feed ye !
    Come to revel, dance, and sing !—
Lovely creature ! Let me lead ye
    Hand in hand, and wing to wing.

THE END.

www.ingramcontent.com/pod-product-compliance
Lightning Source LLC
Chambersburg PA
CBHW031332070726

47496CB00018B/1826

*9 7 8 3 3 3 7 0 0 2 7 9 4 *